The Green Scarf

By Alexander Francis

The Green Scarf

Copyright ©2014 by Alexander Francis

Arcus Verba Publishing
P.O Box 210
De Forest, Wisconsin
53532

www.arcusverba.com

Cover design by Alexander Francis

ISBN:978-1-942420-03-3 print edition

ISBN: 978-1-942420-02-6 e-book

Other Novels by Alexander Francis

Are We A Band Yet?

Mick Grundy….Spy Hunt

Mick Grundy…The Russian Connection

Mick Grundy…Elapid

Geminknot

Beware The Exit

Revenge of Jesus

Table of Contents

In the beginning

My eyes went back to her neck and the fine downy hairs just visible above her collar. She wore her hair up in a braid, piled carefully on her head in a mesmerizing weave of interlaced bundles. Later, much later, she would ask me, her unblinking eyes on mine, if I liked her French braid. Like wasn't exactly the right word, and for the moment, the drone of the professor in front of the room disappeared from my conscious brain as I focused on the hypnotic beauty of her perfect head, balanced on a slender neck. She was seated in the adjacent row, two seats ahead of my own desk. From there I could see the blush of color on her cheek and the occasional flutter of her eyelashes. My eyes wandered over her shoulder, covered by a thin, nearly translucent ivory fabric, down the back of her arm to her elbow, placed delicately on the desktop. An unexpected sound made me turn and look ahead, just in time, for the lecturer was headed toward me.

"Are we back?" he asked petulantly, clutching his legal pad against his chest as if it were either a badge of his office or a shield against possible attack.

Normally, a confrontation of words or fists was something I rather enjoyed…but…I needed the credit for this class, and I immediately decided not to provoke him. Still, I couldn't resist pulling his chain a little. "Back from where?" I asked and leaned back, looking up at him, keeping my face blank.

"Can you repeat back to me what I just said?" he asked.

"Sure. You asked, 'Are we back'. Frankly, I wasn't aware that we had left," I answered calmly, looking into his eyes, trying to not look threatening.

He stooped and turned his head, mocking my perspective, looking directly at Julie. She was watching, her big eyes wide with questions. I could see her face from under his arm, the perfect set of her eyes above full lips which seemed never to need cosmetics. "Were you looking at Miss Frank? Yes, you were, weren't you?" He stood, satisfied with his own answer, apparently not needing my confirmation. "I ask you, is she giving this lecture?" He waited for an answer with uplifted brow as repressed chuckles floated from unknown corners in the room. I shrugged, tapping a fresh pencil against my lips, watching him more intently, hostility creeping into me against my better judgment. With a huff, he turned and scurried back to the front of the room, turning like a ballerina quickly back to face me, locking me in his gaze for a brief second.

My eyes left his face and glanced toward Julie Frank, who was still watching me, her face sending confusing signals. As she turned to avoid my eyes, I looked back to our instructor, who by now was busily writing, clicking his chalk against the hard surface of the green board. I didn't need to look at Julie again. I had by now memorized every visible detail of her face and body, knowing by heart every outfit that she owned, differentiating her from every other woman in the world just by how she moved. Let me be honest…I dreamed about her both in the day and at night. I couldn't get her out of my head. We brushed shoulders one day, quite by accident, and I got a whiff of her scent. Someday, when I am old, I will still recall that perfume, the memories of what it promised by its delicate fragrance.

Another painful truth. Julie and I weren't a we, not even a them. I couldn't pump my courage up enough to ask her out. If she should refuse me, it would likely prove fatal. No sense in diving off the bridge just to find out that you are going to die. Why would some perfect being, the gift of a million years of evolution, ever, ever, consider going out with a me? She wouldn't; I knew it in my heart, so why bother to confirm it? I could feel it when her eyes flashed by, covering my body with a wave of brief energy, leaving to favor some other lucky entity with the soul of her eyes. My turn was always too brief, but one day, if she ever did look at me for long, my intelligence would falter, anything I said would come out babble.

I scribbled my notes, taking the information from the board while listening to the content of today's lecture being read directly from the textbook, my brain elsewhere, currently wrapping itself around the girl seven feet from me who was, in fact, a world away. I endured this class like I always did, probably not learning the smallest item, as was usual for me. There was no need to learn in class, because I could do it so efficiently by reading the book. My grades were as good as any and, I suspected, were at or near the top of the class. I ventured one last look before the bell rang. She was the most perfect thing in existence, and there she was only feet away, one tiny, sparkling earring, winking its rainbow magic into my head.

The bell rang, and the room erupted with the scuffling sound of students getting up and putting books and papers away. I remained in my seat for a moment, letting the eager ones exit, instead of being pushed through the door in the panic to make it to the next class. As I put away my notes, I became aware of a close presence. Someone had stopped at my desk and was waiting for me to look up.

It was Julie. She was holding her books in her folded arms, and her perfect eyes were looking into mine. "Hi!" I said, two or three un-masculine pitches too high.

"Were you looking at me?" she asked, her voice just the right level of feminine warmth. I studied her before speaking. Her face was impassive, her eyes steady. An interrogation, not an invitation, I sensed. Some other students were watching, wishing they could hang around and be flies on the wall. I waited for the right moment to answer what I must. There was no use denying what she likely already knew before the instructor announced it to the class at large.

"Yes." God, I wished that I could think of something to add. I couldn't. She didn't even blink before responding.

"Why?" And she waited.

I decided to make a clean break with my fears, and answer her truthfully. "Julie, I can't help myself. You are so beautiful that I can't get my mind on anything else when you are nearby. I hope that I didn't offend you." There it was, my guts were on the cutting block, and she had the cleaver in her hand. I wanted to say more, but I was already extended farther than I wanted.

"If you are that interested, why can't you just ask me out?" As she spoke, her face still showed nothing which would help me decide what she was thinking.

"Julie, would you please consent to go out with me?" I asked, the desk luckily preventing me from falling to my knees.

"No," she said.

This was what I was afraid of. She had used the cleaver as expertly as a Chinese chef. I could hear the metal still ringing from the chop. "Just a Coke or a walk or just a five minute talk?" I pleaded.

"No." She turned abruptly to leave.

"Why not?" I demanded, just a little too loudly, to her receding back.

"I just don't like you," she said as she went across the threshold into the hall. She never looked back, and I caught sight of her flowing skirt as it disappeared from view.

"RATS!" I said aloud. No wonder I couldn't get up nerve to ask her. Something in me told me what was destined to happen, the inevitable truth. Some cruel fate had dangled what I wanted most in this life just in front of me, then snatched it away. It happened so quickly, I didn't even get a hint of her perfume. As I sat there with a blank mind, new students were starting to drift in for the next class. I had to go and struggled to my feet.

"Hurts, doesn't it?" a voice said. He was a student, familiar to me by sight, but not someone I actually knew by name.

"Sure does. You know her?" I asked, hoping that he didn't. The last thing I wanted to hear about was another man's adventures with the woman I loved.

He laughed. "Not that one. She's likely to give me the same treatment. No, I know how it feels, because other girls have done the same thing to me. You extend your hand, and they cut it off or bite it. Makes you afraid to ask, am I right?"

"You are so right. Ever figure out how to ask and not get hurt?" I asked.

"In a way I did. You ever go into a store and ask the price of something you knew you couldn't afford? They tell you and you walk away. No hurt feelings, you just wanted to know, that's all. Kind of like Julie. Now you know, and you can stop thinking about her. Get past it, you know, move on."

"Wish it was that easy. Tomorrow, I will see her again and my heart will sink like a stone. If lightning strikes her and somehow makes her ugly, I'm sure it won't make any difference."

"You have it bad, all right. Say, I'm Mike Flannigan, your name is Rick, right?" He offered his hand, accompanied by a winning smile.

I took his hand and said, "Rick James. Glad to meet you, Mike." We shook briefly but were nearly pushed out of the room by the late crowd pouring around us in the last moments before the bell. I looked at my watch. Two more hours before the next class. "Mike, want to get some lunch, or do you have to be somewhere?"

"Ever play pool?" he asked with a grin. I instantly knew what he was thinking. There was an old pool hall just a couple of blocks away. Everyone knew that the administration wanted to call it off limits but didn't have legal justification. The college regulars who hung out there never managed to finish school. Usually it took two years, but on occasion, only one. They also had a small snack bar which served greasy hamburgers, fries and a beer if you wanted it. I had time so I readily agreed.

Chapter 2

My new friend

We found an empty pair of stools, both wobbly from years of use, their plastic covers cracked in places. Jimmy wiped his hands on a dirty towel and took our orders, both burgers…the works.

"What do you know about this Julie?" Mike asked, playfully, as if he knew something I didn't.

"Nothing, really. I see her on campus occasionally. We have two classes together so I assume that she is a biology major like me. I don't even know where she lives. Do you know more than that?" I asked.

He hesitated, chewing a big mouthful of burger and holding his finger up to pause the conversation. "I went to high school with her. She was the girl who won every beauty contest, hands down. Every guy wanted her but none ever got her, that I know about. I don't think any of them ever got to take her out."

My head spun. "Ever think that she doesn't like boys?" I asked, hoping he didn't know the answer.

"No, it's not that. Her date for the senior prom was a Marine in a skintight, black uniform. We were all instantly afraid of him. One of the girls said that her father arranged it to keep the boys away from her, and it sure did work. The thought of that guy chasing you down and pounding his big fists into your face was enough to make us avoid her like the Angel of Death."

"So, what's wrong with her?" I wondered.

"Absolutely nothing. Just as you can see, she's perfect. Smart too. My guess is that she's waiting for the right man. If you think that man is you then you should pursue her. Keep asking, maybe you'll get lucky, or maybe the Marines will show up and pull your arms off."

"She was very final when she said 'No'. I don't want to keep getting rejected; my self-image will be damaged beyond what low opinion I already have of myself," I said, picking at my fries and wishing I had ordered a beer and skipped the Coke. Out of the dark entrance to the pool room, there was an occasional crack of a hard ball slamming into its temporary mate. I realized that I knew how the balls felt after collision. Hurts, doesn't it? Turns out that Mike was also a biology major with an eye on admission to medical school someday. We had a lot in common, and for a moment forgot Julie as we discussed various professors and their quirks.

"Buy her a gift," Mike blurted as if he had suddenly uncoiled DNA and laid it out on the dented bar surface.

"You mean Julie, don't you?" I asked looking at Mike's serious face. "What kind of gift, and how would I give it to her?" I was ready to consider any remotely possible route to her heart, no matter how unlikely. My thoughts turned to seeing a Marine, grimacing, pulling hard on my arm, his foot pressed into my chest.

"Something nice, perfume…French…good stuff. Leave it on her desk. She'll know who left it there."

"First of all, I know she already has a choice perfume. I've had it imprinted on my brain. Even I wouldn't want her to change it. Any other ideas, and keep in mind my budget, will you?"

Mike stared at the dirty floor, lost in thought. Someone in the pool area was cursing loudly. "Flowers. Try a nice bouquet of flowers." His face brightened at the thought.

"I'll be laughed out of the school. I won't do it. You might as well stick them up my ass, and let me walk into class. That's where they would end up anyway." The flower idea sucked, but I could think of no other alternative, and I crassly started mulling it over.

"I've got it!" Mike announced, standing up excitedly, slapping me on the back. "A silk scarf! Small, expensive, something every girl wants. Perfect?" Yes, I knew he was onto something. Silk scarf? I tried to recall any previous associations I may have had with silk scarves, but there were none. They existed, I had seen them in movies, but that was about it. I had no idea where to buy one or what they cost. Still, I could see it around her neck, jaunty, tied with one end longer than the other. Perfect. Green. She liked green and had three blouses predominately green. It was entirely perfect. Exactly the right gift.

"You have something this time, Mike. I'll try it. Thanks a million. If it works, I'll buy the beer. If the Marines kill me you can cast it on my coffin as they lower me——be sure to shed a tear or two."

"I've got a feeling that it will work. How could she refuse a man with such class and *élan*?"

The word, *élan*, brought images of a well-dressed and dapper Frenchman, wooing a bosomy French girl with bright red pouty lips. Mike was right. It couldn't miss. At least it would make her friendly, even thankful. If I could just talk to her, convince her of my sincerity, my love, my passion for her. My mind started thinking of women's clothing stores nearby, and a chill went through me. I would have to shop in a women's store, where they would treat me like dirt. I might even have to stand by the pointy bras while I paid. All the points would be directed at me like a chamber of nails, closing in for the kill. It would all be worth it if Julie liked her scarf, but what if she didn't? I would be poorer and even more humiliated than today.

Chapter 3

The ladies store

They saw me as soon as I opened the door and the little chime sounded. The larger one, behind the counter, looked at me over her half-glasses. Across from her was a tall thin one, cursed with a sagging neck, who also was looking intently toward me as I made an effort to look like a casual shopper. I looked right and left, taking in the merchandise, most of which appeared suitable for a matron of society, not a ravishing brunette about my age. To make the dreaded approach seem believable, I occasionally paused, fingering some garment which would make even Julie look like the wife of a nineteenth century president. At this moment I saw myself as a caveman walking down a Parisian fashion runway. I looked up, toward the crouching lionesses, who waited to spring, contempt plainly visible in their body language. In a moment of sarcastic inspiration, I was tempted to ask about ladies underpants and the location of the condom machine…but perhaps it wouldn't be wise, not this time at least.

"Hi!" I said brightly, looking over the half-glasses from the other side. "I am looking for a ladies scarf….in silk." Plain as the time of day, I thought.

"What do you want it for?" the large one said.

Taken back by her response, I looked from side to side trying to find them for myself. "For a lady—to wear," I reluctantly clarified.

"Well, of course, young man. I mean for what occasion?" She

laid aside what she was working on and gave me an up and down look.

"What price range?" the other one said from behind me. I turned and threw a stiff smile at her with no obvious effect.

"Price?" I repeated. "I was thinking green. Do you have green?"

"It makes a difference, you see," the heavy one said patiently. "We have some imported from China and some imported from France or Italy. You might imagine that they are differently priced, can't you?"

"A nice one, in green," I decided. She rolled her eyes and sighed.

"Come with me," she commanded and motioned for me to follow like a small duckling behind its mother's wagging tail. And I did.

She reached behind a wooden counter and pulled out a rack filled with colorful scarves. "This one," she said, pointing to a smaller one at the left end. "This one is two dollars, without tax." She looked to see if I flinched. "This one," she said, lifting the one on the far right and letting it slip between her fingers like she had scooped water instead of silk, "It goes for just under two thousand dollars. Get the picture?" I wanted to run away but instead swallowed hard. My brow must have crusted in sweat, or my color changed. I could tell because of the way her eyes became sympathetic. I looked back and forth and then at the middle. Simple math should show, I hoped, that the ones in the center were of in-between prices. There was a green one right in the center. It softly gleamed up at me.

"May I see that one?" I pointed. Hesitant at first, she deftly pulled the shimmering green one out and spread it for me to see. It was bigger than I expected and trimmed with one single strand of gold thread all around the edge. A magnificent scarf, if you happened to be into scarves. It was just what I thought I wanted, but I dreaded asking the price. The practical part of my brain was having problems with a twenty dollar scarf, since Julie was apt to reject it or even throw it away once she was out of my sight. I sighed deeply, letting it slide over my hand as the clerk had done over hers. It felt as I imagined the skin of Julie's arm would feel when I touched it, if I ever did, that is.

Impatient, the clerk finally asked,"Do you like this one?" Sure, I liked it, the question was, would Julie.

"Yes, I like it. How much?" My voice sounded too curt when I spoke, and I was instantly sorry. What if she jacked the price up just to spite me? I remembered that someone once told me that if you really like something, never admit it. They will just realize that you aren't willing to haggle over it.

"One hundred fifty two…dollars," she said, knowing it would hurt and it did. "Plus tax," she added and watched me in case I had to sit down to recover. Imagine, this sheer, virtually transparent, little thing of silk weighing less than a single penny, but costing more than a thousand of them, much more. I did need to sit down and glanced quickly behind me hoping in vain for a close chair.

"I assume that this one isn't Chinese," I said, trying to sound continental and urbane, whatever that is.

"No…it's French. More at the entry level, however." There was a trace of haughtiness in her voice. I had it coming. A man, or very nearly so, in a woman's world. When we are out here buying this sort of thing for them, and taking punishment and humiliation for doing it, why do they hate us so much? Why do they despise us? There is a most simple explanation after all, I thought. It's the old seller's market theory. They have what we want, and to get it we have to pay the price. Same as corn futures. If you don't like the price, you can always buy peanuts.

"I'll take it," my mouth blurted before my brain caught up. "Can you put it in a small box?" I added, then wished I had left the store instead. The dryness of my mouth was interfering with my speech.

"Gift wrapping included?" I foolishly asked as we walked back toward the looming cash register.

"Six dollars extra. Still want it?" she asked over her shoulder. I did. In for a penny, in for a pound. My mind wandered, escaping from the present, trying to remember who had originally said that, as we pulled abruptly up at the desk.

"Oh! I always liked that one. I assume that your lady friend has red hair and green eyes?" the tall one asked, affectionally feeling the scarf as its box was being fetched.

"No. She is a brunette." I said and smiled at her.

"Heavens!" she said and shook her head in a negative fashion. She disappeared behind her own counter, giving up on me and my poor judgment and fashion foolishness.

I will say that the box was very finely wrapped with gleaming gold paper, bound in restraint with a small red ribbon. It was a delicious little package, one meant to be handed over in a quiet booth, glinting its fineness in moving candle light, offered beside a long stemmed wine glass. Unfortunately, I planned to just put it on her desk and hope for the best. No *élan* and no class, but it was the best I could do.

Chapter 4

The gift

The gold box tied with a red ribbon was burning a hole in my pocket. I could feel it's presence through my clothing like a tribal god was inside struggling to be free. The plan was to arrive early, at least before Julie, set it down carefully on her desk, aligning it to reflect the blue glow of the overhead florescent lamps. It looked magnificent there, all by itself, waiting for it's new and possibly proud owner. My nerves were on edge hoping that someone would not sit there by mistake or even snatch the prize up so I watched it as if it were a crab that would suddenly move sideways. As the room filled, my nervous energy went up like a boiler being fired for steam. I was about to puff a column of smoke out of my ears when I heard her voice from behind. She was, at least, attending class today. I held my breath and my steam and watched out of my peripheral vision as she moved closer to the desk. She stopped, looking down at the package as if it were some small terrorist bomb planted to maim and kill at random. She slung her sweater over the back of the chair and sat down, looking intently at my gift. I didn't dare look directly at her. Would she know whom it was from? Would she realize that it was meant for her? If she did, it wasn't detectable for she carefully placed her notebook under the slender package, opened it and took out her pen. She wasn't going to even touch it! RATS! I felt like sliding out of the desk onto the floor, slithering away into the first available floor drain.

Dr. Gibbs, Gibbs to his class, was punctual as usual. He singled my face out for scrutiny and lingered on it long enough to give me a warning that he was watching. Today, for the first time since Julie captured my entire intellect, I was going to pay attention. The reason?…there was no longer a distraction, an object of pursuit, a living creation of art to rivet my attention away from Gibbs. He was all I had, and I was his, at least for the next fifty-nine minutes. Yes, I could still see the gleam of the undisturbed offering without looking at it. The meaning was as clear as if it were written on the big green board in foot high letters. "You are a loser, and your stupid gift means nothing to me. Nothing." Perhaps my mother would like green for Christmas. She, at least, would say thank you.

The lecture, as read by Gibbs, could not hold my attention after all. My thoughts were on IndoChina and a possible transfer to Ho Chi Minh City University. I wondered if anyone there could speak English, and how long would it take me to learn a new language. Should I bring the green scarf with me? Some nice girl there might appreciate it, bringing it home to show her parents what the nice American boy gave her. Of course, her people would be connected to a manufacturing facility which would rapidly duplicate the scarf, depriving the French of their expertise and a portion of their income.

Gibbs was tapping at the chalkboard again and looking at me. "Are you on drugs, Mr. James?" he said to the laughter of the class. "Did you hear my question, or should I call the nurse?"

I had enough of Gibbs, and I stood. "I don't really care what you do, Gibbs, but I'll tell you that if you insult me again in front of this class you will get a demonstration of what I do when I'm angry." I continued to stand, aware of the flickering feeling of my pounding temporal pulse. It always takes time for me to cool down after I get my blood up.

"Please take your seat and my apology, Mr. James. I was only trying to give you your money's worth. You, after all, have excellent test scores, and I'm not sure that you even need to come to this class. You can skip if you desire. That doesn't apply to the rest of you, however," he said pointing to all the others. Gibbs had backed down in front of everyone. It must have hurt, and I expected him to try and get even in some way, if not now, later. I sat down slowly, with effort. The first public appearance of my evil temper, and it had to come out in front of the girl I wanted to win over. Fat chance of that now. Uncharacteristically, I didn't cool off but instead remained wound like a taut spring, my hands clenching and unclenching. I didn't handle any of this well. First, a gift to a girl who doesn't desire my attention and then a confrontation with a tenured professor, treating him as though he was a pesky barfly. I wanted to become invisible, forced to live in a cabin without running water, and I deserved no better.

Why can you always tell when people are looking at you? Is it a force, a projection of waves or simply mental telepathy? Who knows, but you can always tell. I became aware that Julie was looking at me at that moment, her face a perfection of absolute symmetry, her eyes a window into a magical kingdom. For the first time, we locked eyes and she didn't look away. It may have taken only ten milliseconds, but the effect was one of minutes, days or even lifetimes. She had looked at me as a person, not an insect, and I felt my body returning to normal as if she had stroked my head and closed my eyes with her long fingertips. A warmth came over me, and I relaxed. She looked away, but it was a gift from her to me, and we both knew it. I had given her an unopened box of French silk, but she had given me much more — I was a person, and I had worth after all.

Gibbs tossed his chalk into the tray and looked furtively toward me as if he wanted to say something. I was no longer angry, and if he had indicated it, I would have come to him. He didn't, though, and he left without another word or look.

I felt a hand on my shoulder. "Good work, Rick. Wish I had the nerve to say something like that. You sure put him in his place," Mike said, smiling down at me. "I have to know, Rick. Did you mean it?"

"What do you think?" I asked.

"Gibbs believed it and so did I," he said.

"I did too," I confessed. Just as I spoke, movement caught my eye from the direction of Julie's seat. She was gone and so was the package. I suddenly became limp.

Mike caught the change but not the reason. "What's up, my boy? You all right?"

"The gift you suggested. She took it," I said, nodding toward her empty chair.

"Well, that's a start! Now don't get too excited yet, it's still likely that nothing will come of it. She is a different sort of girl, and no one knows exactly what makes her gears work. Be patient, won't you?"

"No other choice," I admitted.

"Again, nice work, and I'll catch you later. We have to get together again soon. Double date or something?" The way he fled for the door, I realized he must have had a class commitment. I got up, collecting my books, almost reluctant to leave. All the energy I had moments ago was spent, leaving me with apathy. My watch said that I had another hour before my next class so I slowly sauntered out.

She was waiting in the hall for me, her eyes finding mine, pulling me toward her like the opposite ends of a magnet.

"You gave me this gift?" she asked, gently lifting the end of the gold box from the depths of her bag. I nodded that it was me.

"Why?" she asked simply and without emotion. It was just a

question, one to the other.

"I wanted you to have it. There is no expectation, no obligation, and no thanks needed. It's just a gift to a girl that I bothered, hoping to just get close enough to talk to her. I guess it worked, after all," I said, giving a little nervous laugh. How do you talk to an ideal? I didn't feel worthy to even be standing this close to her. There were no words that I had stored up for her, because I never really felt that I would have an opportunity to use them. My eyes wandered over her face, soaking up every detail, every millimeter of skin and hair. There were hints of tears to come and a flicker of emotion that I hadn't expected to find. Her eyes went back and forth between mine, and it seemed that she was trying to extract some truth, some insight from them. Before I could say what was starting to form in my head, she turned, walking away from me, pulling my life force with her, stretching it farther and farther as she disappeared into a crowd, leaving me leaning into the wall with my shoulder, aching to have gone with her.

Chapter 5

Too hot to handle

*M*ike leaned across the small table and cupped his hand like a small megaphone. "What's going on with Julie?" he asked above the loud music. I squinted at the thought of trying to describe a delicate matter by out-yelling the speakers. No go. I waved him off.

"Later," I shouted. Actually there wasn't much I could tell him. Gibbs had cancelled the last two classes, and the only other class I had with Julie didn't meet. I hadn't seen nor heard from her for over a week. That didn't mean, however, that I had stopped thinking of her. Now that I had memorized her face, I used her memory to dwell on every chance I got. Was the scarf tied around her lovely neck? It seemed that I would have to wait it out until tomorrow. There was only one other small tidbit that I had come across. She had a dorm room, and I, indirectly of course, knew her roommate. Actually, I only knew her roommate's name, but I did know someone who knew her roommate. Well, it's closer than I had been. Was this what they call stalking? If it was, I sure didn't feel that I was doing something wrong. It was all by chance that I knew as much as I did, and frankly, I hungered for more.

The music died down for a moment, and I seized my chance to talk. "Are you holding anything back?" I asked Mike bluntly. I could see that my arrow hit the mark, because he did a tell…wiped his upper lip with the back of his hand.

"This is the truth, Rick, all I have is rumor. You really want to hear rumor? I mean, I don't think I have ever actually spoken to the girl. My high school girlfriend sort of knew her, and Julie was always an interesting person because of her singular looks, so I heard gossip."

"Such as?" I asked, cupping my ear.

"Julie's mother died when we were in the sixth grade. It was in all the newspapers, and they speculated that she had been murdered. Then, just like that," he snapped his fingers, "it was gone. No more talk. None."

"What did people make of that?" I asked.

"Pull. They said pull. That's all I know."

"Anything else?" I persisted.

"Her father is, or was, I'm not sure which, an officer in the U.S. Marines, a colonel. He is reputed to be a very tough man. Very tough. I once saw him come to school in his uniform, full of medals. He had his hair so close-cropped that I thought he was bald."

"And?" I levered.

"That's all I know." Mike said and put his hands on the table palms down.

"That's nothing at all about Julie. Is that all you know?"

"Absolutely all," he assured me. I sat up and looked at him. Disappointed? Yes, sort of, but also very glad that he had heard no rumor or negative facts about Julie, not that I would have believed him. I had her on a pedestal, wrapped in ivory-colored marble, mounds of flowers piled at the base. I remembered a lecture last year where I learned about the Ancient Greek view that beauty consisted of symmetry, proportion and harmony. As far as I was concerned, that was Julie. I wondered how green silk looked against marble.

Mike tapped the table to get my attention. "You, my man, are in luck. I told two of the finest babes in town to meet us here, and they should be along any time now. Wait until you meet Carol.

She'll make you forget Julie in a heartbeat, I promise."

Surprised? Yes, I was. First of all, I wasn't needy along those lines, and I knew some attractive girls who always seemed eager for my company. The other reason is that I didn't want to be seen with other girls right now. At least not until I found out if I had even a slim chance to be around Julie. Saving myself for her? I guess that's about it. Mike pointed to the door, and two slender, long-haired girls were walking toward us. Walking is a loose term and that is how they walked…loose. He was right about the attractive part. We both stood as they approached.

Sally, the girl that Mike claimed, wrapped her arms around him and kissed him hard on the lips. I could tell that even though it was not a new experience, Mike lost his concentration a bit and had to force himself to think about the two other people standing there. Carol and me, that is.

"Carol, this is Rick, Rick meet Carol," he said with compactness, returning his attention to the attractive Sally.

"Hi, Carol," I said and pulled a chair out for her. "Are you a student here?" I asked, expecting that she probably was.

"No…Rick is it?…no, Rick, I work downtown. Sally and I share an apartment. You are a student though, aren't you?"

"Pre-med," I said with some satisfaction. That always got them. They could see the prestige and the dollar signs down the road.

"Oh, that means that you don't have much money for dates, doesn't it?" she asked coyly. I must admit, this girl got right down to the now of things, and she was right on target. I had very little surplus money. I sized her up in a glance. Attractive, even pretty. She had long shimmering blond hair, a bit darker at the roots, and lots of makeup. She was used to being around men, and I don't mean so-called college men. No matter how pretty a girl is on the outside, the inside gets changed by the company she keeps. My bet was that this one had kept a lot of company. There was a hard edge to her, a knowing look, a hint of experience. She was not what I was looking for, but I already knew that from what Mike said before they showed up. Perhaps, how he said it. Carol was the kind of girl who assumed that the men she dated expected a sexual encounter fairly early in their relationship. All they had to do is to spend a little money and time with her. A sort of guarantee built into the date. Call me naive, virginal, or old-fashioned if you will, and it will be sort of true. Although I have a well-deserved reputation for being quick with my fists, a hothead who was frequently in trouble, I was aware that most thought me to be somewhat timid with women. But I wasn't timid at all. It was only that I want a long-term relationship with a girl who is worthy of all the devotion that I am prepared to show her. That narrowed the field a lot. Really, it excluded about every girl out there but, hopefully, not Julie.

"Where do you usually take your dates?" Carol asked in a lull between the frolics across the table from us.

"I enjoy long walks, conversation and holding hands," I said, hoping that this would put a merciful end to our budding relationship.

"Oh," she remarked and started looking around the room, obviously hoping to find a previous encounter hanging around.

If the toilet doesn't flush the first time you pull the chain, try again. "What do you like to do, Carol?" I asked.

"Me? I like a noisy place where there is dancing, action and a few drinks. Want some suggestions?" she asked, raising one crisply drawn eyebrow.

"Wow," I said in my best farm-boy voice. "That's exciting! I was about to suggest that we go to a free lecture on Roman Architecture. Doesn't that sound interesting?"

"Very!" She said with mock enthusiasm. "Say, I've got to find the girl's room, be back quick." She got up and rapidly disappeared, leaving me with the certain feeling that we wouldn't meet again.

"What happened to Carol?" Mike asked when he came up for air. He had a blush of red on one cheek matching the color of his date's lips. She came up a bit wild-eyed but kept her hand on the back of Mike's neck.

"She saw someone she wanted to talk to. I expect she won't come back, so I'm going to leave the evening to you two. Be good, or at least, don't get caught," I said and threw a five on the table to cover my previous drink. I felt their eyes track me for a short time until they found each other's face again.

It was a nice evening for a walk, and it gave me time to think. Want to know the first thing I thought about? You're right. I couldn't get her out of my mind. Even after all my probing about her, I still didn't know the first thing that mattered. Seeing the emotion in her face the last time I saw her was perplexing. Hurt? Angry? Interested? I still couldn't guess. If I only had her phone number, I thought. No. There's got to be an invitation from her, even if it's subtle. She has a right to reject my interest, I wouldn't want it any other way.

The next day, I was early for class and stood in the hall waiting for the previous occupants to vacate, my shoulder in about the same place as when I saw Julie last. Finally, I was able to enter and find my desk. There was no assigned seating in this class, but the usual people took their usual seat, with few exceptions. I took mine and glanced at the empty seat which always had been occupied by Julie. This was it, the day it would happen or not happen. The room slowly and noisily filled and still her chair remained empty. When the second hand was approaching vertical, she appeared and slipped into her chair. Around her neck was a glimmering green scarf, tied just so. Not much can make a beautiful girl look better, but this green scarf did, at least to my mind. I waited, but she never glanced in my direction, not even once. My eyes were burning a hole in her back, and she had to feel that I was looking at her, but she obviously wasn't going to turn and look. It didn't matter. I was as happy as a kid with a new bike. She wore the scarf so that I could see it on her, knowing how it would make me feel. Life is wonderful.

Chapter 6

Invasion

Life settled into its rhythm, which for me meant lots of study after class. It was now three weeks since Julie wore her scarf for me, and since then I've never gotten a glance from her, plus the scarf wasn't seen again. I gave up and started the slow process of getting her out of my mind, a difficult task requiring effort each new day. The books I needed were spread out in my little cubby in the library, my notepad at hand, as I worked through the assignments. Mike and I were still friends, but he no longer offered dates for me, and it was what I preferred. Footsteps were coming toward me, light, soft ones. Not many came down here in what we call The Stacks, a smelly area of old books spotted with little serious study caves. In my first semester, I learned to stay out of the dorm when I needed to do some hard mental work. Too much noise and too many distractions. The footsteps stopped, which got my attention, and I leaned out and looked both ways and saw her. As soon as she recognized my face, she headed right for me making it apparent that I was whom she was looking for.

"Hi," Julie said, standing beside my desk, her topcoat over one arm. "Mind if I sit?" she murmured. It was like someone asked me, "Mind if you win the lottery?" There was only the one bench, just wide enough for one large or two slender people. Tight quarters. I struggled to my feet, picking my bag off of the bench.

"Please," I said, indicating the free bench. She slipped in toward the rear, and I perched on the end to keep away from body contact. My pulse went up considerably, but for some reason, I didn't seem afraid of her. Perhaps the intensity was diminished by the delay in our meeting. She piled her coat on top of the table and turned to study me at close range.

"Is this a chance meeting or did you know I was here?" I asked.

"I came to talk with you. Isn't that what you wanted?" she responded.

"It sure is. Hi, my name is Rick," I said smiling and offered her my hand.

"Hi, Rick. My name is Julie." We shook lightly, me with a broad smile, her with a straight face. I waited for her to talk, to break the ice or to give me a clue of why she sought me out, noticing right away that there was no green scarf tonight. She seemed to be waiting on me so I spoke first.

"Julie, have you had supper yet?" I asked. It was 9:00 p.m., but you never know.

"Yes, as I'm sure you have." True, but I was finding this awkward. Delightful but still awkward.

"I have been wanting to talk to you since the first time you came to class." I said.

"I know."

She was here with me, sought me out, but still she was a mystery in almost every way. There is nothing that can take the place of simple truth, and I decided to use a dose of it in this little private booth.

"Can I admit to you that you intimidate me, and that is the reason that I haven't tried to talk to you previously?" I asked, again the smile.

"Why?" she wondered. There was no mirth in her eyes. They were breathtaking but blank, as if she were a perfect robot in human form.

I sighed deeply, hating to admit my weaknesses, especially to her. "You are so beautiful that it makes me feel inferior. It's the fear of your rejection, I assume."

"Don't be silly. I'm not any more perfect that you are. You are just enamored, and you forget your own attractiveness."

"Surely you have been told over and over how special you are, Julie. You know the appeal you must have to men."

"Yes, I've been told. You don't know how hard it is living up to that kind of expectation. Because a person fits some other's idea of beauty, it doesn't mean that she feels that way also. I don't like to be singled out because men find me attractive. I'm a real person just like you. Can you accept this?"

"You will certainly find me accepting," I said. "Was there a reason that you are here tonight?"

"Yes. I came to talk to you, to find out if you are someone that I want to be friends with."

"This is a nice place to talk, but we could go out for a snack or a Coke if you want." I offered.

"No, here is just fine. I also want to thank you for the scarf. You went to a lot of trouble for that. I didn't say anything until now, because I wanted to be sure that you meant it as a gift with no strings. It's obvious by now that you did." I didn't respond because I actually, sort of, in fact really did, mean it as a bribe to get her to at least try me out. It worked, but I couldn't say it to her. Her version was better than mine.

"Are we ever going to go out together? You know…dining, dancing, riotous fun, movies. Things people do together?"

"I've never done much of it with someone, so I'm not sure what I want." she said.

"Can I ask why a girl who is so attractive never dated much?"

"Much? More exactly, not at all," she corrected. "There is a small issue with my father. He doesn't want boys in my life. He can be a problem."

"He isn't around here, though. Can't you do what you want now?" I asked.

"You should be warned that he keeps an eye on me. He might already know about you, and if he does, you will have a shock coming."

"I am prepared to do anything it takes to be around you." I said, meaning it.

"No, you are not. You don't know what you are saying," she said, shaking her head for emphasis.

The Marines. They were going to dismember me. She was right, I didn't realize what I was getting into.

We strolled together, passing under yellow sidewalk lights, taking our time chatting about nothing. Turns out that Julie intended to become a biology teacher, and we were destined to take more courses together over the next five semesters. She was wearing the intoxicating perfume that I mentioned previously, and when it wafted into my nose, it stuck there becoming a permanent and pleasant memory. We didn't hold hands, and I kept my arm to myself, even though I was aching to touch her in some way. She was slightly tentative when she asked if I was attached or had been previously attached. I assured her that my past was nearly as unencumbered as hers. It was true in that I had formed no serious relationship with a girl, but I had dated a number of them, a fact that I avoided mentioning. She asked if I spoke any language other than English, and I had to confess that wasn't exactly a strong point in my résumé. Julie, on the other hand, is fluent in several because of her father's posting abroad. German, Polish, Italian, French are close to being mother tongues, and she knows enough of others to get by. It was enough to make me feel inferior again, and for a moment, it clammed me up. I searched my history for something I did, or learned, of which I could boast or at least point to. Ordinary, I was only ordinary, plain brown paper-wrapped ordinary. The most exciting thing I had ever done was to see the Grand Canyon from the rim…once. My father was a tradesman, and my mother a homemaker. I had no brothers or sisters to be proud of and for that matter, no distant relatives either. At least we had that in common. Julie was also an only child. She was talkative, bright and very well-informed on any subject we touched, a delightful companion. She wore her hair down in a long swaying ponytail, by itself mesmerizing, but it was the way she walked, the sure-footedness of a dancer, that caught my attention.

Our path was straightforward, taking us past closed shops and down the practically deserted sidewalk which sparkled from small flakes of quartzite that long ago some city architect had specified. The late October night was mostly still, but the occasional brown leaf crunched under foot as a puff of cool air rattled others collecting in the gutters.

We crossed a small side street about halfway back to her dorm, and I looked quickly over my shoulder to avoid any turning cars when I saw something that made me look again. A half block back behind us was a man walking in the same direction and speed as we were. Not surprising in a college town, but there was something different that caught my eye. He was unusually broad shouldered, as if a plank was under his jacket, and he walked with the ease of an athlete, using firm bouncy steps. He was looking at us, and for some reason, I got an odd feeling. I glanced at the other side of the street and keeping pace was a similar man, also looking our way. I wanted to tell Julie that we were being followed, but I hesitated, remembering what she had said about her father finding out about me. Were they stalking us or protecting her? If they had wanted to harm us, they already had plenty of chances, so I had to assume that she was the object of interest, therefore I was likely the prey. I had never been in a dangerous situation previously, and I had absolutely no training or experience to guide me. Unconsciously, I accelerated our pace as I looked for a place still busy with people. Julie didn't seem aware of what I was thinking so I continued our idle chitchat as if nothing troubled me. We could see her high-rise dorm just ahead, and the couples scattered up and down the street trying to stay together until the last minute of closing curfew. We were safe for now, so I stole a glance behind, surprised to see that both men were gone from view. My imagination again running wild, I thought. We slowly approached the entrance to the women's dormitory, both of us seemingly reluctant to part. Julie turned toward me, close enough to feel her presence and close enough to search her face with my eyes.

"Thanks, Rick, for walking me back," she said. I perceived that she wanted to touch me in some way, and I silently willed that she do so. But she didn't, and I dared not touch her. This was a special relationship that would be built on trust and would take a long time to nurture. I was ready to be patient and was thankful of just being able to actually talk with her and be at her side.

"Can we set a date or time to see each other again?" I asked, trying not to seem overanxious.

"We'll see each other in class tomorrow," she responded. Was it avoidance or humor? I wasn't sure.

"Then tonight I'll think about where I would like to take you when you do accept my offer. Tomorrow, Julie," I said, wanting to at least peck her on the cheek. She suddenly stuck out her hand for a handshake, and I accepted it. Her hand was small, delicate and a bit cool from the evening air, but it was skin to skin contact, and I didn't want to let it go. If eyes can speak, mine screamed that I was captured by her, loved her, and would love her for eternity. Her's were blank, beautiful, but blank. She withdrew her hand, and I let it slide out of mine, prolonging the contact.

"Well, goodnight then," she said and turned toward the big bronze door. I stood and watched, taking in every motion of her body, every sway of her long hair. She glanced at me through the wire mesh window just before she disappeared from view. So close and yet… She was like the wild bird that you want to land in your hand just so you can have a close up view. You don't want to capture it, depriving it of it's freedom. You desire to be near for a moment, to have a wild beautiful creature of nature make contact with you, one on one, equals in life. The brief moments that she and I were together made me long for more.

After getting off the dingy elevator, I turned the corner toward my room, glancing at my watch. Late. Howard had probably turned in long ago, and I would likely wake him by entering. I had been lucky to draw Howard as a roommate. He was very clean and very studious, setting a good example for me. However, he was, perhaps, a bit on the neurotic side, but so much better than the slob I shared a room with the first year. Occasionally, I became angry at Howard when I attempted to sleep while he studied, discovering that his absolute worse habit was pencil sharpening. Sounds innocuous, doesn't it? Not at 2 a.m. when he is attempting to sharpen all his pencils to exactly the same length for whatever reason his compulsion dictated. Usually, I could get past it, but my anger management was as poor as his control of being compulsive. On occasion we clashed, and there were a couple of times that Howard slept downstairs on the lounge couch. I saw the light under the door and was relieved. Howard was still up and studying.

Clearly, there was something amiss because of the way Howard looked at me through his thick glasses when I entered. He was behind his desk, but even from the door I could see the uncharacteristically disorganized scatter on his desktop.

"What's wrong?" I asked.

"Plenty," he said, looking more frightened than angry. I waited for the rest as I took my coat and flung it on the bed. My side was disorganized also, and my footlocker was ajar. Something had happened in this room since I left.

"Tell me, Howard."

"Just after you left for the library, there was a loud knock on the door. It opened before I answered, and two really big guys came in and pushed me aside. Both were as big as football players but weren't fat like most of them. One pointed to my bed, and I got on it and sat there while they searched the room. They went through everything, every paper, every drawer, without saying a word. I asked what they wanted and why they were here, but they ignored me. Just as suddenly, they left. Do you know what they wanted?"

"They wanted to find out about me, I think. Did they take anything with them?"

"Not that I saw, but they could have put something in their pockets. Why did they want to find out about you?"

"I'm not sure about anything, Howard. Did you report this to the monitors?"

"No. I was afraid that they would come back. I wanted to talk to you first. Could they be cops?"

"Not cops. Cops would have said who they were and shown a badge. I think I saw them on the street. Big guys, hard looking?"

"That's them. Will they come back?" Howard asked, hoping my answer was no.

"My guess is that they were checking me out because of my interest in a certain girl. Her father has a history of antagonism toward any suitors. I don't think…I know…that they didn't find anything bad about me. How could they?" I was asking myself that question, but the answer was still they couldn't. There wasn't anything to find, even I couldn't find anything negative about me.

Clearly, I had unleashed forces of unknown intentions by my interest in Julie. She did warn me, however, and she said that I was in for a shock. By now, her protectors must realize that I am harmless, and surely any father would want his daughter to be happy. I reasoned that I was past the worst of it now that they knew more about me. Boy, was I wrong.

The Green Scarf

Chapter 7

At last

I didn't sleep well that night for several reasons. Part of me remained alert to the possibility that big men would burst into the room, snatching me away for mistreatment of some sort. The other part of me was still fantasizing about Julie. For either reason, I woke up drained. I looked cautiously out our window toward the large patio area expecting to see two lurking shapes in the shadows, but it was empty, to my relief. After wolfing down a quick breakfast at the little coffee shop in the basement of the dorm, I headed out toward the classrooms, a brief walk. It was comforting to be among my schoolmates, the first time I had really appreciated being with them. The color, noise and random patterns of student life were never more apparent and wonderful than this morning. I was going to see Julie again in less than an hour, and there was spring in my step, joy in my heart. This was the first morning I had awakened with more than a glimmer of hope for a relationship with her. It was a strong possibility, I believed. I just had to give her enough space and the right kind of attention. Being early for class, I chose an unoccupied bench and sat down, prepared to study. Instead, my thoughts came back instantly to Julie. I was on the verge of understanding the whole picture, and it was hovering out there just out of reach. Julie's behavior, the aloofness, the hesitancy to engage me, could be because she didn't want to reach out to someone and be cut off again as likely had happened previously. Or she could be trying to protect me, not wanting to make me another target for her overzealous father. It was too late. I wanted a relationship with her, and I felt that deep down, she wanted it also. Maybe this time, they would let it happen.

"Excuse me," the lady said, leaning toward me. "Are you Rick James?" I looked up to see her standing there, and I seemed to recall her from the Administration Office.

"Yes, that's me," I said and stood. She had a paper in her hand that obviously had something to do with me.

"We have a request for your grade transcript from the USMC. I need your signature to send it out. May I ask if you are joining the service and leaving school? After all, you are one of our best students."

"No. I don't intend on leaving school," I said and took the form from her, looking it over. It was a simple request for grades, like a graduate school would request, or another college. I shrugged and signed it. No harm. Let them see that I'm a good student. The lady from administration thanked me and left, leaving me to my thoughts. What's next…my physical measurements, I wondered? This was getting out of control. How dare they…or he…push into my life like this. It made me angry, but I was careful to separate Julie from my feelings about her father and his methods. It wasn't her fault. She was more victimized than I, at least so far.

I sat there in a deepening funk, so different than only moments ago. Moods can change fast, especially mine. Then I saw her coming, winding her way through the gathering throngs of students waiting for the bell, green shining from her neck like a spotlight. She has a way of walking, her hips swaying in a restrained manner so like her whole personality, that sets her apart from the other girls, at least in my mind. She had her eyes fixed on me, and I prayed that I would see at least a suggestion of a smile, the first I would have ever seen, but there was none. She sat beside me, careful not to touch, continuing to hold my gaze.

"Hi," she said.

"I know you don't want to hear me say it, but you look wonderful this morning," I said, meaning it from the depths of my being. She ignored the compliment. I could feel that she wanted something else.

"Anything happen?" she asked. She knew, of course, that something would happen, eventually.

"We were followed last night, and they also searched my dorm room. I got a request for a transcript from the USMC this morning. Other than that, nothing happened."

"How does it make you feel?" she asked.

"I have nothing to hide from anyone. If it makes them happy to check me out…fine. You are the only one who can chase me away from you."

"There will be more."

"I'll take anything I have to," I said. She was silent, but I could see a slight softening in her eyes. That's what she wanted to hear. I had passed her test, if not her father's.

"Want to eat dinner with me somewhere?" Julie asked.

For a moment, I contemplated doing cartwheels in the hall or just a somersault in place, but instead, I calmly said, "I would love that. Thanks for asking."

"Six all right?" she asked. To me it didn't matter if it was 2 a.m., and she wanted to dine in Moscow, I was ready and willing.

"Pick you up at your dorm. Six o'clock," I confirmed. The bell rang, and the door to our classroom burst open emitting a stream of students glad to be free of the mental gymnastics of class. Our turn. I stood just behind Julie to keep her from being pushed, and we found our chairs. After we were settled in, she turned to look my way. Her eyes said it all. I was someone she wanted to be with, to get to know and perhaps trust with her affection. My eyes would have said gratitude if I had my way but likely only said surprise.

Gibbs bustled in and quickly got to the board, writing formulas which were duplicates of what was in the study chapter. I tried hard not to look at her, I really did, but I couldn't help myself. Her long hair was up again exposing that wonderful neck. For the first time I actually understood what the ancient Roman and Greek sculptors were trying to re-create. The human female form is the standard for beauty. All of our ideas about beauty derive from it and for good reason. There is simply nothing in nature or created by man even close.

Gibbs never even glanced my way. Of course my attention was elsewhere, and I could have missed his look, but he never publicly commented on me, and gratefully, the class finally came to an end. We got up to leave, and when she turned around, I finally saw it. A hint, a small hint, of a smile directed at me, accompanied by a slight sparkle in her eyes. My day was complete, and I was to see her again tonight. What bliss. I remembered that she had another class convening shortly so I didn't try to hold her up but instead watched as she left.

"I saw the look Julie gave you! You are in, my boy!" Mike said and slapped me on the back. "Told you that the scarf was the right move. Was that what she was wearing, the one you bought?" he asked.

"Yes, Mike. Thanks again for the suggestion."

"I have to ask, are you two a couple yet?"

"No, not anything like that. We are still making connections. It's early yet."

"It might take years to make connections with that one, if ever. You should have stuck with Carol. She would be making you happy by now."

"I can't complain, Mike. How you find them I will never know, but that is your style not mine. I want to live through my heart, not my groin. Silly, huh?"

"You got it. Very silly. You will be sorry someday that you didn't sow some wild oats when you had the chance. Life is short. Enjoy, don't suffer."

"Thanks for your concern, Mike. My time will come, and I can't change what I am, no more than you can."

"As long as you are happy, friend, and as long as the Marines don't tear your arms off," he said laughing. If only he knew that it was no longer a joke.

Chapter 8

The Colonel

Five minutes until six, and I was just outside the women's residence, dressed in my best clothes and anxiously waiting for Julie. I saw the appreciative looks from the other girls as they made their way past, some looking back my way for one more glance. As far as I was concerned, none of them even existed. I was waiting for the moment Julie would come out, and in my imagination, she would rush into my waiting arms and kiss me on the mouth. Yes, I knew that it was fantasy, but such a dream! My watch said two minutes after, and I was starting to worry, just as I saw her face emerge. She looked as though she had been crying, and she was wearing an old hooded sweat. I walked toward her, questions racing through my mind.

"I'm sorry, Rick. I can't go out with you tonight," she said, trying to withhold tears. I wanted to pull her out of the doorway and embrace her, tell her that it was all right, that I would understand no matter what the reason. Before I got anything out, I saw that she was looking past me toward the street. I turned to see that a car had pulled to the curb, its back door wide open. The man standing beside it was one that I had seen the previous night, and he was motioning for me to get into the car. I turned back to Julie, but she had withdrawn, and the door was closed.

"Who the hell are you people?" I challenged, approaching the car. My anger had finally boiled over, and I was ready for confrontation.

"We are the ones who can do this easy or hard, your choice. Get in the car," he growled. I could see that the other one was behind the wheel, also glaring at me, his big arm over the passenger seat. I was no match for either of them. Not in my wildest dream. They could actually tear my arms off and likely would enjoy doing it. There was really no choice. If I refused now, they could always grab me somewhere else. Might as well find out what they want, I thought, and I got in as the door slammed behind me.

The car was a plain, black, full-sized model otherwise undistinguished. The kind of car that you can't remember actually seeing. As soon as my keeper got in, it lurched forward and accelerated briskly, turning corners hard enough to squeal the tires.

"Where are you taking me?" I demanded.

"Just shut up, and you'll get there and find out," the driver said. We headed across town to an area that was unfamiliar to me. By the seventh, or was it the tenth turn, I was totally lost. We were in an old factory area, now mostly abandoned and decrepit. A good place for them to murder me and dump my body. The car pulled up to an old garage and stopped. A large metal door slowly opened, creaking and groaning with effort, and our car shot into the open space beyond.

"Out," the first one said firmly, holding the door open for me. The other one got out quickly and was waiting for me. In single file, me in the middle, we went up an old narrow staircase toward my destiny. We stopped in front of a closed door, and I and the one behind me waited while the lead went inside and closed the door. I could hear muffled talking inside, then the door jerked open. The one behind me pushed me in with his fingertips, and I stumbled my way inside. There behind an old metal desk was a middled-aged man with very close-cropped hair which bristled with grey. He was heavily-built but lean with very hard dark eyes which he fixed on me. I noticed that he was crisply dressed in a dark business suit and crimson tie.

"Know who I am?" he asked. The two units behind me assembled, blocking the door.

"I can guess," I answered. "Where are your medals?"

"Smart ass, I see." I didn't respond. He had no idea how far I could go once wound up.

"Want to tell me why I was forced to come here?" I asked

"You weren't forced, you were invited and you came. I wanted a look at you."

"You mean closer than pilfering my room, my grades and following me? So now that I'm standing here, what do you think?"

"Same as before you arrived. You are not good enough for my daughter. You are a nothing."

"Does she get a vote?"

"No. She's young. It's not for you or her to decide. It's for me, and I decided."

"I don't agree. I am good enough for anybody including your daughter. This is America. I could end up President."

"When you become president, call me, and I might change my mind," he said, laughing at the possibility.

"Does it matter that I care for her, I mean, beside the fact that your boys couldn't dig up any dirt on me?"

"If we want, we can always put dirt on you. I don't need your smart lip. Look around where you are."

I leaned forward to make a point and heard a rustle behind me. The two large units moved forward to within arm's reach, just in case. "You should kill me now because I AM NOT GOING TO STOP SEEING HER," I shouted.

"Tough guy, huh?" he said and sat back giving me a new

appraisal. "Attitude like that and you are not in the Corps?"

"Army," I said. "I will enlist in the Army when I get close to medical school so that they can pay for it. It's the only way I can afford to go to school."

He didn't say a word, but continued to look me in the eye. What I said had made a difference, and I suspected that I no longer had to fear what they might do to me.

"Get out of here, kid. If you know what's good for you, you will leave Julie alone."

"One more thing I want to clear up first," I said, shaking loose the hands that had grabbed my arms from behind. He glared at me, indignant that I would presume to take charge of his interrogation. He waited for me to continue.

"Did you murder your wife?" I asked. If there was a question designed to bring the house down on me, it was that one. He stood up, his face turning red. The big hands grabbed me again, practically lifting me from the floor.

"Where did you hear that?" he asked with anger so intense that his lip trembled.

"One of my classmates is from your hometown. He told me that your wife died under suspicious circumstances years ago. Your arrogance today makes me believe that it is possible that you had a hand in it." Literally, his eyes bulged out at me. I had struck a big nerve, a geyser, the main trunk. He walked around the desk to face me. He was taller and heaver than me but with a waist probably smaller. I wouldn't be surprised to see him score a hundred push-ups using only one hand. To say I felt vulnerable would be an understatement. Any one of these big men could drive me through the wooden floor if they chose to, and I may have given them reason to do so.

"No, kid, I didn't kill her. She was my entire life, she and Julie. A damned terrorist killed her because of something I had done in the service of OUR country. That's why it was hushed up, to keep the bad guys from knowing that we were on to them. I killed three of them later with my own hands. That is why I protect Julie. I can't bear the thought of something foul in her life or something bad happening to her." When he finished, his tone was subdued, and the big hands put me back on my feet. I felt stupid for accusing him of this horrible crime, but it did clear the issue in my mind.

"There is agreement between us that we both want her to have happiness, and she deserves all we can give her. Although it's obvious you love her, it is also true that you are snuffing the joy out of her. She never smiles, she is suspicious of people, and she never gets out. No one will ever treat her with more respect than I will. This I promise. I propose that if you ever find that I have mistreated her or made her unhappy, then you can deny me access, and I will comply without complaint. Other than that, I intend to pursue her while keeping in mind that her needs come before mine."

The tension was broken, and her father softened, leaning back and sitting on the edge of his desk, while looking intently at me for any hint that I wasn't sincere. "The truth is, kid, we couldn't find a single thing to hold against you."

"Colonel Frank," I started, "Let's start over. My name is Rick James, and I'm glad to meet you." I offered my hand, and he took it in his massive paw.

"You are OK, James. I like tough guys and you qualify. Of course, a stint in the Corps would really put you in shape."

"Well, I'll have to find out if they will do the deal for medical school, and if they do, I'm in." I got a fierce slap on the back from one of the bricks standing behind me. If they hit that hard when they like you, I don't want to ever get on the wrong side. "Could you ask these gents to take me back to the women's residence so I can take your daughter out like I planned?" I asked.

"Take him back, boys. James, you should know that you are still under supervision. Don't screw this up."

"Yes, sir. I won't let you down. Count on it." We shook one last time but avoided the manly hug which I thought would be next.

On the drive back, the boys were talkative and friendly. Both were active duty sergeants, one named Jurkowitz, aptly called Jerk, the other Graham, or Grey. No first names in the Corps. They adamantly refused to discuss their current duties; likely, I wouldn't have understood anyway so I let it drop. They stopped right where they had picked me up, and Jerk held my door for me and shook my hand. Both waved and smiled as they drove off. Now, getting Julie to like me as much as her father did might not be as easy.

Chapter 9

First date

$\mathcal{I}$ pushed the button marked 'Talk' and waited. The voice that answered was that of an older woman. One who might have had her fill of boys pursuing 'her' girls.

"Yes?" she said, the sound coming over tinny and harsh.

"Hi. My name is Rick James. I have a date with Julie Frank. Could you let her know that I'm here?"

"What?" the voice asked, somewhat irritated. I patiently repeated my request, and for a long time, there was no answer. Had she heard me or had she refused my request? I pressed the button again.

"Yes?" the same voice asked.

"Hi, this is Rick James again. Did you pass my request along?"

"Who?" again the tinny voice. I felt like bashing my head into the glass door.

"Rick James. I'm waiting for Julie Frank."

"I know you are, Mister James," the voice said, more shrilly. This time I did knock my head into the glass, three times.

One last try, I decided, "Did you give her my message?"

"Who?"

"Miss Frank. Did you tell her I am waiting?" No answer. I glanced up at the wall above me wondering if it could be scaled. I could just tap on a window somewhere above and ask one of the girls to find her. The so-called direct approach. I backed up and seriously considered throwing rocks at the windows to attract attention. I was getting desperate when the bronze door opened a crack, and I saw her face. Julie.

"Hi. I'm sorry Rick. I can't see you tonight. Thought you understood."

"Julie, I have met with your father and worked it out. We are buddies. He approves of me. You can go out tonight, and you can be with me. Please?"

"You're not kidding?" she asked, eyes widening.

"No kidding. I'm on the 'A' list with him and his two big sergeants. Can we do something together?"

"Come here," she said, and of course, I did. She leaned out and kissed me on the lips, then smiled. "I'll be right out. Don't leave." Was she kidding? I wouldn't leave if an astroid was due to hit this very spot.

The twenty or so minutes it took for Julie to change went by quickly, because I was still stunned by her kiss on my lips. I don't think my feet were actually touching the pavement, nor was the concrete step I sat on cold and hard. Dinner time had passed, and I was hungry…very hungry…and I hoped that she had not eaten. No snack bars for this date, it had to be real, nice, expensive. That was the part that gave me unease. I was paying my way through college, and my funds were very limited. Now I had the opportunity to take out the most lovely woman in the universe, but what was I going to use for money? It was obvious that nights like this one only come once in a lifetime, and this was no time to fret over details.

At last, she came out of the bronze door, and one glance told me that she was a different person. Her smile was radiant, her mood joyous, and she moved toward me seemingly on her toes, her arms extended toward me. Before I could prepare myself, she wrapped her long arms around me and drew my face to hers, and we kissed the kiss that will last my lifetime and beyond. This kiss goes in the books as one of the great kisses of all time, one to be treasured, copied and studied by scholars. It went from my lips, twirled around in my head, passed through my various organ systems down to my toes which pushed my body slowly in the air as I struggled to absorb all the sensations from touching her in so many places at the same time. She pulled away just enough to allow me to breathe, and those blue eyes were close enough to feel her eyelashes brush mine. The scent of her, her lipstick, her French perfume, and in general, everything about her, mixed and swirled in that part of my brain that never forgets. I almost didn't realize that my hands were on her buttocks, but she didn't seem to notice either.

"Where are we going?" she said in her, previously unheard, bubbly fashion. The answer was clearly that it really didn't matter, as long as I had proximity to her. A cave, igloo, or the top of the Eiffel Tower were all the same to me and would disappear behind her face in a blur like an out-of-focus picture.

"Have you had dinner?" I asked, trying to regain some balance.

"Yes, sorry. Have you?"

"Don't worry about me," I said bravely. There is a little place within walking distance that serves snacks and has a dance floor. Interested?"

"Oh, dancing! I love to dance!" she said and kissed me lightly once more on the lips. Every part of my body was tingling, and I wanted to lean forward for more, but I resisted, trying very hard to show restraint. You know what they say about potato chips—you can't eat just one. I tried to focus my brain on the location of the place I mentioned. Having never actually been there previously didn't help, and I sort of recalled that the music was themed from the '30s. The jitterbug era. Now, I must tell you that I took dance lessons in my youth, so I can usually do well enough to pass, but jitterbug was different. I started to have reservations, even before we got there.

We took off, arm in arm, our heads occasionally touching as we talked in low sweetheart voices, the outside world spinning by unnoticed. Just think, yesterday, I couldn't touch her, and tonight our hips are bumping together as if we had always been close. To say I was in heaven would understate how I felt. It was what I would have dreamed of, if I had enough imagination.

The music brought us to a halt. We had arrived, and jazz was thumping through the door. I looked at the marquee to be sure, Harold's Jazz Scene it read. We entered onto a well-worn wood floor and into a room transported from the past. The place consisted of one large rectangular room with tables scattered around an oval area which was currently engaged by four marvelous couples demonstrating the dancing skills of yesteryear. I could smell frying meat and grease dripping from fries. The only thing missing was white sailor suits with flared pants and little white cocked hats. One of the waitresses pointed to an empty table and we sat down, as close as possible to each other, while we took in the sights. There was a small live jazz band on an elevated stage playing to the rhythm tapped out by a smiling drummer. The mood was infectious, and the rhythms got into our system, and soon we were moving and swaying to the music. I studied the art of the couples brave enough to get on the floor. It would take months or years to perfect those moves, some were even dangerous. I saw that it might be possible to retain some of the style and still have fun.

"Ever dance like that?" I asked Julie. It was necessary to ask her first, because I didn't want to answer the question myself.

Unfortunately, she said, "Sure, just not with a boy. You?"

"I can manage if you don't expect too much."

"You'll learn. Ready now?" she asked. The noise of the crowd coming to their feet in applause caused us to turn back to watch the climax. The question should have been, was I ready to be laughed off the dance floor. The waitress saved me.

"OK, kids. That'll be forty, cover charge. Any drinks or food to go with it?" She was lean and had a large nose. Kind of a gritty look, appropriate to the surroundings. 'Ruth' was stitched onto her uniform.

"Want some food?" I asked Julie.

"Just some fries and a Coke," she said.

"No Cokes, dear. Only beer in this joint," Ruth said.

"Very well, beer then," Julie said.

"Can I get a burger with my beer?" I asked. Ruth didn't answer, just rolled her eyes and disappeared. I dug around in my wallet and found three twenties and put them under my glass hoping that would be enough. There was a lull in the music, and we saw the band standing up and stretching. Our food and drinks slowly came, and it turned out that I was short another four dollars. My wallet was nearly empty.

I looked at the beer in front of Julie and had a bad feeling about it. "Have you ever had a beer before or even any alcoholic drink?"

"No. But I'm looking forward to it," she smiled. This and I promised her father a solemn oath that I was going to look after her.

"I sort of promised your dad that I would protect you from the world and especially from me. I'm not sure I want you to drink that beer.".

She smiled an impish little smile and took a long swallow of her beer, the foam remaining on her upper lip. "Ready to dance?" she asked and pointed with her thumb toward the musicians who were picking up their instruments. This was one of my penny for pound moments, so I got up and extended my hand. She rose easily, weightlessly, and gave me a wink. The music started, and we commenced to move with it. At first, we were the only dancers, but our restraint convinced other teams to venture out on the floor, and before the number was over, we were bumping shoulders with them. Seeing Julie's face was worth every bit of effort I was putting into it. Coming past me, she allowed her face to pass closer and closer to mine knowing what effect it would have. Dancing with a woman allows contact during motion that almost no other activity outside of the bedroom does. A societal freebie that highlights the difference in the sexes and stimulates romantic interest, as it was doing for me. As far as we were concerned, the dancing could last all night, and it nearly did. At the end of the last number, Julie threw her arms around me and kissed me with passion.

"Thank you, Rick. I have never had a better evening. You persisted, and you won. I'm yours from now on. Anything, anytime."

"Wait a minute, Julie," I stammered. "That's over the top. Too much too soon. Please allow me to win you over, step by step, pleading with you, begging you, earning your affection one day at a time. I want to feel that I'm worthy of you and that you love me, because you know me like the back of your hand."

"Don't worry that I'm going to be cheap or easy to get. I expect you to take me out every night, spend time and money on me and keep looking at me as if I were your dream."

"And study?" I asked, including the second most important reason we were both in school.

"That's right, forget study. I have a strong desire to experience life, and now that I am yours, you are going to show it to me. You are willing, aren't you?" She touched my nose with her delicate finger for emphasis. It was as if a distinguished committee asks if you want to become president of the U.S. Such an honor, but at the same time, such responsibility. You might hesitate, knowing a little of what you are getting into. I didn't, hesitate, that is.

"Of course, Julie. I am so honored, truly honored, to be able to be close to you. Anything I have or can do for you is yours." Perhaps it was a little thick, but it was how I actually felt. My dream girl of all girls, and she just said that she was mine. Beautiful, vivacious, delicate, smart Julie was mine.

I glanced at my watch. Two hours past curfew for her dorm. My pulse started racing. The very first night, and I had grabbed her buttocks, fed her alcohol and kept her out too late. Not to mention all the vigorous kissing we had done. Grey and Jerk may yet pull my arms off and beat me with them. What had I done?

"We better get back, Julie. It's late," I reminded her. Her face said plainly that she didn't care at all, and she wasn't ready for the evening to end. Disappointment from her I couldn't stand, and I searched my brain for alternatives. There were none. This was a college town, not New York, and the place was dead after midnight, and it was well after midnight. "No choice, Julie, we have to start back. Have you figured out a plan for getting back in the dorm?"

"I don't….can't we just spend the night together?" she said with her head pitched down and her lower lip in a slight pout. I almost fell off my chair.

"No, we can't. Remember Father? He is likely watching every move we make, and he is probably all ready angry about how your first outing went. Want to get me killed this fast?" I heard myself talking a beautiful girl out of spending the night with me. Our two-parted brains, especially male ones, are separated into thoughtful, cerebral portions and the animal limbic system. My limbic system was running around the room panting and rolling its eyes at me, as my cortex was trying to pull on its leash.

The Green Scarf

Chapter 10

Induction

*W*e walked close together, her head on my shoulder, over the sparkling sidewalk and under the sparse street lights which gave their warm yellow blessing to us. I put my arm around her waist, and she did the same to me. It was like I had known her from childhood, knew her moods, her secrets, her desires. Her voice was already part of me, soothing and melodious. Her head was just the right height to rest my cheek against and so we walked toward her dorm and toward problems we didn't want to think about. We passed dark shadows, hidden chambers, alleys and doorways, and there was only the occasional car, illuminating the dark for a brief moment. During one such instant, I saw a flicker of movement which gave me a small start. There was a man watching us from an alley, and he moved toward us as we passed. I turned my head and watched a shadow, a silhouette, move out onto the sidewalk behind us. Trouble. No cops, no other people in sight, and we still had five blocks to go.

"Don't turn but there is a man following us," I whispered.

"Oh, that's probably one of Dad's men. Don't worry, he won't hurt us," she said, unconcerned.

"Not this one. He's too small to be one of your dad's. More like a vagrant, a street person." I listened and could hear the soft footfall behind us. He was keeping pace. Another twist of my head for a quick glance. Only twenty feet, but he was in deep shadow, the light behind him, and I couldn't get a good look.

"Let's walk a little faster," I suggested. I heard the footsteps behind us pick up pace, again matching ours. The idea of confrontation didn't bother me, I can handle myself, but Julie was with me. She is more precious than anything, and she was my responsibility. Already I was figuring where and how hard I was going to strike the man when the moment came. Surprise, aggression and the will to win are always better than passivity. I decided to wait for a threatening move from him, then explode with force. Just as I prepared to turn and start the seemingly inevitable process, I heard a grunt, like air escaping, then silence. I turned toward the noise, and the street was empty, the man was gone. We stopped and waited, both looking back the way we had come. The shadow was gone, evaporated, as if I had imagined a threat, not seen one. Our romantic moment had also evaporated, and we walked the remaining blocks with some determination but at least without a pursuer closing in on us.

I stood with my hands in my coat while Julie pushed the button by the bronze doors. It took several tries but at last the voice came on. "Yes?" it croaked.

"This is Julie Frank. Let me in please."

There was a delay, which by now, I expected. "What is your room number, Frank?" the voice asked.

"223."

There was another long silence then a loud buzz, and the lock snapped open.

"Ten demerits, Frank," the voice noted without emotion.

Julie opened the door far enough to place one foot in, blocking it, and extended her free arm toward me. I quickly moved into her arm and felt her warm breath on my face.

"This was the best night of my life, Rick. Thank you from the bottom of my heart." She lifted her face, and I found her lips for one last goodnight kiss, the kind that makes you unable to sleep the rest of the night. Then she was gone, and I was standing alone on the steps, feeling that something was missing, some part of my body had been stolen from me.

A car skidded to a stop not ten feet from where I stood and the back door swung open. "Get in," a voice commanded. Friends no longer, it seemed.

We did the eight, or was it ten, tight, screaming turns toward our warehouse destination. The two in the front weren't in a talking mood. I had screwed up, big time. "Out!" Grey commanded when the car came to rest. They didn't hold the door open this time. Putting some spring in my step, I went up the stairs, two at a time in front of them, wanting to get it over with so I could get back to bed. Opening the door myself, I entered before Jerk could push me in. This time Colonel Frank was dressed in his uniform, full of braid and medals, pacing the floor in front of the desk. He didn't look pleased to see me again.

"We had a deal, James. You didn't live up to your end of it. What the hell do you think you are doing? I don't remember giving permission for you to go hog-wild with my daughter, your dirty paws and mouth all over her like a disease!" I noticed that the two big units behind me had closed the door and were standing within reach. Colonel Frank stopped pacing and came toward me, putting his face two inches from mine as he finished his speech with punctuation. "Do you read me, kid? Am I clear enough?" The spittle seemed to accumulate just under my eyes, making me want to wipe my face, a move I dared not make.

"Sir, please. May I explain?"

"There is no explanation, James. You disobeyed an order. If you were in my command, I would make you eat two pounds of dirt." If I needed to give any thanks to Heaven, it was that I wasn't under his command, at least not in the military sense.

"Sir, Colonel Frank, if you or your men were watching us, you would have seen that I never once made a move. It was all Julie. She has been so pent-up, she is exploding. I tried to restrain her all night. I even refused…I promise I refused…her offer to spend the night with her. I even tried to get her not to drink the beer. I did the best I could, sir. She is happy, and I showed restraint. I did what you would have done, sir."

"Is this true, Jurkowitz?" he asked the large shape behind me.

"It did seem that your daughter, forgive me sir, was the aggressor. He may be telling the truth.

"You still kissed her…on the lips!" He could have added a nice adjective like 'rodent' or 'cockroach', but he didn't, and I was somewhat grateful about it.

"Could I have refused, sir? Her feelings you know. I had to respect her feelings. How could I refuse her? It's not like I asked her to do it. Not once, sir. I didn't ask for a kiss even once." I was doing pretty well defending myself, and I could see the furor dissipating, though he had resumed pacing.

"If the night was a little longer, you would have been in bed together. What the hell are your plans for her at this moment? Can you answer that for me?" he asked, watching my face for any tics. A lie right now would prove to be painful for me.

"Honestly, sir, I have only her happiness and well-being as my first desire. There is a problem, though. She wants to be entertained, wined and dined, as they say. I can't afford your daughter, sir. I just don't have enough money to do what she wants. I hope that I don't lose her because of it. We can't blame her a bit to want what others have had, but I don't think I can do it." The truth hurts sometimes. I had hold of something that I couldn't have anticipated. A tiger by the tail. I was more fearful of disappointing Julie than angering her father.

"There is the other thing, Colonel," Grey said from behind me as a reminder of something.

"Oh yes, James," The Colonel said, remembering. "Were you aware that you were about to be mugged a while ago?"

"Yes, sir. I was preparing to defend us, and the fellow disappeared. I assume that these guys took care of him for me."

"Yes, we did. It takes six weeks for a bone fracture to heal. Longer for two. You won't meet him again until next summer," Grey laughed.

"Thanks, Grey," I said over my shoulder.

"If you were as fit and as well-trained at they are, you wouldn't need their help. They can't always be expected to bail your skinny ass out of harm's way," the Colonel said.

"Yes, sir. I expect that's true," I admitted.

"Well, I have a solution, James. You are going to get that training you need starting tomorrow. We can't take any chances with my daughter, you understand."

"Am I to join the Marines, sir?" I asked.

"You should, but we will be forced to take stop-gap measures for the time being. You are to meet these two promptly at 0600 hours for training. That means four hours from now. Understood? By the way, the training will continue until I decide that you have the skill and muscle to adequately protect Julie."

I groaned, squeezing my tired eyes shut. I was going to be a Marine, at least a junior version. "Understood and will comply, sir." I really wanted to salute but figured that it would be sloppy by his standards.

"That will be all, James. This will serve to remind you that I am keeping an eye on you. Screw up and the brick wall will fall on you. Dismissed."

They drove me back describing the training regimen that they had worked out for me. We would start with what they called wind sprints, which sounded exotic but difficult. When the car stopped and I got out, I realized that, once again, they had deposited me right in front of the women's dorm. I had to walk the mile back to my own, thinking of doing wind sprints in three hours. Life is a bitch at times.

Chapter 11

Dean's office

The loudspeaker could be heard above the class bell and the commotion and clamor of the rushing students. "Rick James…Rick James…Report to the Dean's Office." The message was repeated three times, and each time more eyes searched me for any sign of danger or disease. I knew it was coming. Life couldn't continue at the present pace without some consequences. Perhaps I do have a disease and its name is Julie…and her father. In the last two weeks I have been near constant exhaustion because of rigorous dawn training with two big brutish Marines. My evenings are spent entertaining Julie…a task hardly tiring…but it has become expensive. After getting back to my dorm, I mean to study, but the intensity of my time with Julie exhausts my energy reserves, and I usually fall into bed.

There never was a better example of gentlemanly behavior than how I treat Julie, and it's not because I am afraid of her watchful father. Not at all. I not only love her, but I revere her. Last week, I finally got up the nerve to actually tell her that I love her, not that I have heard the same words from her. She enjoys my company, and she is very free with her kisses, so I have really nothing to complain about. Thinking about her all the time as I do, I can't help wondering if she loves me in return, but regretfully, I have come to the conclusion that she doesn't and presently I wonder if she ever will.

The door was marked "Dean of Student Affairs", and I paused for a moment thinking that the letters referenced my kind of affair. Perhaps this was the right office to be called to, and I opened the door, looking forward to some adult supervision.

Dean Stewart was at her desk, looking at me over her half-glasses with something other than encouragement and respect.

"Rick James, Dean," I said, "You requested me to report." As I spoke, I was aware of the futility of supplication. The Dean was going to kick my ass, and I deserved it.

She held up a small stack of papers and waved them at me as if my face were full of pesky insects. "Know what these are?" she asked and then didn't wait for me to say the obvious. "They are reports about you. None are favorable. You have fallen asleep in class, even snoring on several occasions. Your test scores are down, your work is late or missing. You look disheveled, unkempt. It is the picture of someone about to fail out of school. You! One of our best students, and you are about to be kicked out of college. In my long experience there are only a few reasons students start this kind of downhill slide. Drugs, partying or illness. Which is it, Mr. James?"

"None of those, Dean," I said. "Love…that's the truth."

"Miss Frank, she the one?"

"Yes, Dean, she's the one."

"So I've heard. Her grades are fine, by the way, and she doesn't fall asleep in class. You're different. Any explanations?"

"I have been training in the mornings with two personal trainers who leave me in a state of exhaustion before my day really starts. But there are no excuses, Dean. It's all my fault. I got what I thought I wanted, and now it's destroying me."

Dean Stewart didn't look up from her papers for awhile, obviously thinking about my predicament. "Mr. James," she started, "I see that you were headed toward medical school. Is that still what you intend?"

"Yes, Dean."

"You'll never make it unless something changes. There are choices in life, Mr. James. This is your chance in life to go in a direction that you choose. I hate to put it this way, but you can always find another girl to court and to love, but if you drop out or are kicked out of school, you'll never get another chance. Your record indicates that you may be marginal in your financial reserves. Has that changed?"

"No, Dean. This affair with Julie Frank has me almost broke. You are right saying that I can't have both…college and Julie. I have proven that to myself as well."

"Will you give her up, Mr. James?"

My brain whirled with the vortex which was my present life, spitting out parts and debris of thoughts as it made its way into the distance. "I love her, Dean. I love Julie. To separate from her would be the same as dying."

She took a deep breath and let it out slowly through her nose, tapping her fingers softly on the polished wood desk top. Reluctantly, it appeared, she leaned back with a squeak from her chair and looked at me for a thoughtful moment before speaking. "Mr. James, can you answer one question honestly?"

I nodded that I could.

"Does Julie Frank love you as you love her?"

That question was one I was ill-prepared to answer, even to myself. I wanted so badly to have Julie love me, and I had devoted everything I had, every hope and care I could muster to that end. Had it been enough to earn love from this beautiful, wonderful girl? Only she knew for sure, but I suspected that while she was willing to give me the outside of her, the inside was held a bit tighter. "I'm not sure, Dean," I admitted.

"You mean she hasn't actually said, 'I love you'?"

"No."

"I shouldn't have to bring this up, Mr. James, but often, in similar circumstances, there is a child conceived which decides everybody's fate for them."

"We have resisted that level of intimacy, Dean. There is no chance of pregnancy," I assured her.

"You are quite a decent young man, Mr. James, and Julie is a very lucky girl to have you in her life. Nevertheless, something has to change. If she loves you, she will understand that you have to prepare for your future together. She should let you back away for a breath, now and then. If not, you are wasting your life on a one-sided dream."

The frank truth is always obvious but having it printed in bold and held out as a banner floating in front of your face helps to bring it into focus. The Dean was right, absolutely right.

"Thank you, Dean, for this talk and your sage advice. I am going to make an effort to come to my senses and get back to my studies. If I don't succeed, it won't be because you didn't try but because of my inability to let Julie go."

"Look, Mr. James," she interrupted, "If your grades go up and the complaints stop, I'll put in a good word for you for a college loan. It might be needed to get you back on track."

I rose to my feet and extended my hand to her. "Thanks again, Dean Stewart. I'll do my best." A resolve to try welled up in me, but could I live without Julie in my life? At that moment, I remembered the last kiss she and I had shared. Her soft lips, the taste of her lipstick and the feel of her body against mine was something I didn't want to be just a memory of what was.

"Hi," I almost whispered into the telephone, picturing her on the other end, her long legs crossed, leaning back, lounge like, against the headboard.

"Hi Rick James," she whispered back. It was one of those times that her voice came into my ear slightly hoarse, a little cracked, low and personal, her voice thrilling, arousing, as if I just woke up, turning over to find her beside me, looking at me with those wonderful eyes.

"Do you mind if I study tonight instead of going on our date? I was called into see Dean Stewart because of sleeping in class and some bad test scores."

"Heard your name over the speakers. Wondered what it was all about," she said languidly. Every utterance she made went through me like a surge of tidewater slipping between black rocks.

"Then would it be OK with you if I didn't see you tonight?"

"I'm feeling adventuresome just now. You'll miss a lot, Rick."

"I already hate myself for it," I said, speaking truthfully, already regretting my decision to not be with her.

"I was looking forward to seeing you all day, Rick. Now this. It's very disappointing for me, but I don't want to force you to see me if you don't want to." Her words left me with the impression that she was forcing me. She was signaling that she was hurt and that I had done something intentionally designed to harm our relationship. I braced myself for the sledgehammer blow which might come next. "You shouldn't feel that you have to harm your career just to make me happy. After all, there are many boys who are anxious to take me out, and I'm sure you won't mind a bit if I go out on rare occasions when you are not able to be with me."

"Julie, I thought that we were a couple now. Couples just don't date around. It would cause a terrible problem for me. Are you serious about seeing other fellows? Truly serious?" The panic was rising, and I was struggling to keep my voice calm. Anger would be sure to follow, and it was the last thing I wanted to happen.

"Rick, of course I don't want to hurt your feelings. You mean a lot to me, but I don't want to be alone just now. You seem to be so understanding with me, so I know it will be clear to you how I feel."

"You remember, don't you, when I said that I love you?"

"Of course."

"Did you think that I meant it?

"Rick, only you would know if you meant it."

"Julie, do you love me?" Yes, it was stupid of me to box her in, asking her a question which could so quickly set me up for agonizing pain. It was a toss of the dice, and it could come up seven or snake eyes.

"Really, Rick, that's too personal for the telephone, don't you think?" Snake eyes or at least a three. She had avoided the answer, not even very neatly. To me, she meant a clear 'No'. Dean Stewart was right again. It was a one-sided love affair.

"Pick you up at the usual time then?" I asked, the cravenly, cowardly part of me taking charge of both the phone and my weak brain.

"Thought you might," she giggled.

Chapter 12

High style

How, exactly, do women learn to use their assets on men? What makes them understand how a curve of flesh or a turn of their head impacts a male brain? Somewhere in their teens the process begins to grow into purposeful activity, specifically designed to cause attraction. No one tells them to do this or that or say this or that, but most of them are well on their way by the end of high school. Julie was an accomplished master. She should be awarded a PhD by a leading university for understanding the full scope of attractiveness. Perhaps a Nobel Prize for outstanding attractiveness.

Then there is the male…me. What is it about our brains that sees women, some especially, as objects of desire? Why do we see almost any of their curves as wonderful, marvelous and sexual? A flutter of her eyes, a turn of her head, her captivating voice. It's a switch of some sort. A hunger switch. When mine flips, it makes hot sparks, and I can almost smell the ozone. I am helpless before it's power and there is no possible way to shut it off.

The dreaded button beside the bronze door awaited me, and I pushed it with reluctance.

"Yes?" it croaked.

I pumped my chest out and almost shouted into the small

speaker, "This is junior Marine James here to consort with one of your princesses, the so-named Julie Frank. If it pleases you, you may inform her of my presence without."

"What?" the voice crackled, irritation coming out with the sound.

"CALL JULIE FRANK AND TELL HER THAT HER SLAVE IS HERE," I said. No response. By long experience I knew not to attempt further conversation with the button and so I waited.

By now, I suspected that a long wait is a key part of a master plan. During the wait, you have time to consider what you are waiting for, something so desirable that not only is the waiting worth it, but necessary, because the she is so much more important than the you. And she was and she is. If I walked through that very same door, not a single person would look twice at me. I would disappear into ordinariness. When Julie came through, there was an opening in the clouds allowing one angled ray to light her up as if it were a grand stage, a vast audience below producing deafening applause and shouts of joy just because of her radiant smile.

"Hi! Waiting long?" she said and pecked me on my cheek, looking up at me with her big eyes, little girl like, innocent, ever intensely beautiful. No, Dean Stewart, I can't do it, I can't stay away from Julie Frank. Perhaps I am destined for a short life, one day bursting into flames, consumed on the spot, but at the same time relieved of responsibilities, struggles and low points. If you seek not only shelter in life but also happiness, then I have arrived at the end point and need go no farther. When I am with Julie, I want nothing else that life offers. She is enough.

"Are you ready for some food?" I asked the by now familiar question.

"I have an interesting spot picked out. Prince's. Ever hear of it?" I had. It was the place the older crowd, the moneyed crowd, went, dressed in extravagant evening wear. High end and expensive. The kind of place they expected you to arrive in your Rolls so the doorman can assist you inside, earning his fabulous tip. My bank account, the sum total of it, wouldn't cover the evenings dessert, or the tip. I swallowed hard and stammered even before I spoke.

"Rick, are you feeling well? You look a bit pale," she said, her smile indicating amusement, not empathy. "I know what you are thinking, and you should stop worrying because this evening isn't going to cost you a cent!"

"How so?"

"Later," she said, dismissing my anxiety with a graceful wave of her hand. She was looking for something or someone, and her head turned back and forth as she looked up and down the street. I saw it as soon as she did. Some sort of telepathy, I'm sure. The glint from a flat windshield above chrome got larger as a big antique car approached the curb in front of us. It crept to an elegant stop emitting a purr, the big motor turning over as smoothly as an electric fan. It was a long, black Rolls Royce, and a man in a grey, fitted uniform jumped out and opened the rear door, brass buttons gleaming from his tunic.

"*Monsieur, mademoiselle, s'il vous plaît*," he stated, showing his perfect teeth and giving a slight bow as he tipped the brim of his cap. A small crowd of students accumulated on the curb looking back and forth between the car and us.

"We better go, Rick," Julie urged, tugging my arm toward the big car. She entered first, and I slid in beside her as the door clicked softly shut. The inside was finished with polished mahogany and soft cordovan leather. Everything seemed new; the smell, the finish, was perfect, flawless. Without any instructions to the chauffeur, the car smoothly lifted away from the curb as the University buildings, the gaping students, slid silently by the windows.

"Julie! What…" She cut me off by placing her finger over my mouth.

"Later," she said and then leaned toward me with puckered lips and closed eyes, her perfume gently entering my consciousness. Either I was dead and in Heaven or I was dreaming. There couldn't be any other explanation, and I voted for my dead version. I accepted her kiss which crackled into my brain as some sort of digestible delight, some food that you can't get enough of.

Prior to arriving at the posh restaurant, I had a moment to assess my and Julie's attire. Before I left my dorm, I had taken care to dress as well as my meager foot-locker of clothes would allow. My best sweater was over my best shirt which was tucked into my best pleated pants which broke over my best black shoes. No tie for me. I realized in panic that I would not even compete with the bus-boys in Prince's regal establishment. Julie was noticeably the better dressed. She was mostly in white with gold accents on her dress, a simple but form fitting number which showed her graceful body just enough to be alluring but decent. A shimmering green scarf around her neck was the perfect accent. She wore her hair long and full, and she occasionally brushed it behind her ear in an absent-minded feminine flourish. Her eyes sparkled with mischief and happiness.

"Julie, I just realized that I will be underdressed. They may even have a dress requirement, you know, coat and tie?"

She reached forward and clicked a small compartment which fell softly open. Her hand disappeared in the recesses for a moment, then she pulled out a small package and laid it in my lap. It was a bow tie, in black, just right for the occasion. "Need help tying it?" she offered, looking coy. I nodded that I did and she began to fuss with my collar. While she worked, she frequently looked up into my eyes, and I noticed the similarity between dressing and undressing. The experience was nearly, but not exactly, the same.

After she pulled the bow straight, she gave me a quick kiss, leaving me longing for more.

"I don't have a jacket. Got one of those in a compartment somewhere?" I asked.

"They will provide one. Not to worry," she answered.

I settled back in the enfolding leather seat and looked her over from a new perspective. Her looks hadn't changed from the first view I ever had of her, but she was different, very different than I thought. Julie was no wallflower, deprived of life's adventures, just waiting on a savior named Rick to open the pages of a better story. There was more to her than I had realized. She was quite at home in this upscale world that had so far avoided my presence. Her grace and beauty matched her poise and confidence, and she would not look out of place in Monaco, London or Paris. How was it even possible that I was in her life? No wonder she didn't answer my question about love. How could she? I thought that I was only outclassed by biology, now I realized that I am also beneath her in circumstances and experience. Worldliness, in a word.

"You are thinking, I can tell," she said and laid her hand in mine.

"I am thinking that I'm not good enough for you, Julie. The wrong side of the tracks. Something like that."

"You big silly goof. Any man I want, I can have. I chose you, you didn't choose me, you just think you did. From the first time I saw the intellect in your eyes, I was in love with you. It was all a matter of time and of timing. We belong together…we make flames when we kiss…we will always be together…we will never part." It was another sledgehammer blow, but this one felt really good. I felt my eyes go wet and I hoped that it wouldn't start running down my face. Julie expertly wiped my lower lids with the pad of her finger, smiling warmly at me as she did so. "You need to shut that brain of yours off tonight and just enjoy. Want to try for your Julie?" She said and patted my cheek playfully.

The ponderous Rolls came to an elegant stop, and I looked out to see the tuxedoed doorman rushing toward the rear door.

Chapter 13

Prince's

We were seated in grand fashion in a corner area, partially hidden from the other diners, likely the most sought after spot in the restaurant. As Julie promised, I was wearing a black tuxedo jacket, complements of the house. The menu was French, written in French, but my table partner was fluent, *par extraordinaire*. I looked across at her beaming face and realized how important tonight was for her. She had it all planned, and I almost threw a monkey wrench in the gears.

"It's most impressive, your planning and your manipulation, my dear Julie. You have swept me off of my feet, and I confess that I will submit to your every whim."

"You already do, my dear Rick," she smiled, raising her cut crystal glass toward me.

"What are we celebrating tonight?" I asked.

"Tonight," she smiled and the little wrinkles around her eyes appeared briefly. "From the vast collection of peoples of the earth, from the thousands of choices we each could have made, we have chosen each other. I have chosen you, and you have chosen me, and I couldn't be happier about it. All my life I have been waiting for you without knowing it. Of all the things I have done, the one that makes me most complete is being with you." She raised her glass a little higher and took a drink without looking away from my face.

"Julie, you don't know how much I wanted to hear you say that. Until tonight, I must admit I had doubts about how you felt about me. There were times I was in agony about it. Thank you from the bottom of my soul for telling me that you love me."

"You understand that I attract boys and men like flies to honey. I had to be sure that you actually loved me as a person. It's harder for attractive girls to know when there is only lust in a man's heart. You persisted, you suffered, you nearly went bankrupt and kicked out of school for me. You resisted my offers of sexual encounters, and you would protect me at the cost of your safety or your life. Looking is over for me. You are the one."

I sat there mesmerized, not knowing what I should say or how I should act. Part of me wanted to get down on the floor and kiss her feet, and the other part wanted to stand on the table and howl like a wolf. My arms burned to hold her and feel her heat against me, while covering her mouth and face with hard kisses, inhaling her sweet smells. Instead, I just sat there and looked at her, immobilized by love.

The waiter coughed out a polite little sound to get our attention. He had been waiting patiently for the order of wine and food and took this moment as his opportunity.

"Mademoiselle, Monsieur, êtes-vous prêt à vous commander du vin maintenant?" He gave a polite bow and smile. I knew he had asked about the wine, and he was looking at me to decide. There was a blank space in my brain which should have been filled by knowledge of wine, but currently, it was only pulsating, not processing. I knew less about wine than I did scarves. A quick glance at the menu came up empty, because it had no wine list. I felt a sense of impotence come over me, a sort of helplessness.

"Permit me, Rick," Julie intervened. *"Comment faire un bon Riesling de la Moselle comme Prüm ou Reinhold Haart?"*

"Très bonne, Mademoiselle. Un excellent choix." He scurried off to fill her request.

"How is it that you know so much about wines?" I asked.

"We traveled a lot in Europe."

"Forgive me, Julie, but I have met your father. I can't picture him being enchanted with French food or fine wines. He looks more like the shot of straight bourbon type to me."

"And he is. My mother was French. Born in Paris to a wealthy family. She was the cultured tutor who taught me several languages and gave me the privilege of extravagant living for a time." Her mood changed, and her eyes went to the table, lost in the past.

"Forgive me, Julie. I didn't mean to bring up painful memories."

"Pleasant memories of things unfortunately past, Rick. She was a grand woman, one who was both elegant as well as beautiful. I have tried to copy her but have not been especially successful."

"Again, forgive me for asking, but how is it that a woman like her would be attracted to your father?"

"Opposites. That's frequently the case."

"You and I. Are we opposites?" I asked.

"More than you know." Her answer gave me pause, and I studied her face for signs, but there weren't any. That might have been the clue, but at the time I was too innocent to notice. Later, it was obvious to me that Julie's face was what she wanted it to be, a mask for public consumption, the real Julie hiding deep inside.

The ordeal of ordering the food was made easier by the hints and suggestions from the other side of the table, the experienced and sophisticated side of the table. In part, I was stunned by the prices to the right of the French text, but just as inhibited by the strange and unfamiliar descriptions. The tab was mounting higher and higher, but Julie didn't seem to mind. She was more focused on having a quiet, continental dinner with me than what it was about to cost. Her choices were elegant, right on target, and the food was superb. What was especially superb was watching this gorgeous creature across from me, the candlelight flicking from her hair and eyes. How I wanted to present her with a huge diamond ring for her left hand just then. I wanted her to be mine forever. She took charge of our conversation and talked about Paris and all the things to do and see there. My focus was on her, but she managed to intertwine her images of Europe with the view of her that I was seeing, constructing a woven quilt of beauty, history and tradition. It was as if I had been transported to France and was to sleep tonight in the Rue de Something or Other with her at my side.

Our waiter was actually from France and delighted in conversation with her to the point that I started to become jealous. Julie noticed and smiled at me in a motherly way, calming my rough edges with her soothing voice.

"It takes me back, talking with Philippe. A happier time for me. Someday I want to return there with you at my side. You will go, won't you?"

"Nothing would make me happier. Of course I will, and anywhere else you choose." We were pretending, of course. There was a lot yet to do before we could jet off to Europe and dine on escargot in wine sauce in a quiet cafe in Paris. A little thing like school stood in our way, and I wasn't making any headway dining in extravagant elegance with a beautiful companion, no matter how much fun it was. It was like a little nag, pulling at part of me; a small dog attached to my pants leg, growling when I paid attention to it. Before I met Julie, I was on my way. Success was out there like the little circle at the end of a train tunnel. As long as you can see it, you will eventually arrive. My train had taken a sharp turn, and the end was no longer in sight. I had only thoughts for her, and the passage out of the tunnel was forgotten for now. An unmentionable, for this was not the time to bring up unpleasantness. This evening she had schemed to pull off for me was really about and for her. I was happy with a hamburger as long as she was close enough to touch. Her happiness was all I cared about, and if this evening, this pretend excursion to Paris, was important to her, then it was important to me as well.

"There is one more thing which would make my evening complete," Julie said, the candlelight being captured by her white teeth. The little hairs on the back of my neck were alert, waiting for what I had been expecting to hear. "You and I are incomplete. There is more to our love than sharing a meal. *Vous ne comprenez, n'est-ce pas?*"

"*Oui.*" My only French word came out of me, and I heard the sound distantly like someone else was speaking. It was the alternate me person, who would throw care to the winds and eagerly, passionately, hungrily, take Julie to bed, taking freely of the best that life offers. There could not be anything I wanted more than that. It was recurrent in my dreams, frequently awakening me in the grip of fierce desire, her image floating out in the darkness just out of reach. I yearned to see and feel parts of her that so far I was only able to imagine. Her hint caused my pulse to accelerate and my mouth to become dry. For a young man, an inexperienced one such as me, her hint was the winning ticket to the lottery, the grand prize of grand prizes, the promised trip to paradise.

She waited on more from me, her eyes glinting over the rim of her wine glass, her mind penetrating mine. Softly, she sat the glass down and casually folded her arms against the edge of the table, her ripe, red, perfect lips hovering like a beacon of sexuality. The next move was mine.

"You know the answer. There isn't anything I want more than that," I said quietly, in a coarse whisper as hormones surged into every inch of my skin.

"But? Say the rest," she commanded, just as softly.

"I can tell you that I know what love is. Being near you makes me comprehend it for the first time in my life. It's scary, a little bit, the passion love creates, the longing, the urges. At the same time, love makes me aware of the risk, the risk of losing someone I love so intently. Should that person be lost, the person that I love so much, the rest of my life would seem empty, the void too large to fill. Love that intense makes me cautious, because the risks of losing are so large. The union between a man and a woman can be the ultimate expression of love or the ticket for the train to elsewhere. It's all about the timing of such a union. Too soon and the intensity is diminished and the risks high. The right time and you achieve what love was meant to be, and the experience will last the rest of your life and beyond."

"Now you are the wise one, the worldly one, Rick. It's what I saw in your eyes, the thing that attracted me. I do love you, more than I thought possible. There is a part of me which yearns to make you happy, to seal our love, to zip it up, and I'll do anything it takes to keep you."

"And I was just looking at you, wishing that I had a diamond ring in my pocket. If I did, I would ask you to marry me, tonight if you would agree. And it's the same for me as it is for you. I will do anything to keep you. Unfortunately, I'm just a poor college student and truly not your match, at least not yet. Love by itself isn't enough. I'll have to wait for that honor, Julie. I'll have to earn it, and I'll have to wait until there is something tangible to offer you."

"Une merveilleuse conversation, mais puis-je offrir le dessert?" the waiter said with a little discrete smile.

"Apportez la chocoate panier, s'il vous plaît," Julie ordered, giving him a hard look. He had been listening to a very private conversation and he should have guessed that his tip would suffer as a consequence. In a moment, he came back with a large cart of

various fancy chocolate desserts, and we selected one that we could split.

Philippe looked concerned, likely because the value of his tip had plummeted. He folded his hands together much like a prayer and said, "Please forgive me for my impertinence. I couldn't help but hear. Truly, the beauty of your sentiments made me cry." His French had fallen away like a bath towel. Julie was angry and dismissed him with the little French flip of her hand. Her eyes momentarily went cold and hard, then recovered as she realized that I was watching intently. It was a revealing moment, one that I would frequently remember later. I saw her glance at her wristwatch briefly and realized for the first time that it was small, but well endowed with little diamonds, a glittering glory of reflected warm candlelight.

She noticed my appraising look. "Mother's. It's the first time I ever wore it. In some ways it's painful to see it on my wrist instead of where it belonged." The emotional mention of her mother left her with shiny eyes, and I decided not to comment.

"Do you have any other entertainment in our evening plans?" I asked.

"I certainly did." We were back to that again. I resigned myself to spending an uncomfortable night tossed between regret and lust when we parted. Instead, I could have accompanied her to wherever rendezvous she had planned for us. Why was I being so perverse? This abstraction of her I had formed wasn't correct at all. Julie knew what she wanted and where she was going much better than I did concerning myself. I wanted to be with her and she with me, and the universe had tossed us in the same little pot. I was a fool.

"I'll go anywhere and do anything, Julie. I have no limits when it comes to you. All I want is to not lose you."

"I know," she said as she looked at her watch, figuring out some mysterious item or itinerary.

"The limo will be here soon. We can talk then. More privately, in fact." As she added the last part, she glanced at Philippe who was gathering the plates.

Julie's eyes went past me into the larger room behind us. She was watching something or someone, and again I saw that hard look creep into her face.

"*Apéritif... cognac,*" she snapped at Philippe who gave a quick bow and scurried away. She was looking intently over my shoulder, and as I watched, I saw her fingers curl into a tight ball.

"What's the matter, Julie?" I asked, tempted to turn around and find out what she was looking at.

Her eyes came back to mine, but her face took longer to change this time. "Sorry. I was thinking about something. She looked at her watch again, then back to me. One brief flick again over my shoulder then back to me. There was someone of interest in the other room, and I had to know who it was.

"Don't turn around," she ordered. "I'll tell you about it later." The hard look again, this time at me.

Philippe returned with our after dinner drinks and avoided eye contact with her. She snapped her fingers in front of his face to get his attention.

"Is there a way out without going into the main dining area?" she asked him.

Philippe rolled his eyes for a moment, likely thinking of how as well as why. "To be sure, miss. A bit awkward but Philippe will lead the way when you are ready." He had almost redeemed himself, at least in his eyes, and was most anxious to please this ravishing but authoritarian young woman.

"Not yet, Philippe. I will signal you when we are ready," she said, and her face softened for a brief instant. She glanced again over my shoulder, and I was burning with questions about it. Someone was out there she wanted to avoid, badly wanted to avoid. An old lover, perhaps? Would I ever discover his name? I waited, watching her face, her beautiful but taut face. We slowly finished our drinks, and she continued to flick her gaze over my shoulder. Eventually, she ordered another round of cognac and we waited, our conversation nearly nonexistent. I suspected that our limo was at the curb by now waiting for us as we waited for the unknown happening over my shoulder. Julie's pupils dilated ever so slightly as a new wave of emotion came surging over her like a shadow of a cloud passing beneath the sun.

Julie snapped her fingers and Philippe instantly was beside the table. "Now, Philippe," she commanded and started to rise, making an effort to keep me between the line of sight from the other room. We left that way, Julie sandwiched between myself and Philippe. He led the way into an arm of the kitchen, the staff there both surprised and irritated to see us invade their domain. Philippe reached the back outside door and held it open for us. Without a word, Julie put three one hundred dollar bills in his shirt pocket on her way to the outside.

"That take care of the bill, Philippe?" I asked.

"*Oh, oui, oui,* more than generous! *Bonsoir, monsieur, mademoiselle.* Please to come again," he gushed.

We carefully picked our way past the scattered cans and street trash and made for the outside street. As we turned the corner, the shiny black Rolls was there, crouching, smoke slowly curling out of the rear end. As we came into the light, the chauffeur jumped out and held the door for us as before. His tunic was unbuttoned, and on my way into the backseat, I saw the handle of a large handgun sticking out of a holster under his arm. I took another look at this so-called chauffeur, and I saw a very fit body, topped by a hard chiseled face. Marine? I wasn't sure, but it seemed plausible, even likely. By this time, I was in 'the ask no questions' mode and just along for the ride.

The door softly clicked closed, and the driver went around and got behind the wheel. There was a pause as if he were waiting for directions.

Julie pushed the intercom button. "Take Rick to the men's dorm, please." The car didn't lurch forward but remained stationary, idling, hovering in place. She pushed it again. "Change in plans. Men's dorm." This time the car responded, and the trip home for me started.

"Want to talk?" I asked.

Instead of answering me, she put her slender arm around my neck and slowly and deliberately pulled me down on top of her. We were nose-to-nose, chest-to-chest, and I felt her breath on my face. As we kissed, she put one hand on my buttocks and held on. The experience was intense, and I became breathless. She thrust her hips into me and pressed her face ever harder into mine. Father Time, are you listening? If you are, please stop until I give you permission to move ahead.

"Did you have a good time?" she asked in my ear. Her free hand tousled my hair, and the other one was still engaged where we both wanted it to be.

"A truly marvelous evening. I can tell that it would have only gotten better except for my big mouth. Can you forgive me?"

"It wasn't you that shortened our evening. You would have gone with me. Something else came up."

"Shouldn't I know about it?"

"You aren't ready yet. It has nothing to do with our relationship. I know your little brain is imagining a previous lover. Stop that right now. There never has been a previous lover, never, never. You are the only one, my only love." She made her point by another long passionate kiss. My body was ready for more, a lot more, but it was used to denial by now. Another night alone wouldn't kill me, even though parts of me would never forgive the rest of me.

"Our driver has a weapon. Is it customary for chauffeurs to be heavily armed?" I asked.

"Depends on the circumstances….later, we'll talk later." Another later and I may grow old waiting on the latest later to expire.

"You love me, and yet there is something that you are not telling me."

"That's right, Rick. There is a lot I'm not telling you, and it's for your own good. You'll just have to trust me." Her hand withdrew from my buttocks, and we sat back up looking into each others eyes, the flash and motion of the street lamps going past playing on our faces, the shadows moving slowly across. For me, the effect was to make her even more radiant than ever, especially since our evening was about to end. I pulled her toward me for another kiss, but I could tell that her mind was elsewhere, and though she allowed the kiss to happen, it was one-sided. The big car slowed and then came to a full stop. The men's dorm was in sight and waited for me like a pharaoh's tomb, ready to take me in, separating me from the world, plunging me back into the harsh reality of study and fast food. RATS!

Reluctantly, very reluctantly, I got out of the car by myself, and when the door closed, I placed my two palms onto the door glass in an effort to…I really don't know what that was supposed to accomplish. The car didn't care that my hands were still in contact with its window, and it started to move away with the inevitable force of a planet turning in space, majestically, timelessly, moving away, getting smaller as I watched. RATS!

I started for the door of the dorm and something caught my eye. A yellow cab was parked just in front of the building, waiting for something. A moment of inspiration seized me, and I sprinted for the cab, tapping on the drivers window.

The window came down partway, and I could see the driver's eyes under his hat. He was looking at me with interest.

"Say, can I hire you for a quick trip out and back?"

"Where to?"

"Prince's restaurant. I have to return my dinner jacket. Won't take long."

"Get in, pal," he said, and I heard the back door unlock at the same time the motor started. This trip was a lot faster and rougher than the one in the limo, but of course, my mind had also been occupied by my companion. As we approached, I decided to proceed with some stealth and directed the driver to stop a half-block short. He gave me a look but did as I asked.

"Wait here please, I'll be right back." It was close to a plea, because I didn't want to be on foot for the long walk back. Besides, I had another reason to want the cab to wait. As I promised, I sprinted the distance to the entrance, pulling my jacket off as I ran. Once inside, I tried to calm myself but at the same time remain alert. There was something in there of interest, and I intended to discover what it was. The main dining room, the one Julie was careful to avoid wasn't in full view from the reception desk, but I could at least see part of it.

"Yes? The manager said, looking me over carefully, ready to toss me out.

"We were here earlier. I forgot to return the jacket," I said as I offered him the coat. He snapped his fingers, keeping his hands behind him. From somewhere, a small woman appeared and took the coat from me. I wanted to have a look in the room behind him, very badly wanted a peek, but he stood defiantly blocking my way, as if he divined that was what I actually wanted.

"Anything else?" he asked, ready for me to take my leave of the place. I took a step forward toward the dining room, and his hand shot up to block my way. "Rules, you see. Our guests demand privacy, and we aim to please. Unless you want another meal?"

We both knew that I had been fouled, and I could see the look of satisfaction in his overbearing face. I gave a little wave and went back to the cab and got in.

"Wait here for awhile, please. I want to see who comes out."

"The meter will be running. It's your dollar," he quipped. I hoped that I wouldn't have to wait too long, because I only had a twenty with me and I could see seven dollars was already used. As we waited, the grind of the little gears counted out more and more money that I could ill afford to waste waiting for a party I wouldn't recognize even when I saw them. I started to panic a bit when we went over the ten dollar mark. A few customers filtered out now and then as new ones entered. This was getting me nowhere. My eyes blinked hard when recognition finally struck me. There was someone I knew, because I had seen his face for months, three times a week. Biggs. He was coming out of the door, buttoning up his long coat. He put his arm around another man in a very friendly way, around the man's waist, not his shoulder. I got a good look at the other man when they walked right by the cab. He was smaller, darker and wore a short beard. Both men were expensively dressed in evening wear and both wore brimmed hats. I shrunk away from the light as they passed, but I could feel their eyes penetrating the darkness of the cab and probing my turned back.

"Driver, back to the dorm, please," I said, relieved that the two men had passed by without comment.

Chapter 14

Mike?

Grey positioned the hand markers very carefully, making sure that my face would come down on the pile of fresh dog dung. Grey and Jerk were having a good time at my expense, and it could only get worse. I was soaking wet from my own sweat, having carried a large bag of sand as I ran up the stairs of the bell tower and back down. The second round was agony, especially coming down. Now, shit in the face push-ups.

"Ready, junior Marine?" Grey asked with delight. "Put your hands on the markers, boy, and have at it."

I did as he directed, the pile directly below my nose when I dipped. There was a strong incentive to not dip past a certain point, but…as you tire your face goes lower and lower. Besides, the big burly coaches are there to make sure you tire.

"Give us fifty, and count them out so that we can hear you," Jerk ordered. I started slowly, methodically, trying to conserve my strength. "Faster, boy," Jerk shouted, causing me to pick up the pace, exhausting my muscles faster as I did so. I made it to thirty-eight, by my count, and knew that my face was about to hit the pile. Instead, I rolled to the side, collapsing in a fetal position, holding my painful chest with my painful arms.

"That won't do, junior Marine James. That's going to cost you fifty jumping squats. Get to it."

A groan and a roll brought me to my feet, and I started squatting and jumping so that my feet cleared the ground. I made it to 50 but with my last breath of effort.

"Back to the push-ups. Assume the position," Grey shouted in my face. I got in position, my arms quivering from previous exertion. This time there was a surprise. The aptly named Jerk positioned a sandbag across my shoulders. "Fifty. Start."

It was a game that I was destined by design to lose, and after a count of eight, my face hit the dog pile, just as they wanted.

Grey threw me a wet towel when I stood. "Good work James. Don't feel bad. We all go through that same torture at some point, and you did better than most. Congratulations, you have graduated to small arms training, starting in the morning. This time we are going to pick you up outside of your dorm to save time. Ever done any handgun work?"

"No, never," I said from under the towel. Would the stench ever come off my skin and from inside of my nose? I accepted their back slaps in good humor and started trotting back to my dorm for a much needed shower, my poor legs quivering with every step.

At last, I entered my room and saw Howard straining his neck to get a look at me.

"God, Rick! What is that smell. It's like a barnyard!"

"Oh, nothing. I just had my face mashed into a big pile of dog manure. Other than, that I stink from my own sweat."

"Why…?"

I cut him off. "Don't ask Howard. Later." I headed to the showers, clutching my kit, the wet towel still draped over my face. I found the showers empty, and I got under a hot stream and just hung there giving me time to think. It had already been six weeks of supervised hell each morning. I had gained nearly twenty-five pounds, and I, and every other person who knew me, noticed the difference. My arms and legs were thicker and muscles more on the surface. My posture was better, and I had more energy. I was forced to admit that the training was working.

Julie and I never again had a night like the one with the Rolls. Our passion had not cooled, but we curtailed our outings, and my grades shot back up. There was a bond between us that remained unbroken and unspoken. I knew that someday, when the time was right, we would wed. The certainty of it gave me immense calm, and I could clearly see that my future was going to be much better than my past. Julie was part of my life and would remain so forever. My day was not complete without seeing her at least once. The eye contact we made, even in class, was comforting, satisfying, reassuring. She was mine, and I was hers.

She never mentioned how that evening was paid for and her 'later' never came. Nor did she ever give me an explanation of why sighting Biggs caused her so much concern. We went back to being ordinary college students who were in a deepening love affair.

The hot water pounded my neck and back, and I had a hard time shutting the water off. Two more issues were still nagging at me. I found one morning that I no longer had a problem with money. Twenty-five thousand dollars had been added to my account, and so far I couldn't find out who did it or why. Julie denied any knowledge of it, and I believed her. The list was not long, and I suspected it had something to do with her father, but I had not seen him in some time. The other issue was Biggs. Why was he interesting, and why did she avoid him seeing her? I didn't want to admit to Julie that I went back to the restaurant that night, so I was reluctant to discuss it with her. The other possibility was that Biggs was not the one she was looking at after all. Finally, I had enough and turned the shower off as my stomach signaled that it was my next priority.

My usual breakfast of eggs and sausage was smoking in front of me as I hurriedly studied my notes for the last time prior to this morning's test. I took a sip of coffee and realized that someone was sitting down across from me.

"Last minute cramming! You always set the curve Rick. Back off for a change!" Mike said as he sat down.

"Hi, Mike. Does that comment mean that you have already crammed this morning and are here to bother me to keep my grade low?"

"That's exactly what I intend! You knew!" He put his cup down and continued to look at me with a grin.

"All right. Tell me why you are actually here. You don't even live in this dorm, right? That means that you are looking for me, doesn't it?" His face went funny when I said that. Not angry or humorous but uncovered or unmasked. There was a reason for his visit, and it had nothing to do with friendship.

"Passing by, Rick. Say how are you and Julie doing? Making it yet?"

"If we were making it, Mike, I would never tell you about it. We are doing well. We are a couple, you know that." I looked at him trying to discern his motives. "That reminds me, Mike. How are you and Sally doing. Making it with her yet?" I countered.

"Old hat man. Of course we are doing it. From the first date we are doing it. Good body, sweet lay. I need to move on soon. She's getting tiring."

"Thinking of moving in on Julie then? Your question, you know, brought this up."

"No man. She's yours. Ever meet her father?" This question was not one I had ever heard from him previously, and it caught me by surprise. Out of the blue, as they say.

"What makes you think that I have met her father? Isn't he in the Armed Forces? He doesn't live around here you know." Counterpoint or check, something like that.

"I saw you working out with a couple of big guys a couple of times. They sort of look like Marines. Made me wonder, that's all."

"Oh, them. They are the ROTC and football types. They are just helping me get into shape. Buddies, you know."

"Kinda looked like they were slapping you around. Made me worry about you keeping that kind of company."

"How is it that you are up that early and over at the athletic fields Mike?" The sparring was more obvious as we went on. Mike had dropped his smile, something I had never seen him do previously.

"I jog that way some mornings. Gotta stay fit for the ladies, you understand. That why you are working out so hard?"

Ignoring his response, I tried a different tact. "You are a runner? I didn't know. Want to meet for a run together some morning?" I saw him shift his position, a tell. The runner excuse wouldn't fly.

"No man. You are outa my class. I can see how fit you are getting." Then, what did he actually want, I asked myself.

"Say, Mike, now I have a question for you. I asked Julie if she remembered you from high school. She didn't. Didn't you tell me that you went to school with her? You seemed to know a lot about her." He rubbed his face briefly, another tell. A lie was coming my way.

"I'm not surprised. She and I had little in common. Different circle of friends, different classes. She's really stunning and I am sort of…ugly. She would never have even looked my way." He stopped for a moment studying my face before he spoke. I felt that the reason for his visit was finally coming. "She ever discuss her mother's death? Why it was hushed up so quickly?"

The truth never hurts. "No, Mike. We never discussed it. I'm sure that it's too painful to talk about. Perhaps someday but not now." So he was mostly interested in Julie's parents and not Julie. I wasn't sure that he even knew Julie. Something was fishy about the whole thing. I felt a little invaded, and my back started going up.

"Anything else Mike?" I asked, picking up my study papers indicating an end to our conversation.

"No. Just wanted to say hello. Good luck with the test, Rick." He bolted the last of his coffee, threw a quick grin my way and left as quickly as he had appeared. Another blasted mystery. All I wanted is to study hard and go to medical school then I found Julie and the tornado which surrounds everything she does. I put down my papers and finished eating in a hurry. There was something I had to do.

Chapter 15

Investigation

"Jees Rick, this is going to use a whole tank of gas," Howard whined.

"Will you quit complaining? I said I would buy the gas. It's not much farther," I said while studying the map. "This turn, Howard." He pulled into the school parking lot, the square red brick building hovered off to the left. "Want to come in or wait?" I asked.

"No thanks. I went to high school already, and I swore I would never come back. I'll wait."

"Shouldn't take too long," I said, pulling my wallet. I tossed a couple of twenties on the seat. "Go get gas and buy some food. There's a burger stand we passed a couple of miles ago." Howard looked delighted and relieved, scooping up the bills as I headed toward the school. It seemed strange to be back in this environment again. I felt so much older, and the kids looked so much younger. The office location was well-marked, and the path to it outlined with yellow tape, just in case you were confused.

"Hello. Can I be of assistance?" she said, tossing her long brown hair over her shoulder. Cute and giving me the eye. She came up to the counter, looking me over, smiling a patronizing waxen smile.

"I was told that you keep all the past annuals here."

"In the library. There's a whole section. Someone in particular you want to see?"

"Two people actually. They graduated two years ago. You attend school here?" A good guess given her apparent age.

"That's when I finished. You didn't go here, did you? If you had, I would have remembered," she said, her smile genuine this time.

"Julie Frank." Remember her?

"Of course. Everybody would. Prettiest girl in school. Best grades also. She was here for two years. You know about her mother?"

"I heard that she was murdered. Is that the story?"

"That's what was in the papers. We never heard if the killer was caught, and Julie never talked about it. Do you know her?"

"She and I are classmates at college. Friends also."

"Lucky you. She never dated, you know."

"I heard. The other one was also a student here. Remember Mike Flannigan?"

She repeated the name very slowly as her eyes searched the ceiling. "Mike…Flannigan…I don't think he went to school here. You sure about that?"

"It's what he said, and that's the reason I'm here."

"He could have gone to one of the other schools. Hold on a minute and I'll check." She went to the computer terminal and started typing. "No go. No matches. No Mike Flannigan went to school in this county during those years. Could the name be wrong?"

"Something is wrong for sure. Could you show me the annuals for those two years so that I can look for faces?"

"Sure. What's your name, sweetheart?"

"Rick. Rick James. I'm not from this town."

"I gathered," she said as she led the way to the school library. "I'm Marsha. "What are you studying in school, Rick?"

"Pre-med."

"Doctor, huh? If you ever get tired of Julie, look me up will you?" We found the stack of annuals, and she pulled two off and we sat down together.

"Is Julie a real close friend, if you know what I mean?" Marsha asked.

"Not that close. We've dated a bit."

"I'm relieved to hear that and also surprised that she dates anyone. We worried about her. Rumors about her father being possessive were circulating. Meet him yet?"

"Yes. Tough guy. Apparently I passed inspection."

"You pass my inspection, but I wouldn't mind a closer look."

I busied myself turning the pages as Marsha watched me closely. She managed to rest her hand on my arm in a casual way, and I noticed her big smile each time I looked up. Julie was the Homecoming Queen, the Prom Queen, the winner of the Beauty Pageant and so on. She was younger looking but radiated from the page with her familiar smile. My Julie-arousal mechanism was functioning perfectly and rang loudly each time her image came up from the page. Oh my God, I love that girl. If I could have only been her classmate, it would have extended our time together by years. Mike's photo was not in the two annuals we reviewed. He had lied. Still, he told her history accurately, so he did know about her. I never asked Julie about Mike, even though I told Mike I had. It was time to tell her about him and see what she had to say.

I had seen enough. "Marsha, I need to read what the local newspapers had to say about the murder. Are there any collections here?"

"No dear. You need to go to the public library. Want me to come with?" She smiled again and looked very endearing.

"I had my roommate drive me, and he's waiting in the car. Just point me in the right direction."

"I have a better solution," she said and took my arm in hers.

"My daddy is Chief of Detectives. He'll know all about it. Want to talk to him?" The idea was tempting, but it was going to step on a lot of toes and would likely get back to Julie's father. If there were terrorists involved, like her father said, I would get noticed for asking, perhaps even investigated. Sleeping dogs barked at me.

"I don't want to probe that deeply into something that's really none of my business. Just interested, because the subject is too painful for Julie to discuss. I wanted to know a little more, that's all. No need to bother your father, and I'm sure he wouldn't or couldn't tell me any more than was printed in the paper."

Her interest was piqued, and I watched her eyebrows raise. It was the female competitor coming to the surface. "This Mike you are looking for. How does he fit in?" she asked.

"He was the one who told me Julie's story. He seemed to know all about her and said the same things you just said. I have no idea what that means. He lied, it's obvious, but why is not obvious."

"This is an unsolved murder! Every fact is interesting! You must discuss this with father before you leave town. You wait right here, Rick, and I'll give him a call." She quickly left the room, leaving me sitting, looking at Julie winning another contest. I contemplated just leaving because I was getting in too deep. Nervously, I continued flipping the pages, not really looking at the endless photos of people I didn't know. Howard would be upset by now and would likely be considering leaving me here and driving back to school without me. Rats! The same old story. Julie's life was a complicated mess. How could a sweet girl who looks like a goddess be…. My thoughts were interrupted by the sounds of a police siren getting closer. It didn't take long to realize that Marsha's father was headed my way. I walked down the hall toward the entrance and toward the siren to wait for his arrival.

A uniformed policeman pushed open the double door and that's when I realized how large he was. Thickly made, mostly muscle and bone, with military-style close-cropped hair and aviator glasses. His large chrome handgun glinted at his side. He stopped when he saw me and looked me up and down.

"Your name James?" he asked.

"Yes sir."

"Come to my car and we'll talk," he said and held the door open for me. At least I wasn't under arrest, at least yet.

"Just a moment," I said. "I have to let my driver know so he'll wait for me." I started to head toward Howard's car but stopped when I heard his command.

"That'll have to wait, James. This way," he said and started walking toward the waiting patrol car. Unfortunately, Howard's car was parked around the corner, out of view. I was shown to the backseat, and Captain Rodgers sat in the front. He didn't introduce himself, but I saw his metal name badge.

He cleared his throat and put his arm on the back of the seat. "Marsha said that you were asking questions about the Frank case. Want to tell me about it?"

"I don't know the first thing about the Frank case. I am dating Julie Frank and wanted to know more about it. That's about it."

"She mentioned someone named Mike. Who is he?"

"He is a classmate at college where both Julie and I go. He claimed to be a former classmate, but his photo is not in the annual, and his name isn't in the computer. That's all I know about it."

"Give me a description of this Mike and his last name."

"His last name is Flannigan. He is an ordinary college student about my age and height. Brown hair and eyes, lives in another dorm. I see him on occasion, but we are not close. Last time I saw him he brought up the Frank murder. He seems to know Julie, but I haven't asked her if she knows him."

"That all you know?"

"He likes girls."

"What college boy doesn't?"

"Since I'm here, can you tell me anything about the murder?"

"Have you met Colonel Frank yet?"

"Twice."

"When I was in the Corps, he was my Captain. If you met him, you know that this is personal for him…real personal. Any information you get has got to come from him." Captain Rodgers was silent for a moment, thinking about something. "What's your opinion about this Mike?"

The spotlight was on me. "I thought he was all right until he started asking questions. That caused me to come here to check him out. I'm in love with Julie and anything that concerns her concerns me. The impression I get is that her father likes me, at least a little. Otherwise, I would have been found crushed into the street by a tank."

"True, James. Crushed like a bug," he laughed. "Here is the straight truth. I can't tell you anything about this case. It's been classified, sealed and taken out of local hands. What I can do, however, is to send out feelers about this Mike. If I hear anything, I won't be able to tell you, but I will be sure to pass it along to the Colonel, and I will give you credit. From now on, don't get involved in this case. You and Julie stay out of it. Understood?"

"Yeah. Terrorists. Right?"

"This is bigger than you, kid. Leave it alone."

Chapter 16

Explanation

oast," I said and raised my wine glass toward her. The glass wasn't cut crystal and the table cloth only plastic, not linen. The waiter was grubby and unconcerned, but the restaurant was private, comfortable, dark, and there was just the two of us.

Julie raised her glass smiling, her warmth jumping across the table at me. "To us?" she suggested.

"To a union made in heaven and which will last forever," I offered. We touched glasses and drank, watching each other with love in our hearts.

"This place is nice, Rick. How did you find it?"

"Accident, just luck really. Not approaching the level of Prince's but more in line with my expectations in life."

"You can't mean that!" she said, wagging her finger at me. Her usual remark when I said anything even slightly negative, especially about myself. It's not that I don't like expensive or refined things, but more that I have learned to live without them and still manage to get along just fine. Julie had been exposed to that side of life by her mother and certainly didn't feel out of her element in opulent circumstances, as I do. Besides, a singularly beautiful woman like her should expect the finest things in life to surround her. After all, she is one of the finest things in life. My guilt, that I could never provide an upscale life for her, hung around my neck like a dead albatross. This was one of the times I could smell it.

"Julie, are you aware that I meet with two of your father's men each morning?"

"Yes."

"I wasn't sure you knew. The training is supposed to enable me to protect you from something. At least that's what I was told."

"Yes."

"If you know all that, please tell me whom I am supposed to protect you from?"

"If I knew that, I would tell you, but I'm not the one who asked you to protect me. Ask my father." Her voice had a tone of finality, hinting that the subject was, for now, closed.

"Please, Julie. There are some things bothering me. Could we talk about them for just a bit?"

"Such as?" The final note again. It was obvious that I was pushing against a brick wall which could come down around my head.

"Such as when we were at Prince's and you avoided someone. You said to ask later. It's later."

"Not yet it isn't," she said.

It's what I thought would happen, but I had to find out. I decided to push in a different direction. "Did you ever hear of a fellow named Mike Flannigan? He told me that he was from the same school that you went to."

"I've never known anyone by that name. You sure he went to my school?"

"Actually, I don't think he did. He just said that he did." This got her attention and I saw her pupils dilate slightly for a brief moment, and her face took on a far away look.

"Where did you meet him?"

"Right here in school. He's in one of our classes. The one taught by Biggs." Her face fell just a little and worry crept into her eyes.

You would have to know her really well to see it, but I was a student of her face, its moods, its joys and its sorrows. Her face was better known to me than my own, and I had committed to memory every possible nuance of it.

"What does Mike look like? Describe him."

"There isn't any distinguishing feature, I'm afraid. He is medium everything with brown hair. Oh, and he smiles a lot."

"Point him out tomorrow in class. I'll see if I remember him."

"One last question, if I may. What is your father and his men doing in town?"

"You might ask them." She seemed to summon up something deep inside of her and penetrated me with one of her looks. "Rick, you might as well let all of this go. It's really complicated and…when the time is right, we'll discuss it, not before." My mind wouldn't let it go, I knew, but for now my lips were sealed tightly shut, and I resolved to change the subject.

"You don't look lovely tonight, Julie, you are way beyond lovely. I don't have a large enough vocabulary to describe you adequately, but it is one of life's treasures to just sit here and look at you."

"Thank you Rick," she said. There was distraction still on her face and in her eyes which occasionally searched the little restaurant even though nothing had changed and nothing had moved. It was unsettling for me once I realized that she wasn't comfortable. It would explain her terse answers and her lack of return compliments.

"Julie, is there a problem? You seem to be tense."

"I'm not at all tense, Rick. It's your imagination."

"Then did I say something wrong?"

"No, Rick. We are here to enjoy. Start enjoying." The tone was more of a command than a suggestion.

"Your attention is elsewhere, Julie, your thoughts are not in this restaurant but someplace else or about someone else. Since we had our outing at Prince's you haven't been the same. Is it me?"

"For the last time, Rick, it's not about you, otherwise I wouldn't have come."

"Julie, I don't have more to give toward our relationship than what I have done or am doing. Are we about to part?" I wanted to say more, to pour it on, but we were in a public place. My comment had an instant effect, and I saw her lower lip start to tremble and her eyes moisten.

"You have to believe me when I say that I don't want us to separate," she said.

I did believe her, with all my heart I believed her, and I wanted to hold her and kiss her unhappiness away. "Thank you for saying that. I just want to say that there isn't anything that you could possibly tell me that would change how I feel about you. Forgive me for picking at you because of my fears and ignorance."

The food came, and the waiter put it on the plastic checkered tablecloth with a clatter. Oh well, it wasn't costing as much as a meal at Prince's either. He put the small bottle of wine between us, his open hand suggesting that we pour our own as needed. We ate quietly, both digesting our feelings and our thoughts. I had made a nice mess of this date, and I wished I could start over with more understanding toward Julie. There was so much I wanted to ask her, but all of it was off-limits.

"Want to go dancing after dinner?" I asked casually. It was always in my plan for this evening, and the suggestion previously never failed to get a smile from her.

"Not tonight, Rick." Her face had resumed the placid mask hiding every emotion and thought. I wasn't aware when I first met her that her face was beautiful enough to cause me to be distracted by it, not seeing Julie hiding underneath. The more I was with her, the more I understood that you could only see Julie, the real Julie, on rare moments when she wasn't in total control. The rest of the time, you only saw what she projected or what you wanted to see. The perfect movie actress who was convincing in any part because you wanted to believe, wanted to keep watching her, the enchantment of her physical form captivating you, hypnotizing you.

"Of course, Julie. We'll catch a cab back to your dorm after dinner."

"No. I have other plans," she said, the mask pulled tightly over her face. I didn't respond, because it seemed that every time I had asked a question, it was the wrong one. She watched me like I was a bug going aimlessly back and forth trying to find a small crack to in which to hide.

"Tonight is later," she blurted, and I felt my intestines tighten a bit. Did she mean that the information I wanted was about to be delivered or did she mean a romantic liaison was about to happen? My eyes widened, or bugged, as they say. My face was no mask and even people down the street could tell what I was thinking, especially Julie.

"No. Not sex. Not tonight, at least," she added, reading my soiled little mind. Were we to go somewhere for this exposé of knowledge? Was it to be a quiet place or just on the sidewalk as we strolled?

"Better drink your wine, Rick. You might need it." Now I was really concerned. The information was obviously bad, worse that I assumed, and my mind had already assumed the worst. My first thought was that there was another man after all, my absolutely worst and most dreaded fear. The image of Julie with someone else caused me to drain my glass and reach for the bottle. Julie snapped her fingers at the waiter who eventually responded, wiping his big hands on his soiled apron, making me realize that I should have spent the money for a better establishment. He flipped the check on the table, giving me a sideways look, probably because he saw

Julie taking charge. He had earned a minimal tip, and I folded it and the rest of the payment around the ticket and tossed the wad back on the table.

We left together, not arm in arm, but at least she allowed me to hold the door open for her. Standing at the street curb for a moment, it was apparent that she was waiting for something or someone to come along and we didn't have long to wait. A, by now familiar, dark, nondescript car slid silently out of the shadows and stopped at the curb in front of us. Jerk waved at us from the front seat, and we got in and closed the door.

"Good meal, kids?" he asked from across the seat in a way that was more perfunctory than inquisitory, neither of us bothering to respond as the car sped away into the dark. I put my arm around Julie to draw her close, but I felt her muscles tighten so I slowly withdrew it. Her mind was not on me, it was clear. The corners came one after another, and the twisting car pushed her close to me at times. I felt the heat from her thigh and her shoulders, which braced off of mine, but at this moment we were farther apart than ever before. We were not a couple any longer, just a man and a woman uncomfortably sharing a back seat.

I knew the route by now and expected we were about to meet her father in his decrepit warehouse. This might not be a rewarding meeting, as if any of my previous meetings had been so. Julie was in her own world, staring out at the dark city streets passing by us, the infrequent street lights playing in her hair. Suddenly, my impulse was to get everything out in the open, before we met with her father again. "I was told by your father that your mother was murdered in revenge for something he had done. Do you mind talking about it?"

Her face had a cloud pass over it, a mean, black, threatening one. The change was quick, a chameleon changing colors, but returned to normal just as fast. I would have missed it if I had just met her. The sensation it aroused in me was unsettling. I didn't know Julie Frank as well as I thought. I saw her looking at me and wondered if she was trying to determine if I had seen her brief emotion. She took a long deep breath, her eyes fixed on mine.

"Hezbollah. My father's mission ran afoul of Hezbollah in the Middle East. There was innocent blood shed which necessitates revenge, and they never forget or forgive. It was two years before they found us, and we still don't know how they did it. One day, three of them showed up at the door after Father left. Mother shouted for me to run, and I did, out the back door and over the fence, hiding at the neighbors. She was tortured before being killed. They cut her open, leaving parts of her all over the house." She paused, and looked around blankly, reliving the horror once again. "Father and I both swore revenge. So far, he has found three of them. There are more, some may possibly be Americans, whom we will eventually find even if it takes forever." Moisture filled her eyes, and she stopped, coming slowly back to this world. This was not the girl I thought I knew. This one was filled with hatred, horror and hardness on a scale I couldn't imagine. I was angry at myself for ruining her evening, hated that I knew more that I should ever have known.

"I'm sorry Julie. Truly, I shouldn't have asked. I'm very sorry."

"You had to know sometime. I didn't have to tell you tonight so I'm sorry also. The story is part of who I am, and I hope that you and I are not pulled apart by it."

"Not in the least. I love you more than ever, Julie. I'm for you through thick or thin, and if I can help you and your father resolve this horrible crime, I will." As quickly as the storm arrived, it left, transitioning a complete change of scenery without a drop of the curtain. She was back to being the Julie she wanted me to see. What was going on in her soul was private and off-limits even for me. A great and towering wall of stone was in her heart, and she could be on either side of it just as quickly as a blink. On which side of the rocks I stood was an open question, but Julie, the consummate actress, had regained charge of her emotions, at least as far as anyone could tell, and at least for tonight.

The car paused as the ancient door lifted, creaking, as if it were a drawbridge of a medieval castle. Grey was there to open the door on Julie's side, extending his arm in a gentlemanly way to assist her. I clambered out clumsily and followed them up the well-worn, creaking staircase.

As before, her father was waiting, dressed in his black full dress uniform, complete with medals and braid. He stopped pacing as we entered and accepted a hug and kiss from his daughter. During their brief embrace, I saw his dark eyes play over me, like I was a piece of military hardware there to use or discard as needed.

"Did you have to pick this particular evening, Dad?" she asked, pushing away from him.

"Things have to be said, Julie, like it or not. James has to be brought in, and this is the time for it." Standing erect, he turned to face me, his face roughly chiseled from granite.

"James, you must have become aware that we are keeping a close watch on Julie and you, correct?"

"Yes, sir."

"I got a call from a old subordinate over in Fayetteville. You know whom I mean?"

"Yes, sir."

He cleared his throat and started to pace again. "This Mike you were looking for. Have you seen him lately?" The question made me flip through my memory of recent classes, the faces there rapidly going past my mental eye like an old film strip. Mike wasn't in there.

"No, Colonel Frank. He has not been in class for a few days."

"Just as I thought. He wasn't registered as a student and was never officially in class. At this moment, we don't know where he has been living, but it wasn't in a dormitory."

"Who is he, sir?"

"I'm not sure, James. Not whom he said he was, that's obvious." He turned toward his daughter and put his big hand on her shoulder. "How much does he know?" he asked, obviously referring to me.

"I told him about Mother's death a few minutes ago. That's all he knows," she said. They both were watching me intently. Both big Marines were blocking the door behind me, their presence weighting that side of the room.

Colonel Frank walked around me slowly, his hands behind him, while I stood waiting. "You are a good man, James. You keep your word, and you have shown my daughter respect and restraint. My sergeants tell me that you have not slacked in your training and that you are coming along." He continued to circle me, occasionally looking into my face and soul. I felt like a captured gazelle being circled by a big cat, the loops tighter and tighter leading up to a grabbing moment.

"Sergeant Graham," he snapped. "How is his firearms training progressing?"

"Well," Grey hesitated. "Starting from nothing, as he did, fairly well. He hasn't had combat training yet and no work with long arms, but he is hitting the targets."

"That has to continue, Sergeant. Step it up a bit," he commanded.

"Yes, sir!" There was a snapping sound as a crisp salute was given behind me.

He stopped in front of my face, and I braced myself for whatever he was going to throw at me. "James," he started. "Why do you think you are being trained by these men?"

"To protect Julie, sir," I stammered, feeling the need for a salute but not giving one.

"And why does Julie need protection by you?"

"I wasn't sure until tonight, sir. I guess it is to protect her from terrorists?"

"Your half assed knowledge and your skinny little arms wouldn't protect her from a grandmother, James. That's clear at least, isn't it?"

"Very clear, thank you sir." I was nearly in the Marine mode in spite of myself. Take whatever is dished out and never complain.

"Look, James. Try as we might, we can't be there every single second to protect Julie. We might need you to do what you can someday, as little as that would be. Am I understood?" He managed to not spit in my face this time.

"Very clear, sir. I will do what I must, whatever it is." When I finished, something hit me in my stomach, knocking some wind out of me. I reached down and felt the hard cold outlines of a large handgun.

"Take this wherever you go, James. Hope you won't need it," Colonel Frank said. "Start training like your life depends on it and it might."

"Yes, sir. May I ask a question or two, Colonel?" I inquired. There was silence, and I assumed that I was being given permission to speak.

"Mike said that your wife was killed when Julie was in the fifth or sixth grade. Was that correct?"

"No, James. It was three years ago. Julie changed schools twice after that."

"Perhaps we should check out the other schools. Mike might have been there."

"We did. He wasn't."

"Why is there a continued threat? They have had their revenge."

"I'm afraid not, James. They were after Julie. My wife was only a convenient substitute in her place. My mission in Lebanon caused the death of one of the daughters of a Hezbollah chief. He won't let it go."

"So you are after them, and they are after Julie?"

"That's right."

"Why not move her far away. Even change her name. Why put her where they can find her?" I asked.

Julie answered for her father. "Because I want my revenge, and it is the only way to finally stop them. We have to finish it."

"Won't they just keep sending men? It's never going to stop as long as you both are alive," I said becoming agitated.

"We think the Hezbollah commander is going to try and do it himself," Colonel Frank answered.

"That's just fine and dandy," I said, feeling the ground move under my feet. "Why here, at this college?"

"There is a link. This town is a base of operations for them," he said.

"Why am I involved. Did you think that I was one of them?"

"Not a chance, kid. You are here because you wouldn't get out of the way…and because Julie fell in love with you."

Chapter 17

Carrying

Got your gun?" Grey asked as we drove away from my dorm. Sure I did. I could feel it pressing against my spine, letting me know that I had it, but it also had me.

"I do."

"Different training this morning, bubba. You'll like it." He laughed an evil laugh, one that I heard previously when they made sure I didn't like it.

"Where's Jerk?" I asked, hoping he had been sent to Afghanistan since our last meeting.

"He is preparing the site. This is about combat, not targets. You will be using live ammo, so don't get careless and shoot one of us by mistake."

"I would expect bullets to bounce off if they managed to hit you," I teased. I couldn't resist saying what I had been thinking for so long.

"Don't be a smart ass. This training is serious, and someday it might save your life. And Julie's."

He was right, I knew. I had nothing to offer but naivety, but what I had learned from them so far was starting to change me. Seems weird to say, but somehow I was starting to enjoy the massive amount of pain they could inflict on me. It made me realize that I could become just like them with training and perseverance.

The Colonel's well-worn gun at the small of my back was aggressively digging in with its many sharp edges. I took it out and laid it on the seat beside me. "Colt 45 Cal." the engraving read. A rather formidable weapon, rich with history, tradition, even a touch of glamor, and one which kicked back harshly when fired. I spun it so that I could look into the opening of the barrel. The business end, as Jerk put it, was large enough to accommodate my little finger. I couldn't even imagine what a slug that size would do to a soft human body.

We turned off the highway onto a dirt road leading toward a large stand of trees in the distance. Grey stopped in a small clearing, and I could see through the windshield the ivory color of a wall of glimmering rock on the other side of the trees. A perfect backstop for bullets. Jerk walked toward the car with a big smile.

"A private shooting range, just for you!" he said as I got out, holding my new weapon in my right hand. "This morning you are going to learn to shoot at targets of surprise. Not everything that pops out at you will be something you want to put a bullet in, such as children, women and good guys. The bad guys will try to shoot you first, so you have to be accurate and fast with your fire. Hesitation usually proves to be fatal. Got that?"

"I think so," I said but didn't really understand how this was going to work.

"Alrighty then," Grey said. "Load your weapon and come with me. I'll go through the first time with you. You aim and fire when I tell you. Quickly. Very Quickly. Keep in mind that if you shoot without aiming, you will miss, and that's not good. Slow and accurate is better than fast and missing. Fast and accurate is best. We are training your reflexes this morning. You already know how to aim."

Grey pushed me from behind, sending me stumbling toward the

start marker. After I regained my composure, I crouched down a bit like I was shown, my senses on high alert, and together we went toward the trees full of bad guys, interspersed with the occasional no shootums. After just a few feet, the first target suddenly leaned out from behind a large tree. It was a life-sized cardboard cutout of a big man holding a gun which pointed directly at me.

"Shoot! Shoot!" Grey screamed at me from behind and I rapidly leveled the big gun at the target's head and squeezed the trigger. No explosion, it was a dud.

"That was a dead round to teach you not to close your eyes. You anticipated the noise and squeezed your eyes closed, then pulled the trigger. The first mistake of a beginner. You can't shoot with your eyes closed. Back up and we'll try it again."

The rest of the morning went by in similar fashion. We went through the trees and every time I did something stupid, Grey was right there to correct me, occasionally delivering a slap to the back of my head when I did something particularly egregious. Eventually, I managed to put several cardboard fanatics away with kill shots. In hindsight, it was the first time I had fun training with those two and the experience made me want to continue.

"Tomorrow it gets harder," Grey said. "We'll move into the quarry, and you'll be required to crawl through the course and shoot from a horizontal position. Next week, we start amid the rocks and perhaps also a little fun in the mud. At the end of three weeks, you'll be able to handle yourself a little better."

"Is this the same kind of thing you do in training?" I asked innocently.

"Ours is more like ten hours a day for three months. In our courses, the targets actually shoot back at you. No, it's not the same, but this is the best we can do for now. Don't get overconfident. The people you could run into are very experienced and completely savage. I wouldn't rule out a suicide bomber or two."

The thought of that kind of fanatic woke me up. My life story so far had not involved contact with even the smallest trace of real evil. I was unprepared and innocent, and I was being asked to protect the one person that I most loved against forces seeping from the darkest recesses of the brains of men who dealt in death as a way of life. But what could I do other than try to get ready, hoping that the occasion would never arise?

While riding in the back seat on the way to my dorm, I put the pistol in its place against my spine, tucked into my pants, an extra magazine in my right pants pocket. I wasn't ready for action, yet I carried around with me the possibility of it, as if it were a thing lurking somewhere just out of my sight. That kind of thinking gets into you like a poison. You start to notice people more, studying their faces for intent, always watchful for anything unexpected. It's a tense way of life, and one that leads away from trust and more toward seeing everybody as a potential adversary. I was a walking time bomb with a large gun. My brain noted every shadow, every flicker at the end of a long hall, and heard every footstep. My palms sweated and my underarms stunk from nervous anticipation. I tried to tell myself that I wasn't the only one protecting her, that actually, I was the last resort, the one last firewall before they got to her. And if they got to her, it would be a mutilating and painful death. I had to prevent that at all costs, whatever it took. Part of me wanted to go back to just being a college student, studying hard but still able to toss a couple of happy beers in my free time. The transformation was happening before my eyes; I was rapidly growing up, seeing the world as it really is, sensing its immediacy and its callousness, its indifference.

There was one problem that I didn't anticipate, and his name was Howard, my roommate. He had always watched me closely. Previously, I had ignored him, but now this invasion of my personal space raised my hackles. I was trying my best to hide my big black gun from his penetrating eyes, but I had to shower, and during those times, I was forced to leave my gun in our room, secreted away in my bedding. What I needed was some distraction for this little book-worm who seemed to have no life of his own. I needed a willing female to pay him a visit, one that would make him grow up and focus on his sexuality and not on what I was doing. It was time that Howard found out what all his parts were really designed to do. And…it was excellent blackmail material in case, some day, he did discover my gun. Unfortunately, I didn't know any loose women and especially any who would accept payment for services rendered. In my limited world, the only person who would know was Mike and he was likely on the run, thanks to me. I did remember Mike's girlfriend, Sally, and the one he fixed me up with…named…Carol, her name popping up as I thought about it. Either one would do, or they might know the right girl for what I wanted. Besides, I might get a line on Mike. The question was, how do I find them?

The more I remembered about those two women, the more I could imagine the kind of place they would be drawn to. Several rough joints were near campus, but the better students would never frequent them, because their patrons would likely not be very nice to clean cut college students. Like me. These particular bars catered to heavy metal enthusiasts or perhaps the motorcycle crowd. I decided to go pay a visit and see if I could run into Sally, Carol or who knows, even Mike.

Chapter 18

Sally and friends

The sign was just ahead, swaying slightly in the wind, renting the night with its harsh neon lettering, while blinking erratically like a loose Christmas tree bulb. "Pete's Pub" shouted out in bright red from one side. The other side had been broken for years, and from the slight downward angle of the whole assembly, I could foresee that one day the entire sign would crash to the street. The feeling of going into this bar was giving me an out of body experience. Why, again, had the fates conspired to make Julie's troubles part of my own? Why was I walking into a seedy bar carrying a large pistol and trying to look tough enough to ward off bullies? Couldn't I have chanced to fall in love with any other girl among the many choices walking provocatively around school?

The door frame spoke volumes of what was likely inside. The wood was chipped and dirty, a shade of brown, especially where many hands had rested, pulling their owners across the filthy threshold. A brass, or what used to be brass, push plate was outlined in green with brown streaks, suggesting something that had crawled out of the toilet area and landed on the door, instead of making it outside with its previous donor. It was the music, the harsh gurgle of rough singers pretending to sing using words you hoped you couldn't understand, which was repelling me the strongest, and as I pushed the door open, I got the full blast. The air column pushing past my face was laced with stale alcohol, sweat, cheap perfume, harsh guitar chords and the guttural laughter of big men in leather jackets entertaining hard women. I stepped in and looked as some of them looked back, making me feel not only out of place but small, vulnerable and alone. The room was dark, illuminated largely from the bar area which lay across the left side of the room. The bartender was a trim woman with red and purple streaks in her hair, complemented by bad teeth and a skin rash. Not wanting to stare and create confrontation from the patrons, I decided to stop at the bar and casually look around, peering into dark corners using quick glimpses.

"Haven't seen you here before. You lost or something?" she asked, wiping the wet areas before me with her dirty cloth. I looked at her with more interest. She would have been pretty, even glamorous…once…though no longer. Too much seedy life had passed under that bridge to ever regain even a semblance of attractiveness. She was looking at me with indifference, not hostility.

"Hi," I offered. "Draft beer please."

"Oh, even a please. Don't hear that much in here. You sure you should be in here, college boy?"

"Just out of prison. Returning to my old haunts and looking for old friends," I said with a tough guy smirk.

"In your dreams, sonny. Better can that story. Some in here have been there for real, and they would enjoy spinning you around like a kid's toy. What kind of beer?"

"Regular," I said, not understanding my choices. She shrugged and rolled her eyes but went to the tap and pulled a foamy yellow froth into a tall chipped mug, sliding it across to me before turning her back. Down the long bar, looking with some interest at me, were two women on bar stools, their loose garments barely concealing heavy, drooping breasts which moved slowly back and forth as they drank from long stemmed cocktail glasses. One raised her eyebrow at me when she thought I was looking at her, and I quickly looked away. These women were not what I was looking for. Howard wasn't ready for medicine that strong. I leaned back into the bar rail and casually inspected the flock. In one particularly dark corner was a young blonde girl sitting with two large men wearing half denim jackets, their backs emblazoned with colorful embroidery. Motorcycle club or gang members, I didn't know which. Both men wore ragged short sleeved shirts and displayed extensive tattoos on their muscular forearms. When she turned her face, catching the light just right, I thought she might be Mike's girlfriend, Sally. I wanted to keep watching to make sure but didn't want her or her friends to notice. Too late. The girl stood, looking right at me which caused her male companions to twist in their chairs, also looking toward me with interest.

"Well, college boy, you're in the soup now. Better not tell those two your little fable about prison, because they really did just get out. How about paying for your drink while you are still able," the bartender said from behind the bar to my back. I put a ten on the bar as I watched the blonde make her way toward me followed by two menacing men behind her.

"If it isn't Mike's friend," she said. It was Sally for sure. I had found what I wanted, and it reminded me of the old adage "be careful of what you wish for, you may get it". "You down here slumming or something? As I recall, you seemed to be too good for Carol or me last time we met." Her big friends looked over her shoulder like some creatures from an old movie.

"I was actually looking for you, Sally," I said, trying hard to look unconcerned, and taking another swig of the diluted beer to bolster my confidence.

"You're too delicate to be down here, handsome. You might catch your death!" All three laughed huskily. "Just what do you want?" She put her hands on her hips and squared off at me.

"Seen Mike lately? He seems to have gone missing," I inquired.

"That asshole! He dumped me ten seconds after you left! I haven't seen him since that evening. But if I ever do…." She waded up her little fist and formed a frown.

"Funny. He said that you and he were a thing. Made a big deal about it," I tattled.

"You know, I don't think he had what it takes in the man department, know what I mean? Had to leave before it came out." She laughed a coughing sort off laugh and nudged one of her companions with her elbow. They laughed also.

"Mike told me some big lies. I wanted to see him again to straighten it out."

"You are looking in the wrong place…say what is your name, little boy?" This was good for another round of laughs. Their smiles and laughs contrasted with their eyes which were full of hatred.

"My name is Rick," I reminded her. "You must remember that your friend Carol left me standing, Not the other way around."

"Yeah. I remember. Carol doesn't like to be bored very long."

"You guys still buddies?"

"What's it to you?

"I'd just like to start over, that's all" I said. Sally looked me up and down for a moment, sizing me up as if I were a dog for sale, a used one.

"Maybe. Did you know that Carol is one of those kind of girls who gets paid for a date?"

"No, but sounds like what I want. How can I get hold of her?"

"What's in it for me?" Sally asked.

"How about a ten?"

"More like a twenty," one of her large friends said.

"Yeah, twenty for each of us," the other said.

I was in a bad spot, and it was getting worse by the second. "I don't carry that much. Sorry. Ten's all I have." It was more or less true, I didn't have more than twenty in my pockets.

One of the big fellows gently pushed Sally aside, towering over me. "What if we pick you up and shake you. See what falls out?" he said as Sally grinned from the sidelines. I was tempted to draw my gun, but there were too many at the bar watching me. But I couldn't let them find it on me, not without some struggle. The front door slammed shut, and all of us looked around instinctively. Another big fellow had come through. He was dressed in jeans and a tight black T-shirt, his ample muscles bulging out of and under his shirt. A large 'USMC' tattoo was showing on his arm, and his hair was cut very short. Sergeant Graham. He gave me a small wave and leaned against the bar with one big arm, surveying the room with narrowed and experienced eyes.

"Well, hello Rick. Strange place to meet you," he said, grinning his knowing grin. The three in front of me didn't look as sure of themselves as they had. There was a sort of a standoff, two against one and one half, until the door opened again, and Jerk came in with the same little twisted smile. He nodded to me and stood beside Grey. These two Marines could easily clear the room and everybody knew it, just from a glance at them. The two ex-cons in front of me starting backing up, leaving Sally by herself.

"Rick, give me a number and the ten, and I'll have her call you," she said and held our her hand. I put both in her hand and thanked her.

"Tell her I look forward to hooking back up," I said. "I'll be waiting for her call."

The three of us left together, me in-between as usual. Once on the street, Grey shook his head disdainfully.

"Did I actually hear you trying to link up with a hooker, James? Tell me it isn't true."

"It's not true, Grey, and thanks a million for saving my butt just now." He reached behind my back and patted once.

"Got your piece. You shouldn't have had to worry, sport. You can shoot, can't you?" he laughed, poking Jerk with his elbow with this little joke.

"I was nearly forced to resort to it. You saved me or them, I don't know which."

"Looking around the bar, James, it would have taken a whole magazine. That's a rough place. Explain."

"Two reasons. One, I was looking for Sally and found her. Mike Flannigan lied to me about her also. She hasn't seen him for some time. Her roommate is a girl named Carol. I met her briefly, previously on a blind date set up by Mike. She is a hooker all right, and I plan to pay her to connect with my introverted and nosy roommate, Howard, in case he needs to be silenced." My little explanation gave them a big laugh, a laugh than continued until they were both red in the face.

"Howard! We met him! I almost want to be there when this girl grabs hold of him!" Jerk guffawed and slapped me painfully on the shoulder. "That's a great idea, James. You are learning fast!" Each man put a large hand on my shoulder from either side, and we walked the two blocks toward their car, parked invisibly ordinary at the curb.

Just before I got in the back seat, Grey leaned toward me in a serious manner. "James, you were in a kill or be killed situation back there. Learn from it. In a call of Duty or Honor, it's all right to die, that would be honorable, but never die for nothing." His words would ring in my ears for a long time to come.

Chapter 19

Howard's surprise

his is Carol. You wanted me?" Her voice came pleasantly over the telephone, not at all corresponding to my memory of her.

"Thanks for calling, Carol." My mind went blank. How was I going to broach the subject of employing her for sex? Offering to pay a woman for sex is something I never, ever, considered that I would do. Not only that, it wasn't even for me.

"I've got an uncomfortable question to ask, but first, I want to find out if you have seen Mike lately," I tentatively said.

"Mike and I were never…you know…personal. He gave me a Benjamin for what he said would be pleasant work with you. Luckily, I got it in advance. You looking for me to earn it?"

"Something like that. Willing?"

"Sure. Especially if you throw a little more into the pot. Want to make it a threesome?"

That would really release the demons in Howard. A threesome in the dorm room. The management might have to renovate following that romp.

"The other party have a name?" I asked.

"Sally. She all right?"

"She'll do nicely. What about seeing Mike? Have you?"

"He's around. Saw him last week but didn't talk. Aren't you friends?" she asked.

"I guess not. Another question?"

"Shoot," she said.

"I want you to hook up with my roommate. His name is Howard. You'll have to use our dorm room. I should mention that Howard is inexperienced. Very much so. Get the idea?"

"Sounds like a lot of fun. Sure we'll do it. Shouldn't take more than an hour, if that long. What about…say…another two hundred? You can join in at that price."

"Tempting offer but I have a steady. She wouldn't like it. I'll meet the price but make sure he has a good time."

"About the money. We like it in advance."

"I'll leave it in the room with your name on the envelope. Only one request. Don't scare him."

"Not a chance. He's going to remember that night for the rest of his life," she laughed. "Oh, and when?" she wondered.

"Tomorrow night about seven? I'll wait for you out front and escort you to the room."

"That's a date. See you then," she said, her voice brighter now.

"And, thanks a lot Carol," I said before I hung up.

I stood uncomfortably in front of the dorm, waiting. It was just a bit past seven and Howard was up there, bent over his books, living his lonely little life in the dorm. Things were about to change for him. Too bad I didn't rig a video before it happened.

Their voices came to me before I saw them, chatting back and forth, walking arm in arm like lovers or close friends, their hips touching at times. They looked like typical young college students absent the backpacks full of books. No one would guess that these were women of the street, experienced and ready to do anything for money.

"Hi Rick!" Sally shouted, and they swiveled toward me smiling and batting their eyes. I was relieved that they were both dressed rather elegantly and without excessive adornment. In fact, I was impressed that they both looked particularly appealing as we closed the distance. Both girls were heavily endowed and sported small waists and curving hips. When they arrived in front of me, Sally put her hand on my chest sliding it slowly and provocatively toward my belt line, feeling my abdominal area as her hand moved. "Well, I didn't remember that you are so fit!" she said and smiled up at me. Carol put her hand on my shoulder and squeezed like I was being appraised for slaughter, selecting the cut of meat pre-mortem.

"Wow!" Carol said and patted my chest. "You have to be there too, Rick. I can't wait to pull those clothes off of you."

"You both look wonderful," I remarked, gently backing away from the caresses. "Your money is on my desk, and although he doesn't know it, Howard is waiting for you."

"Please be there too, Rick," Carol said. "I have a debt, and I want to work it off with a real man like you. At least you can watch."

"Those two big guys who were with you the other night. Are they around here someplace?" Sally asked, looking around as if expecting to see them.

"They came in the nick of time, didn't they?" I recalled.

"I'm afraid that they did. Sorry about that," she said, smiling as if to erase her role in helping to provoke the incident.

"You know how to get in touch with those rough boys of yours?"

Sally hesitated in answering, not sure of why I should want to contact someone from that layer of society. I wasn't sure why I asked either. It was something digging at me, some notion of alignment of assets, a just-in-case hypothesis forming like a thickening haze. There could be a time that I would need something illegal done that even tough Marines couldn't or wouldn't do.

"I think so. Why would you want to?"

"At the moment, I don't. Someday I might want a job done. The kind of job that someone would do for a little cash and no questions. I'll let you know."

"There's a lot going on in that young handsome head, isn't there?" Sally remarked to Carol.

"Yes. He's more interesting by the minute. I'd do him for free," she said, patting me again.

The funny thing is that I sort of enjoyed their company and their free uninhibited talk and way of life. I was comfortable with them. What the heck was happening to me? There was a metamorphosis going on, but I wasn't becoming a butterfly, nor quite a wasp, but rather a small angry honeybee.

I escorted both women through the halls, riding the elevator with them standing as close to me as clothing would allow. I admit that the effect they desired was happening to me even though I was resisting with everything I could muster. Finally, and at last, my door was before us, and I put my finger to my lips to silence their chatter. I slowly opened the door and saw Howard at his desk, laboring over some currently pressing study.

"Howard!" I called through the partially open door and watched his head shoot up at attention. His eyes were magnified by his thick glasses making his appearance rather owl-like. "I have a small favor to ask," I said. He continued with his blank look, waiting for the rest. I swung the door fully open and ushered in the two women, watching his eyes widen impossibly more. "My two friends are going to wait here for me for just a moment if it's all right with you. They promise to be quiet, and you can go on with your work. They are both very nice girls, and I want your promise to be polite. Would that be OK?" Carol and Sally smiled their little innocent girl smiles at him, exchanging giggles. Howard swallowed hard, his Adam's apple moving up and down.

"I suppose so, Rick," he said, looking back and forth at them. "Is that permitted? I mean, women in this dorm?" he asked, his voice a pitch higher than normal.

"Oh, sure. It's just a visit. No one minds. It's done all the time. I want you to behave yourself now. I'll be back in a little while, and I'm sure that you will all grow to be close friends in that time." The girls giggled, knowing my opinion was unquestionably true. I winked at them, backed out and slowly closed the door. I started walking down the hall when I heard the first of likely many outcries from Howard. "OH MY GOD!"

I took my time returning to the room, just to make sure the girls were gone, and that I wouldn't be in the path of some self-destructive forces. Standing tentatively in front of the door, I listened carefully before turning the handle and opening it a crack. The room was quiet, deathly quiet, and I was hit with a guilty pang. Was Howard all right? I opened the door fully, sensing the lingering perfume and other female scents still hanging in the air. Howard was on his bed, facedown, one arm dangling toward the floor, his clothing in disarray.

"Howard? All you all right?" I softly asked. Howard groaned, his voice muffled by the bedding. He rolled his head toward me, trying to focus without his glasses.

"What happened, Howard? Where are the girls?" I questioned, seeming to truly wonder what could have transpired in my short absence. Howard groaned again and shielded his eyes against the light.

"Rick?" he quizzed, rolling to a sitting position. I could see that his belt was unfastened and his zipper still down. I had to keep myself from laughing.

"Where are my friends, Howard? Did you chase them away?"

"Rick, something awful happened, and I hate to tell you about it. You are going to be very angry."

"Are you trying to tell me that you offended those two innocent girls?"

"It wasn't like that, Rick," he stumbled, looking for the right turn of words to describe what had descended on him. There was no need to pull the details out, because I knew very well that those two experienced women had gone to work on Howard's previously locked-up appetites, those that he didn't know existed until a couple of hours ago.

"It's all fine, Howard. You don't have to explain. I just hope one of them, or both of them, don't get pregnant from your antics. Think of what that would mean. No one would expect it of you, Howard, that kind of behavior. It's my fault. I shouldn't have trusted you, shouldn't have closed the door. You are such an animal, Howard."

He sat back on the bed looking at the interesting, plain, white ceiling, lost in the memory of the most intense minutes of his entire life thus far. Howard was a changed man, and I no longer had to worry about his obsession about everything I did on the other side of the room. Mission accomplished.

Chapter 20

Picnic

*I*t wasn't very manly of me to complain, but the handle of the picnic basket was digging uncomfortably into my right hand as we walked, so I tried assuring myself that it wasn't much farther. I couldn't switch hands because Julie was holding the other one, and there wasn't any way I was going to turn loose of her hand. The path continued its inexorable climb through the trees with no destination visible, the evening shadows of leaves making patterns on our hair and faces as we walked in contentment.

"Nice day for it," I announced the obvious. She was on my left, rewarding me with occasional beaming looks, her scant lipstick, just enough of it to reflect the yellow light, drew my eyes to focus on her lips every time I looked her way.

"Yes! Sunlight always makes me happy," she said, and for emphasis, swung our arms higher. She was wearing a loose blouse and white shorts under which glowed her tanned legs. Her hair had been let down, and it swung gloriously from side to side as she walked. This particular afternoon, Julie was a light-hearted, insanely beautiful, nymph who was all mine and because of her, I wore the peace and contentment of a spring meadow in my heart.

"How much farther?" I asked hoping that she would take pity and at least slow down.

"Are you having a problem?" she asked, giving me a little sideways smile. She knew that I was suffering, not wanting to show any sign of weakness. My thoughts were on the basket, a very hefty one. How could a picnic basket be so heavy, and so large? There had to be enough food in there for a party of twelve.

"Ahead, there is a side path toward the top. Can you make it?" Julie laughed. I could and did, and when we at last came through the trees, there was a small clearing and a gorgeous panoramic landscape before us. The spot was on a narrow cliff with a precipitous drop on three sides but just enough room to feel comfortable standing or sitting. The evening sun was still up but dropping quickly toward the west hills on the other side of the river, shining off of the tops of the trees and giving the earth a mellowness and warmth of evening light.

"How did you ever find this place?" I was awestruck by its unique location and slowly crept up to the edge, looking down at the forest eight hundred feet below.

"I have a friend that found it. She camped up here a couple of years ago and couldn't stop talking about it."

She opened the big wicker basket and pulled out a large checkered cloth, woven in small red and white squares. We spread it out and sat down. Out of the basket came the food and dinnerware, wrapped in foil and still warm. No wonder the basket was heavy. I also saw the labels, "Prince's Restaurant".

"Wow! You spared no expense, I see. It's going to be worth the trip up here." My stomach started growling as soon as she opened the first dish.

"This is a special evening. One that I want you to remember for a long time," she said and lightly caressed my arm, her eyes sparkling with happiness. Out came the wine, the long stemmed wine glasses and an opener. We dined in exorbitant elegance with the majesty of the setting sun imparting complacence, an indolence of movement, reluctance for an ending and an unspoken wish that the moment could be prolonged forever. A glass of wine tastes so much better on a mountain top with charming company. We lingered until the last rays of day were extinguished, leaving a warm purple glow outlining the hills in the distance as night crept up from its underworld.

"It's a long trip down. Don't you think we better start soon? I asked.

"No, we're not going down yet." She opened the basket again and pulled out two tightly packed sacks from the bottom. "This one is a tent, small, but all we need. The other is a sleeping bag, notice it doesn't have a mate."

"We are going to sleep up here?" I asked with jaw-dropping shock. The realization of how much planning went into her surprise finally hit me. I reached out to her, pulling her gently toward me until we were lying on the cloth, face-to-face, body-to-body and lips-to-lips. My arm slid under her head, and I held on tightly, feeling her breathing, the swell of her chest and breasts against me. The feel of her curves, her perfection, was overwhelming, making me feel that any violation of her was an act against God, a spoiling of nature's endpoint. Yet, this moment was what we all live to have or to dream of, to conspire toward, but usually never to achieve. This moment, and those to follow, was something so important, so fundamental, that I couldn't take it all in, couldn't take it slow enough to savor, defining those memories that I needed to keep for replay over and over in my memory through the years of life ahead.

We laughed as we struggled to erect the simple pup tent in the dark, tripping over the tie downs and fumbling with the unfamiliar equipment. At last it was ready, and we tossed in the single square sleeping bag and closed the basket. I withdrew my large pistol and put it inside, in a corner of the tent. It was time. My heart was in my throat, beating, leaping, reminding me of its excitement.

"I suggest that we disrobe before entering. There's just not enough room in there," Julie said. "This time it's males first." Night had fallen, but I could still see her outline in the blue light twinkling from the vast smear of stars in the heavens. She stood just two feet from me, and I could almost make out the amused expression on her face as she waited for me to remove my clothing while she watched. "Do you need help, Rick?" she chuckled, her teeth shining in the dim starlight.

"Well, I'm standing with a several hundred foot drop just feet away while the most beautiful woman in the world watches me fumble with my buttons in near total darkness while my brain is busy trying to calm down or even think at all. Sure would be nice," I admitted. She laughed a deep soft laugh, tousling my hair. I felt her hands deftly taking down my buttons and my belt buckle, and as my pants fell away, caressing my buttocks. I wadded my clothing tightly, leaving it on the basket, then stood ready to help Julie, but my first touch found her skin bare and wondrous to touch.

"You've already taken all your clothes off!" I exclaimed, not realizing that she was far ahead of me. I had obviously missed an important moment because of the dark.

"Not all," she whispered.

My hands said otherwise until they found her neck, and I realized that the only article of clothing she wore was a singular green scarf tied just so.

My eyes opened a crack, letting in the dim light of morning, just arriving through the dense stand of trees east of us and seeping softly into the little tent. Julie was pressed tightly against me, her head resting on my shoulder, her legs intertwined with mine, her skin against my skin from face to toes, and her warm breath cascading onto my chest. My free hand rested lightly at the small of her back, feeling her body heat pouring from that delightful spot. This is what we humans seek to achieve, diminishing every other moment of our existence compared to this one, where two bodies merge into one being, inseparable for life. My layers of passion had been peeled away leaving the bedrock of unshakable love, the newness replaced by the now familiar and the knowledge that this marvelous woman was to be with me as long as I was to live. And she was all I ever wanted and more than I ever dreamed…

She took a deep breath, stirring slightly, and I knew that soon her wonderful eyes would open and focus on me, the power of her intellect lighting up the world. Once again, I buried my nose in her hair, breathing her scent in deeply, saturating my brain with the essence of her, as if I could hold her in my arms forever and ever in my memory, summoning her to cherish over and over.

I thought about her surprising passion, her lust, her tenderness and understanding, all molded together within the package I knew as Julie. What possibly had I done to deserve to have her in my life? Clearly, I was outmatched in every measure compared to her, even if her fabulous beauty was disregarded. My thoughts were seized with the idea that she would realize her mistake someday and leave me to my ordinary world and my ordinary fate, while she rightly moved into an extraordinary circle befitting what the Gods have ordained for her.

"Hi," she said with that delightful small cracked voice that I had dreamed that someday I would be present to hear. Her eyes remained closed, but she arched her neck and puckered her lips toward mine, which I gratefully accepted as my passion returned in full force. When we parted, our lips clinging together with that last release of human stickiness, her eyes opened, and I felt a wave of her power wash over me, pulling me toward her as if I was caught in a vortex.

"Hungry?" she asked sleepily, half yawning her question.

"Yes. For you."

"I can tell," she laughed. "We're not leaving this tent until you are completely satiated, even if it takes all day. I am yours, and you are mine, and this is the first day of the rest of our lives together. There are no longer any inhibitions between us, and from last night forward things are different."

"Julie, will you marry me?"

"Yes, Rick, but not yet. Later." There was that word again, later. I have come to realize that it translates to "nearly forever".

"If you love me as much as I do you, you would understand that I want to keep you with me whatever happens and wherever I go. I mean marriage as a commitment to you that I will do whatever it takes to do that."

"And so do I. There are some things which have to be resolved first, and you know what they are. We will be together, even though we are not married, at least in our hearts. I married you last night, and I accepted you into my life, and I will never change my mind. You will not lose me."

I searched her eyes and saw that what she said was true. She was mine, inside and out, and there was no doubt in her soul.

"Do you think our skin has glued together like our lips?" I asked.

"I hope so. That was delightful, wasn't it?"

"The separation? I don't want any separation. I like being glued to you. My life is enhanced by you being so near. In fact, it's likely the best feeling I ever had."

"Likely?"

"Yes, likely. Want to know the best?"

"Show me, don't tell me."

Necessity, the natural kind, forced us to consider leaving the tent just before noon. "Are you aware that our clothes are outside the tent, and we are in the tent totally naked?" I asked. "And, it's broad daylight out there, and we are on a cliff which can be seen for miles."

"You just lay there and watch," she said and pulled the zipper on the little triangular flap, allowing the panoramic view to pour through the opening along with crisp air. Before I realized what she meant, she pulled away from me and emerged cat-like on the outside. She turned to make sure I could see her standing in the full light of day, nude except for the green scarf still around her neck, smiling her little devil smile at me. Facing away from the tent, she stretched casually, taking her time and looking like a pink and cream version of some ancient work of art, her long hair caressing her perfect buttocks. Relishing my appreciative gawking, she put on her clothes slowly, making an art of reverse stripping. I was stunned by her perfect body, her timeless beauty, washed in direct sunlight just for me. No wonder the Greeks were obsessed by the female form, for nothing in nature or made by the hand of man ever comes close. She had been in my arms for hours, but I was not satiated. I never could be.

My clothing arrived wordlessly inside the tent, and I could hear her laughter spilling over the edge of the cliff.

Chapter 21

Train like you mean it

The rain came down steadily, coldly, seeping inexorably into my inadequate clothing, accompanied by a stiff, frigid breeze out of the north. My teeth started chattering, a reliable sign of falling core body temperature. I was covered in wet, caking mud on the front, also working its gritty way under my clothing, but unfortunately, I wasn't done yet.

"This time through, James, a new problem for you," Grey said, grinning, while water dripped from the brim of his black DI hat. "Jerk is out there in the trees, hiding and waiting to shoot you when you get close enough. He is using a paintball gun, and I promise you that it will sting when the wad hits you so don't let him get a round off first. You have a laser on your gun, and if you hit him, it will sound out. Game over. You are going to do this over and over until you score. Got it?" Of course I got it. It was a sure thing. Jerk never misses, so I was in for a long morning crawling through the mud over and over until I froze to death or drowned. Either could come first. Fighting Marines on their own turf, with their rules, was hopeless. Jerk might as well use a real gun and put me out of my misery. "Get up and get moving, James," Grey ordered and shoved me on my shoulder, spinning me toward the tree line and my fate.

As before, I dropped to my belly in the fresh mud and slithered along, snake-like, with rainwater spilling off of my forehead into my eyes, clouding my vision. My elbows were yelling that they were slowly shredding into useless pulps with sand grinding the skin off of the bone with every forward slither I made toward the trees. Try to ignore the pain, I was told. Try to focus only on killing your enemy, not on surviving, not on how good a hot cup of coffee would taste. Easily said. I focused every fiber of me on the trees, trying to detect motion, but also trying to guess where he would suddenly emerge, shooting, spraying his lethal paint balls at me. He couldn't see me unless he peeked, and I was determined to be looking for any hint of him, not even blinking, if I could help it. As I crawled forward, I decided to break my pattern and their rules. I veered slowly to the left toward a small bush, off the path. I hoped that Grey wouldn't voice complaint, letting Jerk know what was coming. To my relief, he was silent, at least so far, a sign that he was willing to let me think my way along rather than just depend on my reflexes. Once behind the bush, I had a small advantage of surprise and also shelter from his paint ball. I could shoot through the small branches, but the paint ball would be stopped before it arrived at its target. I held my position but nothing changed. The rain still fell and the wind still blew, but there was no indication of life among the trees. He was waiting me out.

My shaking returned, and I had to move to create enough heat to survive. I decided to leave the shelter of the bush and started creeping toward a large tree on the left. Painfully, my knees and elbows supporting my weight, I moved inch by inch toward the big tree, fully expecting to see Jerk at any time. Once there, I slowly stood, holding onto the wet bark while listening for any human movement. Now we were at least even, because I knew that Jerk was also standing behind a tree, I just didn't know which one. Looking up, I saw an array of small branches leading up to a big crotch. The crotch was protected by an overhanging limb still full of dead leaves, clinging and wet from rain, obstructing observation of the crotch area. My grasp on the small limbs was limited because of the wet bark, but they supported my weight, and as I ascended, no breaking sounds gave me away. Once safely in the crotch, I braced myself in a comfortable position, settling in to wait for as long as needed. Our roles had been reversed, because now I was the predator and Jerk was the prey. Come to daddy, Jerk.

Twenty silent minutes passed, and I waited, patient but alert, gun at the ready. At first I heard every noise, every bird call, all obscured by the patter of rain. The one sound I was waiting for finally arrived, a crack of a small limb underfoot. Jerk was moving. Grey made no noise from behind and I knew that they both always played fair. Hard but fair. Grey wouldn't rat me out, or he would already have done so. This was between Jerk and me. My tension and fear were both real, and I don't believe that I would have felt differently if we were using lethal weapons instead of toys. My right leg signaled that I was about to have a painful cramp, but I dared not move, not an inch. There was another crack from the forest floor, closer this time. My breathing stopped, and I became part of the tree, a part armed with a laser sight bolted to my pistol. There was a suggestion of slow motion coming through the leaves, as if a tortoise was playing death with me, waiting to change into a black leopard, snarling with rage, armed with a paintball gun. I saw a boot-clad foot stop, listening, ready, then very slowly and silently move. Now a leg and part of one arm could be seen under the canopy. Still not enough to chance a shot. It had to be a body or head shot to be lethal and to prevent a missile of paint from coming my way. I looked down the tree, toward the ground, trying to calculate where my body would fall after being struck by paint moving at one hundred feet per second. Better to concentrate on shooting first rather trying to think about the future. He was moving silently forward, one half step at a time. I could just make out his hand holding the gun. His next step would give me the shot, the one I would take before his wary eyes would emerge beneath the canopy, giving my position away. Very slowly, I swung my gun into position, leveling the front sight where his chest would be on his next step forward. The rain ceaselessly ran down my neck into my soaked underwear, dropping my body temperature by the second. I began to worry that he had somehow substituted a mannequin for me to spot and was approaching from the rear, when he took the next cautious step forward.

Three shots in rapid succession radiated from my weapon and three loud buzzes emanated from Jerk. He was dead, dead, dead. I had beat a Marine in one-on-one combat, and from behind me, I heard the yell that I had hoped I would eventually hear. "Oorah! Oorah, James!" Grey screamed and started running toward our position. Jerk was squatting, looking around still trying to find my position. Yes, this was the best day of training, the best feeling of satisfaction of all.

"Up here, Jerk. Don't shoot me," I yelled, waving to him.

"Come on down, James. You won fair and square. I'm not about to shoot you," he said.

The shaking came over me in earnest once back on the forest floor, and I could hardly stand on my feet. I had only minutes to go before total shutdown from hypothermia, and they both instantly recognized it.

"Let's get you to someplace warm, James. You look like you are about to start quacking," Grey said and held me up by one arm. They half-carried me back to the car, pushing me into the backseat to wait as they rapidly cleaned the training site. I fell asleep quickly, curled up in a fetal position, bouncing along in a child's dream like state as they drove back to town.

"Another coffee, James?" Jerk asked politely. It was my third, or was it my fourth? I was using coffee to wash down a steaming stack of pancakes, and it was my second round. The grime and sand in my clothing was tearing at me, but at least, I was warm. They were treating me with deference for the first time, and I could sense that they felt badly that I nearly dropped from hypothermia. But I had done it and hadn't complained, just like a real Marine.

"You did well, James. We are proud of you and forcing Jerk to battle on your terms…well, it's what we wanted to happen. Don't allow the enemy to dictate how you are going to fight. Bring it to him, give no mercy, ignore any rules. You've got the idea, James," Grey said and slapped me on my back again, making me spew some pancake and coffee on the table.

Grey looked at me over his coffee, thinking, unblinking, deciding if I was finally one of them. "James," he began as usual. "You are as well-trained as we can manage, given the circumstances. Both of us are pleased and so is Colonel Frank. Today completes it for us and for you."

"Yeah! Good job, James. Been a pleasure!" Jerk said, thankfully not slapping my back this time. There was a moment of silence, a parting without words between us.

"Now, what am I supposed to do with all this training?" I asked through another mouthful of food.

"Good question," Grey admitted. "Here's hoping that you don't have to do anything at all."

"You both should level with me. I've earned that much, don't you think? After all, I've done everything any of you want and then some. Julie and I are lovers. Her father sort of likes me. Come on now, tell me."

Grey rubbed his chin. A tell? I waited. "We are sergeants, that's all. We obey orders. Someone above us gives orders, and we carry them out. There's a lot we don't know, James."

"Granted, but what do you know?" I persisted.

I heard a big sigh from Jerk and turned toward him. "Here it is James. Abdullah Azzam Nasrallah, or so he calls himself, is on the way here to either murder or arrange the murder of the daughter of Colonel Frank. A revenge killing for something that happened years ago. He has connections, money and friends. He floats around in liberal circles, being acclaimed as a peacemaker, even though he is widely known as a terrorist and a sponsor of terror. As far as I am concerned, the world would be a better place if someone were to just shoot him, but that's not how it works. We have to have provocation or at least catch him in the act. You can expect that he has employed a wide variety of people to help carry out his plan. Some may know more than others. He isn't above using suicide bombers but that would likely be a last resort. Personally, I think he will want to kill Julie himself and with his own hands."

The information that I had previously accumulated, scrap by scrap, was in step with what Jerk told me, so there were no real surprises. Still, the knowledge that an attack was going to happen, instead of just possible, was unsettling. There was going to be action, perhaps soon. At that moment, the image of Julie was floating around in my mind. So wonderful, so perfect. The thought of some harm coming to her was going to drive me mad.

"What would happen if Nasrallah were killed before his plan was completed. Would it end? Would Julie be safe?" I asked, looking back and forth between them.

"You know us, James. We are men of action. Don't you think that has occurred to us and to the Colonel? There are a couple of problems with that plan. First of which is that Nasrallah is an assumed name. We don't know his real name, the name he may be using to travel with, even if that one is real. And, we aren't sure we know what he looks like," Grey said.

"Wait a minute," I asked. "Didn't you just say that he is a darling of the leftists. Doesn't that mean that they party with him, meet with him and publish his picture?"

"Sure. We just think that the one showing up at the parties is a substitute, not the real Nasrallah. You can't just shoot one of them hoping he is the real one. Besides, that would alert him, and he would go underground even deeper."

"Then what is the plan?" I demanded.

"Catch him in the act and blow his head off," Jerk answered.

"So," I summarized, "we are going to try and out-draw him, just like a marshal in the Old West? We don't know who is coming, who is with him, when he is coming, and how he or his men are going to attack? Is that it?"

"See our problem now?" Jerk summarized.

"Here's another idea," I said. "What about using a substitute for Julie? A ringer, one of you?" They exchanged glances, meaning that it wasn't a new idea after all. At first I didn't think that they were going to answer me, but I saw Grey give a shrug as if to say "might as well tell him".

"Do you think Julie would want anyone to die in her place? Does she strike you as someone who would hide? Besides, Nasrallah will employ people to positively identify her before he acts. This isn't Beirut where they can kill indiscriminately. I should think that Nasrallah will expect us to use a decoy. He'll have to proceed very carefully, because he knows that the Colonel will protect his daughter."

"So that was Mike's role. A spotter," I said, thinking out loud.

"Yes, and if, or when, we find him, we'll discover who hired him. When I finish with him, he will turn in his own mother," Grey said with such fierceness that it was chilling.

"So how did Mike know her? He seemed to know all about her, but I couldn't find him in the high school annuals. Can you explain this?" I asked.

Jerk smiled and glanced at Grey. "They have a file on Julie, we're sure. Problem for them is that not many pictures of Julie were ever taken. Those that have been printed are being watched by our people. Nasrallah can't even be sure that we haven't been tampering with the existing photos. He isn't sure about anything, not sure Julie is really Julie, not sure that we are watching. He's got to employ people who will study her, compare notes and zero in on her, right under our noses. Your friend, Mike, was one of those. He was told to find out all he could about Julie. That's why he tried to become your friend. So that he could learn what you found out when you were with her."

Grey spoke up, "It's what we wanted, someone to start asking questions. You were too smart for your own good, and ours. Instead of going to us with your suspicions, you tried to find out about Mike on your own. Something scared him away. Either something you said or the fact that you were looking for proof of his existence. Now he's gone to ground, and we lost a link in the chain." It struck me, what they were saying, and made me recall each time I had met with Mike, going over in detail our conversations in my memory.

"It was me all right. The last time we met I became defensive, because I could tell he was lying to me. He obviously picked up on that. I couldn't tell you about him before I was sure he was a fake."

"That would have done it. I'll bet he was also following you without you knowing it," Jerk observed.

"And you would be right. He watched you training me. Had questions about it," I admitted. As I sat there, something new started bothering me, eating at me, making my entire existence surreal. Was my Julie real? Was she actually Julie or just an actress? If she wasn't whom she said, then does she actually love me, or is she just using me for cover, just waiting for the inevitable assault on her life? In that case, am I but a tool, to be discarded later when

I am no longer useful? There was no need to ask them about her, to betray what I might have figured out. These two loyal Marines would do what they were instructed, and they were instructed to protect the girl going by the name of Julie Frank. I suddenly felt sick, and I looked down at my unfinished food with near nausea. I might be in love with an image, not a real person, and there was absolutely no way to discover which she really was or is. But…I had seen her high school photographs. She was really there, really did win the beauty pageants…or were the photographs altered as Jerk suggested? Even I am not able to tell if Julie is real. Whomever this girl is, I am in love with her. At least that much is real. My love for her is palpable, and I will be willing to protect her at any cost. What is going to happen later is the unknown.

The Green Scarf

Chapter 22

Biggs

$\mathscr{A}$s soon as she came in, I saw the green scarf, that and the smile she wore just for me. It was the smile that said we shared a secret, and the secret was what we both remembered about when she wore the green scarf…only the scarf. She wore it to remind me of the love and excitement we felt, the feeling of our bodies together while the earth slowly turned night into day as we embraced, hoping that night would never end. And I did remember…ever detail was still fresh, and it made me hungry for more, endlessly more.

She sat down in her usual seat, briefly turning, giving me a glance to see if I was still watching. I was, intently watching, remembering her in my arms, remembering her kisses, her warmth. My memory of her will never fade, because it is too intense to fade, and I will never allow any woman to hold that place in my thoughts but her. It no longer mattered to me if Julie's real name isn't Julie, if she is Colonel Frank's actual daughter or not. I loved this woman, her body, her mind and her soul.

Biggs pushed the door open, coddling his textbook and notes in one crooked arm as if they were his child, his delicate baby. On his way to the podium, I watched his eyes flick toward Julie, then to me and back again. It was the first time that I could remember that he actually looked with interest toward her. What did it mean? Was it connected to her sentence of death? He was both an irritating man and an excellent teacher, but I could not view him as a physical threat to either of us. He was prim, proper, even haughty but in some ways delicate, effeminate. He had been in my head off and on since I saw him emerge from Prince's that night. Whom was he with and did it matter? Those questions remained unanswered, but thoughts of him were a thorn and a bur to me. I just couldn't get past the suspicion that somehow Biggs did matter. Call it an unfounded hunch, a poorly formed theory or more likely a waste of my time. While he spoke, my thoughts and my focus were on Biggs, not what he was teaching. I watched his eyes, the key to his soul, and I watched his hands. One time he paused, at first seeming to loose his train of thought, but I followed his eyes, and they were on Julie. He recovered quickly and continued on with the lecture. I knew he would snap his focus on me to see where I was looking and he did, just for a millisecond; he wanted to see if I was watching him look at Julie. He knew that I had noticed, I could feel it radiating from him. We all were aware that Biggs had a personal preference for men. Not only was it rumor and occasionally fuel for humor, but it was obvious. For Biggs to have a visual preference for a girl, a beautiful one at that, was out of character, different than expectations and caused my antennae to point in his direction. All at once it became clear that I should find out more about Biggs. Since I was told that Julie's sworn enemy had the capacity to employ surrogates, I knew that I had to be very careful not to draw attention to myself while I checked Biggs out. I couldn't trust anyone completely, no matter where they worked. I decided to first find out where he lived, how he got home, and who else lived there with him.

While this little play was going on, there was no indication that Julie saw any of it. She remained focused on her work and rapidly took notes as Biggs lectured.

Should I contact Colonel Frank or his men with my suspicion? Not yet, I reasoned. Biggs deserved at least that much respect from me. I had to have more than a simple negative feeling about him. What could I tell them other than Biggs had glanced at one of his star students and that he had supper with a friend at the same restaurant that we had dined in. Not nearly enough to level charges at someone who may be innocent. On the other hand, deep inside me was a clawing feeling that Biggs was on the other side of things. I remembered what Grey said; his words twirled in my head. "Don't play by their rules…bring the fight to them…be ruthless." I intended to do just that.

When, at last, the lecture was over, Biggs gathered his materials and started for the door in his typical bustling hurry as most of the students rose from their seats to head in the opposite direction.

"Dr. Biggs!" I shouted, while rising and moving toward him. He turned disdainfully toward me, seeming to look down his long aquiline nose at me, the insect who dared speak. Biggs was tall, thin and unusually well-attired. His gilded, puffy ascot lay against his chin and hid his slender neck which is likely why he chose to wear that fashion statement. The glimmer of a soft, red waistcoat outlined the opening of his double breasted jacket.

"Well?" he said and stopped, placing a hand, thumb forward, on his hip.

"Dr. Biggs," I began, watching his eyes narrow at me. "I saw you look my way during the lecture. Was I bothering you or had I done something wrong?"

"No more than usual, Mr. James," he said. "Is that all?"

"Is there some reason you don't like me, Dr. Biggs?"

"You mean your inattention in class, your obsession with the opposite sex, also in class, and your general image of yourself as a tough guy? That would give most a reason, don't you think?"

"It's true that I'm not as refined a person as you, Dr. Biggs.

Some things you are born with. Then what about Julie Frank? You seem to be watching her as closely as you do me. Any reason?"

"I don't discuss other students. That entire line of questioning is impertinent. Is that all, Mr. James?" He turned and headed toward the exit door, finished with our conversation.

"One more question, Dr. Biggs," I demanded. His hand was already on the doorknob, but he hesitated and partially looked over his shoulder. "I saw you at Prince's Restaurant recently. Who were you with?" That had the desired effect, and he turned toward me, anger in his face. It was the raw nerve I wanted to touch, to see what that kind of probing would bring to the surface. His reaction could give me a window, an opening, to climb through and rattle him a bit.

"How dare you spy on me! How dare you ask anything about my personal life. Who do you think you are, Mr. James?" He was angry, turning red in the face but knew his physical limits and refrained from body contact with me.

"You shouldn't get offended, Dr. Biggs," I said smoothly, stroking him with calmly delivered words. "I thought I recognized the man and was tempted to say hello, that's all. It was the Middle Eastern appearance that reminded me of a former teacher. He had a small beard, didn't he? And seemed to be very well dressed, just as I remembered. What is his name?"

"I've checked you out, you little troublemaker. You don't have enough money to dine at Prince's. That means you were spying on me! I don't remember seeing you there either."

"No, Dr. Biggs. I was waiting outside in a cab. You walked right past and didn't notice. You had your arm around his waist, as I recall."

"Are you making an accusation!" he bellowed.

"Calm down, Dr. Biggs. I don't care about your sexual preferences as much as you seem to care about mine. We were talking about the man you were with in the restaurant, not what you did or didn't do later that night. What was his name?"

The door slammed behind him leaving me standing alone as the classroom started to fill again from the other side. There it was, I was in his headlights like a deer standing in the road. If Biggs was involved in a conspiracy to kill Julie, I had just made myself a big target, one that would have to be eliminated. Now on to the next step, staking out his house.

Biggs address proved harder to find than I expected. There was no listing in the phonebook, and it wasn't in any public information available at school. Finding it took five days of careful work. The faculty parking lot was visible from the bookstore. All I had to do is to be there when he left in his small white Mercedes. I watched the car as it sped away, turning three blocks away from my position and disappearing from my view. The next day, I was at the corner when he made the turn and watched his car until it was out of sight. I used the same method, day after day, and was fortunate that Biggs was a creature of habit and followed the same route each day. The fifth day, I was in sight when he turned into his drive and parked. From where I stood, I could see him look both ways after leaving the car. It seemed that he suspected that eyes were on him, and it made him cautious, watchful and vigilant. The daylight prevented me from coming too close, but I decided to return about two hours from midnight to see what I could discover.

The first time, I walked nonchalantly on the sidewalk past the house, trying not to be obviously looking toward it. I could see lights on, but the shades were drawn, and the house was silent. This approach was getting me nowhere. At the end of the block, I turned around, deciding to get a lot closer this time. Nearby, I heard a car door close softly, and the hair on the back of my head started tingling.

"James. That means you, stupid. Come here." The whispered

voice was one that I had heard many times before he slapped the back of my head. I turned toward a hulking shadow behind me and recognized the silhouette. Grey.

"What are you doing here, Grey?" I asked. Without words, his large hand grabbed my arm and lead me toward a dark parked car. He shoved me forward toward the back door. I knew the rest, and got in without comment.

"Didn't we tell you to keep us informed? What the hell are you doing, James? Playing cop now?"

"I want to find out who else is in that house with Biggs. It's taken me a week to find it."

"You could have asked, stupid. We have had it under surveillance for a month. Kind of makes me sad, James. We all thought you were getting it. Team play? Ever heard that term? So tell me why, exactly why, you are here right now."

"I had a hunch that Biggs was involved. The way he was watching Julie…and me. There is something going on in his head. It's a hunch I have. Also, I saw him in a restaurant one night with a short guy who had a beard and looked interesting."

"That the night that you came back in a cab? The night that Biggs and this man walked right by your cab? That night?"

"You were there?"

"And this amateur effort to find his house. Pitiful. You were just standing right in the open. We are certain that Biggs saw you. Everyone else did."

"Now I do feel stupid."

"And you should. Think about it. If Biggs is connected to the terrorists, you will be the first one to go. I could have easily taken you out just now if I wanted and so could they. They might even shoot you from a distance. Pop, and you are history."

"All right, I am a stupid amateur. I admit it. What about the man with Biggs? You know who he is?"

"No. On that score, you are right. We haven't seen him since that night. He might be in the house, we just don't know."

"Can't you break in and find out?" I asked.

"James, we have to follow the law. They don't. We need a court order to break in, and there is no reason for one to be granted. No probable cause. If this were any other country than our own, we would just kick the door in."

"Do you think I should tell Julie that Biggs is a suspect?"

Grey laughed, shaking his head. "James, she has been on to Biggs since the first. That's why she is in his class. Didn't you know? Don't you two ever talk about anything other than your sex organs?"

I'm sure my jaw dropped a bit, because I felt myself take a big breath. Julie was not so innocent. She was part of the game. I was cover. "Grey, will you level with me if I ask you a question?" I asked.

"Depends. You can ask though."

"Is Julie the Colonel's actual daughter or a stand in?"

"I couldn't tell you that even if I knew the answer, James," Grey said solemnly. "That answer has to come from a higher authority than me. Sorry. You love her, don't you?"

"More than I can say in words, Grey."

"In that case, you would love her even if her name was Fred. It doesn't matter, does it?" No, it didn't matter. And then again it did. If she wasn't Julie Frank, then I had been told a lot of lies. What was true and what false? It shook me.

"One last question," I said. "Are you working with the city police or the Feds?"

"Not the city blues. We're not sure if there is an inside man. The Feds, that's another issue and one that I can't talk about. Why do you ask?"

"You remember those two cons who were going to work me

over?"

"Sure. Big and stupid."

"What if I sort of encourage them to break in to Biggs house for money. Find out what's in there?"

"James, you can't trust criminals like those. If you can buy them, they can be turned against you just as easily. It's dangerous."

"What if they break in, and it gives probable cause for you to go in after them?"

"You might be on to something. Let me think about it for a second." He sat back and looked around vacantly. "It could work, and it would also send those two back to prison so there could be no reprisals from them. But it might not prove anything other than to find out if our mystery man is actually inside. It won't prove who he is or his intentions."

"I'm no legal expert, but wouldn't it allow you to search everything in the house? That would include the mystery man's possessions, wouldn't it?"

"I don't know, James. We'll have to check it out first, so don't do anything until I say so. By the way, we know that somebody lives there with Biggs because of all the food he brings home. It's being eaten by more than one person. The packaging and waste shows that cuts of lamb have become a staple."

Chapter 23

About Howard

$\mathcal{M}$y eyes opened and saw the morning light streaming through the venetian blinds making horizontal marks on the ceiling. The more I looked, the more I could make out imperfections in the plaster which made musical notation along the path of the light and dark lines. I wondered what music was playing, wishing I knew more about music. Perhaps if I could hear it in my head, it would lead to the discovery of a famous piece of music, one destined to change mankind forever.

"Rick, since I can see that you are awake, can we talk?" Howard asked from across the room. He had been anxious to catch me alone since his visit with Carol and Sally, but I had been gone so much that he never had a chance, even though I could see the querulous look on his face.

"Howard, I don't want to know what you did in this room. It's an invasion of my privacy to know and besides, a gentleman never tells."

"I couldn't help myself, Rick. That's not how I was raised. I feel awfully bad about it. Ashamed, really. I need someone to talk to about it, someone experienced with women."

"Experienced? That's not me, my friend. I have very little experience. You are already ahead of me."

"Come on, Rick. At least let me tell you how it started."

"No. Please don't tell me. Instead, I have a question for you. Did you find the experience thrilling and memorable?"

"I sure did."

"And would you secretly want to do it again if nobody could know?"

Howard was quiet for a moment, giving it some thought. "In spite of myself, yes."

"Then it's settled. You had a good time and leave it at that. No one but me is aware that something happened, and I won't say a word about it."

There was a longer period of silence as Howard mulled it over. I suspected that our conversation wasn't over, and I expected it to take a different turn, which it did. "Rick," he began, "Do you think those two girls would go out with me again? You know?"

"Yeah, I know. You mean to have sex with you, don't you? Listen Howard, those two may not be the best women for you to get involved with. Now that you have developed a healthy desire for female companionship, I suggest that you find a nice girl, one you can make happy and who can make you happy. Love, Howard, is what you are after, not sex."

"Not true, Rick. All I think about is sex. It's what I desire. I know that I'm not attractive, and any girl who would pay attention to me is probably one that I wouldn't want."

"That's sad, Howard, and not even true. Why don't you try dressing up a bit and going where the girls are. Forget about sex, because it'll come with the right girl and will be more meaningful for both of you. If you just concentrate on sex, you will never be happy for more than a few seconds at a time, and it will lead to a desolate life, one without meaning."

"Do you know how to contact those two? Actually either one would be fine," he asked. I could see that I had made a terrible mistake, and my foolish actions might have wrecked Howard's life.

The can was open, and the worms were crawling around the room, nibbling on anything in sight. I didn't answer him and instead got up and started dressing. This was the first morning in months that I had no scheduled training. I was free but realized that I had grown accustomed to the rigor, the stress and the expectations, missing it more than I thought possible. Suddenly, Julie was in my mind. I had to see her, watch her face change by the second as emotions passed over her and became perceptible in the depths of her eyes, hear her voice, inhale her perfume. Before I realized it, my cell phone was in my hand, dialing her number as I stepped into the hall for privacy.

"Rick!" she said, her voice alone enough to arouse me, making me want to pour over the phone and immerse her in myself.

"Have time for breakfast with me?" I asked.

"Love it. Where?"

"There is a coffee shop two blocks from your dorm. That okay?"

"Want to meet there?" she asked.

"Not a chance. I'm on my way to your dorm."

"I'll be there waiting. Love you."

"Love you too." I clicked off and came back into our room to finish dressing.

"Are they going to see me again?" Howard asked. He was sitting up in bed giving me that owl look, the one with the long neck and the magnified eyes. I almost felt sorry for him. No, I did feel sorry for him.

"I didn't call them, Howard. That was my girlfriend, Julie. We are meeting for breakfast." The disappointment in his face clicked some trigger deep inside of me. I had started this mess, and now I was obliged to help fix it. I was going to meet with a woman who lit up the world for me, one that meant more to me than even breathing, but here was Howard, dreaming about the wrong things.

I sat down beside him on his bed and put my arm over his shoulder. "We have to talk, Howard. There are facts that you should know, but I want your promise, your very solemn promise, that you will never tell anyone what I'm about to tell you."

"Sure, Rick. Say we make a trade. You call Sally or Carol for me, and I'll keep quiet." He smiled, convinced that he at last had the upper hand.

"That's the way it is, huh? How about you keep quiet, or I'll tell the authorities and your mother that you had sex with two prostitutes in your dormitory room?"

"They were hookers? Really?"

"Yes. My gift to you, Howard. I thought you needed it, so I paid them. Now you don't have to feel guilty about abusing two innocent young girls. They aren't innocent."

"Wow!" he said, his eyes widening more, not a good sign. "That explains a lot! You are right. I don't feel guilty at all, and now I can tell you that I really enjoyed it and want to do it again. Can you set it up?"

"No Howard, you don't want to do that again. Now I'm the one feeling guilty about it, like I have done something really bad to you. I promise Howard, you don't want to get involved with them for a lot of reasons. They are part of a really rough crowd, and they have no limits on what they will do for money. Think of it as a one-time affair, one that woke you up to what you were missing in life."

"There had to be other reasons that you were willing to pay hookers to entertain me. Want to level with me?"

"That's the other part of the story. I have a gun in the room, but I have good reasons to have it, and they are all legitimate. If, I reasoned, there was something to hold over your head, I wouldn't have to worry what you would do if you found the gun. Call it preemptive blackmail."

"I already knew about your gun. I found it long ago, and I

would never say a word about it. Don't you think you can trust me?" Perhaps it was the innocent look he had, the utter helplessness of Howard that softened me toward him.

"Can you accept my apology, Howard? I misjudged you completely, and I feel really bad that I got you involved with that type of girl. There has to be some way I can make it up to you, I'm sure."

"There is, Rick. I want one more go at them. This time I won't be so inhibited. Please, one more time."

"One day I met their boyfriends. Both are hard ex-cons…desperate and dangerous men who would cut you to shreds for a nickel. Trust me, you had your fun, more would be chancy." I felt his shoulders sag under my arm. It wasn't what he wanted to hear. "How about this. I'll ask Julie to help fix you up with a girl from her dorm. You just have to begin like the rest of us do, courting her, enjoying her company, and if you're real lucky, fall in love. How does that sound?"

"Doing it your way, how long will it take to have sex with her?"

"The longer the better, Howard. The right girl will take a long time. A girl you want to keep will only have sex if she is in love with you."

"I can't wait that long, Rick."

"If I don't get out of here, Julie will be waiting for me. I'll think it over, but try to consider what I said. The kind of stuff you probably want isn't something a nice girl would ever do."

"What does your girl do for you?"

"That's an off-limits question, Howard. Never ask that again. Julie is someone that I love and want to marry. That's how I know what you should look for in a woman, because that's what I have."

"I've thought about it. Call them."

My gait lengthened as I hurried toward the women's dorm. I

didn't want her to be waiting outside for me, not even for a second. Sure, I had become paranoid about her and I realized that I wasn't exactly good protection for her, but I was all I had and whatever came up, I was determined to do my best. As I got closer, I saw her standing alone on the sidewalk looking expectantly toward me. She was dressed in red and visible from Mars. Even at this distance, she was strikingly beautiful, her curves and long hair reminding me that I was the luckiest guy on the planet.

"Hi!" I said breathlessly. "Hope you weren't waiting for long."

"You are worth waiting for. Don't you know that? Her little tease made me laugh. Imagine her waiting on me and thinking it was worth it. Such a dream I'm living. I took her arm, and we strolled toward the cafe, not really anxious to get there, not hungry for food at all, just for each other's company and touch. Every time she turned toward me, and I saw that brilliant smile, those twinkling eyes, I had something deep inside of me tighten up. It's a hard thing to explain to people who haven't experienced it, and I was trying to explain it to myself at that moment. I believe that the feeling arises from love so strong that you know you can't be without it, that it has become part of what you are, intertwined around your soul, inseparable. Tearing it out of you would be bloody, possibly fatal. That's why it's a mixture of wonder and also pain, this thing we call love. It comes with a price, foremostly, the fear of losing it.

We sat down in a little booth, our steaming coffee cups separating us, and our eyes locked on each other. Honestly, it was like we had been married for years instead of only experiencing stolen moments together. I knew her face better than my own, and I knew her moods, her passions and her body from toe to head. She was mine.

"So you finally finished training. Feel like a Marine yet?" she asked, laughing at her inside humor.

"Correction. Junior Marine James, at your service. I learned a lot, but I now know what I don't know, and it's a bit bigger than me." She brought the subject up; I wouldn't have, but it opened up some questions that were nagging at me. "You knew about Biggs, didn't you?" The question caused her face to change, her eyes seeming to lose color. I shouldn't have asked.

"Yes, Rick. He is a suspect. I heard about your efforts from Grey. He probably told you to drop it, didn't he?"

"He did, and I have. There is more to you than I ever knew. I keep discovering more depth every time we meet." Julie remained silent, looking at me from across the top of her mug, analyzing me, probing me from the inside out.

"You have doubts about me?" she said flatly.

"No doubt that I love you."

"Do you doubt that I love you in return?"

"No, Julie. I know that you do." Her eyes softened just a little, but her brain was still working me over, her eyes moving rapidly between mine.

"I just can't tell you everything, Rick. I just can't." Her eyes glinted from additional moisture, her sincerity palpable.

"We've never really talked about this, Julie. Want to know what I want to do?"

"I want to know, Rick."

"I want us to go away together. Run, Julie, before anything happens to you. Please, let me take you someplace where we can be free of this mess. We'll change our names. They'll never find us."

"No Rick. I can't do that. After this is over, I will do anything you want, that is if you still want me."

"Meaning that there is a lot yet left to be discovered. Some more surprises for me."

"Yes."

"Look, Julie, I'm in love with you. I don't care if you are

someone else, you are still you to me. It won't make any difference."

"It's not that, Rick. It's what I might have to do. There could be things that you couldn't abide."

"I can abide anything except losing you. If you are killed in this madness, I might as well go with you, so we can be together after death."

Her tears dried, and her face became taught, her eyes steely. "I don't plan on dying, and I don't plan on you dying either. Others are going to die, not us." I believed her, but her resolve and her certitude frightened me. Compared to her, I was weak and vacillating. I stood on no principle, had no values, no backbone. She was all I cared about, nothing else mattered.

We kissed lightly, as much as public courtesy would allow, in front of her dorm, and with a last, lingering look exchanged between us, we parted. Every time we separated, my heart sank as it did just then. Our frank talk did little to clarify what actually was going on except to confirm that we were playing games which will result in death, likely several. There must be something I could do to protect her or at least find out how to prevent the enemy from striking first. It dawned on me that there was something I could do, and kill two birds with one stone. Last time I talked with Carol, she told me that Mike was still around. She had seen him. If I arranged for her to satisfy my roommates lust, I might get a line on how to contact Mike. If I did find him, I had to prepare a cover story, just in case.

She picked up on the first ring. "Yes?" she said.

"Hello Carol. This is Rick James. Remember me?"

"Sure do, handsome. Ready for a tumble?"

"Very inviting, but no, not this time. I have a friend in need."

"Let me guess. It's the little boy sharing your room?"

"I'm afraid so. He just can't seem to make it through life

without experiencing you again. This time he knows that you are a working girl."

"Who pays?"

"He is, this time."

"Two hundred. Cash."

"I remember."

"In advance."

"I remember that also. Seems fair to me."

"I'd do you for free."

"I'll look forward to that. Say, I need another favor of a different kind."

"Name it."

"Mike. I need to talk to him. Seen him lately?"

"What's it worth to you?"

"I just acted like I was your pimp. Isn't that enough?"

"Yeah, I suppose it is. Mike hangs out at Frisco, the bar on Seventh. If I were you, I wouldn't go in there alone."

"Can you give him a message?" I asked.

"What's the message?"

"Tell him to meet me in the pool hall tomorrow about four. No tricks, and I'll be alone. I just want to talk. I owe you one."

"Consider it done. I'll collect from you later, and it won't be money."

"Oh, and the other thing. Can I tell Howard to meet you outside the dorm at four?"

"I guess. Trying to avoid me, Rick?"

"No, I enjoy your company, Carol. It's just what we have to do."

Chapter 24

Mike's story

At four in the afternoon, the pool hall usually was sparsely populated by devotees of the game. Once, I was told that the late evenings into the early morning was when things happened. During the day, the college regulars were around but cleared out before the heavies rolled in later. I could see that there were a couple of tables occupied but most were available, waiting with balls already racked, the overhead lamp on, the omnipresent cigarette smoke hanging in a horizontal layer about head height.

My watch read thirty-five minutes past four. Mike either didn't get my message or was wary of meeting me. I couldn't blame him, because if Grey or Jerk laid their hands on him, he was in for a really bad time. Leaning over and using my cue to sight the path of the white ball, I saw someone standing in the shadows, just beyond the table. I took the shot and watched as the nine ball spun in the wrong direction after being tapped.

"You should have put more top spin on it," he said from the sidelines.

"Are you good with the stick?" I asked.

"Better than you. Compared to you, I'm a hustler, but I know enough to stay away from this place after ten."

"I've heard. I may have even heard that from you, in fact."

"You did. Want to see me?"

"I thought we were friends, once."

"We still are. I never did anything to you."

"And I never did anything to you."

"Yes, you did. You went looking for me in Fayetteville. Now they are searching for me. What do you want, anyway?"

"I want to pass along something I've learned. It might save your life. That's what a friend will do."

"Holding my breath over here. Spill it." Mike moved into the light, standing beside the pool table, the harsh light casting his face in high contrast. He picked up one of the hard ivory balls, shifting it from hand to hand in a threatening manner.

"Here's the deal, Mike. I'll tell you what I know, you tell me what you know. Sound fair?"

"And why would you do that?"

"Simple. I've been lied to by them and by you. I'm fed up with lies. I want to know the truth."

"There is no truth, Rick. Life isn't about truth, it's about survival, money or sex."

"What drives you then? Did someone pay you to spy and pretend you are a student?"

"I had an obligation to pay off. I never got any money."

"You are putting your life at risk getting involved in this. We are in the tip of the spear hurtling toward a target. It's a clash of cultures bigger than us."

"All right, Rick. You first."

"It's taken me some time to figure out, but I can tell you for sure that Julie is a ringer. I'm in love with her just the same, but she isn't who you suspect she is. It's a big trap. Run away while you can."

"You're wrong. Julie is the daughter of Colonel Frank. She's been certified."

"They changed the albums. They have people in place. This is very big." After I spoke, I saw Mike's face change. Momentarily, his eyes lost their focus. He wasn't as sure as he had been, but he was still determined to let me think so.

"I don't believe you. You are telling me what they want you to tell me. They are trying to protect her and so are you."

"They are not and neither is she. They want you and everybody in this plot to go down. You are marked for death, not for prison. They want you to believe she is the real McCoy, don't you see? As soon as they are sure they can round up everybody at the same time, they will strike. Run away, Mike."

"I'll tell you how I got into this, and you'll understand. Want to hear my side?"

"Of course."

"I was in the Corps and stationed near Kandahar. You've no doubt hear about that part of Afghanistan. It's a tough place, and we never did completely control it. One day I did something real stupid, and I've paid for it since. Our patrol unit passed regularly through a village, and we were expected to make friends with the natives. We were ordered to stay far away from the women, but there was one that caught my eye, a real special one. I managed to get away with her one hot afternoon, and we used her little hut to do what boys and girls have always done. She got into my blood, just like Julie has gotten into yours. Our encounter was all I thought about. I had to have more; it was driving me crazy. The very first time I went off base against orders, they caught me sneaking back in, and I was hauled in front of, guess who, Colonel Frank. He accused me of everything under the sun, including collaboration with the enemy. It wasn't true, none of it. I was simply infatuated with a lovely girl. I had no contact with the Taliban whatsoever. He, Colonel Frank, got out of control and ordered the arrest of the girl, accusing her of being part of the Taliban. They were going to turn her over to the Afghan cops, and

I had heard what usually befell girls when that happened." Mike stopped for a moment, remembering his lovely Afghan woman, looking away somewhere back in time where he could never go again. He continued to toss the ball from hand-to-hand, suspended for a moment in a mental world on the other side of the planet.

"What happened to her, the Afghan woman?" I asked trying to bring him back.

"I slipped away that night wanting to warn her to leave. Before I got there, one of our units, on the orders of the Colonel, took the village by force in the dead of night. Someone blew her head off in the resulting firefight. My woman was dead, and I was AWOL and already accused of assisting the enemy. My goose was cooked. I was about to spend the rest of my life in Leavenworth. There was no choice for me so I fled into the hills. I'm a deserter, the lowest form of life."

"How did you get out? That would seem to be in the frying pan or in the fire to me."

"The Taliban. They quickly captured me, and once they realized that I was worth more alive than dead, they got me out of the country. They hauled me through Iran into Syria and on to Lebanon. I was passed from group to group like a sack of rocks. Many times, I thought I was about to die, and I wished that I had. They agreed to help me return to the U.S. for a price. That price was that I was to do whatever they wanted…forever. This is my first assignment, perhaps my only one. If I didn't cooperate, all they had to do is rat me out to the American Military or the Feds. By now, there is a death sentence waiting for me. Either way, I have nothing to look forward to. For now, I do what they say, and when they told me to identify Julie, I did. Frankly, I don't care if she is the real Julie or a ringer. I hate her father not her, but if they kill her, I won't care a bit."

"Mike, there might be a chance to turn things around. Julie

means more to the Colonel than anything even if she is a decoy. I've seen them embrace, and I know she means a lot to him. What if I can act as a go between? If you become a double agent, it might be possible to turn things around. It sounds like you haven't done anything so far but be a victim of circumstances. There has got to be a way to redeem yourself, Mike." He stopped tossing the ball, looking at me, his face blank. He was thinking it through, teetering on the fence. For the first time, he realized he might have a choice in his life.

"The Corps would never set me free. There is always the desertion charge, and they could add a dozen more if they want."

"A bit of jail time, but better than being dead. Why not take a chance?"

"Look, Rick. They don't know that I'm back in the country yet. If you start negotiations about me, they will start frantically looking. I'd have to try and get far from here, away from both sides. There isn't enough money on Wall Street to do that."

"How did Colonel Frank run afoul of Hezbollah? They are only in Syria or Lebanon, isn't that right?" I asked.

"Not completely. They have sent dozens, perhaps hundreds of men into various battle zones for training and experience. Colonel Franks' men captured some of them, and they talked. The Colonel worked out a plan to take out their command center in Lebanon, identified during the interrogations. The Navy used one of our fighter planes decked out in Israeli markings to make the strike. It worked, but they killed some civilians, the wrong ones, and the game was on."

"They know about you Mike, just not the real you, but eventually they will piece it together. Let me help you turn this around before time runs out. If Hezbollah makes a move against Julie, it will be too late."

"Yeah, they know about me, but it's thanks to you and your

snooping that they do."

"I admit it. You lied to me, though. I was only trying to protect Julie. It doesn't matter about what I did, because they have already fixated on Biggs. You were in his class pretending to be a student. Sooner or later someone would have checked."

"Biggs? I didn't know he was in this. Are you sure about Biggs?"

"I'm not sure about anything, Mike. My entire goal is to prevent harm coming to the girl calling herself Julie. That's all I want. As far as Biggs goes, he just seems suspicious."

"Biggs is a gay blade. Only, he might have picked the wrong boy to play with this time," Mike said. It was a point of view I had not considered. Biggs may have a taste for exotic types and have unwittingly played into the hands of Hezbollah who are just using him for cover.

"What about it Mike? Can you change sides?" I asked.

"Looks like I'll get knocked off either way. If my handler gets any whiff of this, I'm done for. If I don't do it your way, my own people will snuff me. Why don't you ask the right people. Tell my side of things and see what happens."

"I'll see what I can do. We'll use Carol to communicate. Okay?"

"Carol gets around. She's a good choice, but she has her price also. You might find out."

"I got a hint of it. When you leave here, you better have a plan because, often, two Marines are keeping an eye on me."

"If I didn't have a plan, I would never have survived this long. I'm counting on you Rick to do what you promised."

"I'll try, Mike, but you might want to do what I said the first time. Flee. Hide."

"Too late for that. Everybody would want me, and I wouldn't last long out there by myself."

"Good luck, Mike."

"And to you. Thanks, Rick. Thanks for giving me hope, even

for just a moment."

The meeting with Mike was over quicker than I anticipated, and I found myself standing in front of the dorm realizing that it wasn't yet five. Not quite an hour. Carol might still be up there giving Howard his money's worth, a full hour with Carol and her interpretation of male and female physical relationships. Before leaving the room, I warned Howard of how much he was expected to pay her. Immediately, he sat down, methodically calculating what it would cost if he were dating and courting someone. Figuring all the costs, he felt that he was coming out ahead hiring Carol and that way he didn't have to wait for a sexual encounter. Besides, as he observed coolly, he was learning things which would take years on his own with an inexperienced female companion. I tried my old stale arguments on him, my judgment about what constitutes a good healthy relationship and one far more fulfilling. He wanted none of that monkey business. He wanted sex, pure and unfiltered, unadulterated and raw, and I assumed that he was getting what he had purchased right now.

Carol stepped off the elevator, catching my eye as she did. She headed my way, and I could see that her hair was askew and her make up smeared. Carol had been handled all right, a full hour's worth.

"Carol? Is everything all right? You look a bit used," I said, suppressing any mirth. She rolled her eyes at me and fussed with hair.

"It's a hard way to make a living sometimes," she admitted. "That's a different boy than we had the first time. Such persistence. I think we did things that I hadn't done or even thought of before."

"He got his fill, I assume?"

"I sure did, but no, he didn't. I have a regular appointment set up with him from now on. You and I may be seeing each other quite often. It'll give me a chance to tempt you to give me a try."

"Well, the first thing is to get some food into you. Can I buy you dinner, and we can talk for a little while? We never got to know each other."

"Someplace fancy?"

"Cafeteria. This building."

"Better than nothing. I would like that."

We sat across from each other and engaged in polite conversation. Carol was obviously hungry and had selected a large variety of dishes which were spread and arrayed around the small table. She was talkative, cheerful and actually very interesting. I wanted to discover how she had chosen her current line of work, but I resisted asking, instead discussing myself and my uninteresting background. Carol had one year of college, majoring in English. She enjoyed reading and was very current and up-to date with the latest book selections. Her family were all farmers embedded in a tiny Midwestern town which is the reason she escaped. She wanted more excitement, more freedom, but ended up in another small city after all. Carol imagined living in Vegas or New York, because she felt there were more opportunities there. What kind, she didn't mention. She didn't smoke, and avoided those who did, but had a weakness for alcohol which, she admitted, was necessary in her line of work.

"You are a sweet boy, Rick, such a pleasure to sit and talk with and so free of accusations or demands. I wish it were you meeting me once a week instead of your lonely roommate."

"We can dine together every time you are here if I am available. I enjoy your company also."

"I'm in with a bad crowd, Rick. It's not a good place for me, but it's how I live. You understand, don't you?" she asked with raised eyebrows.

"No, no I don't. You are an attractive woman, and I've only seen your face. I think that you should have lots of options. You aren't dumb or ignorant and seemingly can talk about any subject. Your problem is that you are in with people who have no dreams of betterment. What about trying a different lifestyle?"

"Money, Rick. I have to eat and live. And then, there is a job. I have no references, no experience, no training. How could I support myself?"

"If I were you, I would look for a job first, the rest will follow."

"I can clear a thousand a week, when things go well. I can't make that flipping burgers."

"Where does all that money go?" I asked. She stiffened and gave me a look. That was private, off-limits, meaning the cash likely went to boyfriends, pimps or drugs. This was her real trap and the reason she couldn't easily exit without external support.

"I'll tell you what, Rick. You support me, and I'll quit. I promise that I will make the evenings exciting for you. I'll show my gratitude appropriately."

"You have to understand that, financially, I'm barely here, Carol. I don't have any money to spare. You'll just have to settle for my friendship."

"Okay, friends with privileges. I'm happy with that."

"You'll make a good friend. If I can ever help you, call me. You have my number."

"Did Mike meet you?"

"Yes, we met."

"Work things out?"

"At least we parted smiling. Say, we may need to connect from time to time. Would you act as go-between?" Carol stopped eating and studied me carefully, finally nodding to herself.

"So that's why all this friendship? Just so you can use me in some nefarious plot you two have schemed up?"

"You brought up Mike… I never mentioned him. You don't have to agree to help, because we can work something else out, and you don't have to be involved." I could tell that my logic didn't fly. She clearly understood what I was up to, and she was correct. Mike was right, this girl will be problematic after all.

"I'll act as your messenger for a price. Guess what that is?" she said and smiled broadly. I didn't need to guess what she was thinking. Now what a fine mess this was.

"Tell you what, Carol. Let's just drop the whole subject right now and be happy with friendship. I have no ulterior motives regarding you. You make an interesting and enjoyable companion, and I hope you feel that way about me. Couldn't we leave it at that for now?"

"Can I bring my problems to you, whatever they are, and you promise to listen and not moralize about them?"

"Yes. That's what a friend does. May I do the same?"

"Friends!" she exploded, shooting her hand across the table.

Chapter 25

Blinded and going uphill

Two big hands grasped the thick burger full of trimmings and lifted it to his mouth. I was reminded of the story of Odysseus and the Cyclops who would eat sheep, or men, whole. Jerk did the same, and the two burgers rapidly disappeared.

"What did you want, James?" Grey asked, after he wiped his lips of catsup. I could see that both of them were waiting to hear why I wanted to meet and were interested.

"I don't know how to start, Grey. Whatever I tell you will send you over the edge. You have to promise to allow me to tell the whole story before you jump down my throat. You know I trust both of you, that's why I'm telling you the story first."

"Short story, he's screwed something up again," Grey said to Jerk who nodded agreement. "Go ahead, James. We're used to it by now."

After I put my drink down and cleared my throat, I began, "This story goes back to Afghanistan. You both have been there, I know." Both sets of eyebrows went up, sort of like antennae and both put down their food, waiting on the rest. "There was a grunt, name withheld for now, who was commanded by the Colonel and who jumped ship…deserted."

"Well, James, this is going to get interesting, because both of us served with the Colonel and desertion from the U.S. Marines is rare as hen's teeth. We already know the single individual, the only individual Marine, who ever deserted in the last twenty years."

"Yes. Well that's probably the one. His side of the story is that he had a girlfriend and went AWOL to see her but was accused of collaboration by Colonel Frank. He says that she was killed in an action against her village, and he had no choice except to defect."

"This guy give you a name, James?" Jerk asked and resumed eating.

"Mike. Mike Flannigan."

"What a bunch of crap!" Grey said, pounding his big fist on the flimsy table. "I don't know who this guy is, but he's a fake, James. Every time you go wild on your own, we have to come in and save your butt. The Marine who went AWOL was killed and mutilated by the Taliban. I personally took his body back to HQ. He died, James, and his name wasn't Mike Flannigan."

"Can you tell me, at least, what kind of unit you all were in over there?" I asked. Grey looked at Jerk and shrugged.

"Sure, James" Grey said. "You probably should know that. We were all part of Scout Sniper Platoon, Alpha Company, 1st Battalion. Colonel Franks was our Captain. He had also trained as a sniper, back when. We were all snipers, including the Marine who defected."

"Tell us the rest, James," Jerk said quietly.

"He told me that the Taliban held him captive and took him to Lebanon where he agreed to spy for Hezbollah in exchange for his life."

"What earthly purpose did you have in meeting with this man?"

"I wanted to stop them from killing Julie. I wanted to tell them that she is a ringer, not the real Julie. Perhaps they would call off the hit."

"What do you think Julie would say about that. Did you ask her?" Grey questioned.

"No. I didn't tell her, because I already know that she won't back off."

"Look, boy. The entire reason that we are here and Julie is in school is to entice these bad boys out into the open. We want them to make an attempt, the last attempt of their lives, you can be sure. That's the only way we can end this once and for all. When we find the mastermind, Nasrallah, we want to take him prisoner, not kill him, at least at first. During interrogation, he will spill the beans on the others, and we can round them up and dispose of them."

"What if you are wrong, Grey?" I pleaded. "Say they shoot her from a distance, like you warned me about. Or they could blow up the entire classroom just to get her. What if getting rid of this Nasrallah doesn't stop the machine he has in place?" I felt desperate to stop this madness. Julie was the key player, both to me and to the other parties. She was the only thing that mattered to anyone, the lamb tied to the stake, waiting for the tiger.

"How did you go about talking to Mike? Tell us how you contacted him?" Grey growled. They weren't going to let it go, I could tell. Before I answered I thought about my contact, my new friend, Carol. She might have been in on it from the first, part of the other side's team. Since she was the only possible link to Mike, I had to keep her from discovering that I suspected her. Play her as she was playing me. I wasn't about to rat my only link to Mike out to these two.

"I might have been duped, fellows. My link might be a spy, not a stooge. If I give this person over to you, you won't get another chance at finding Mike. If you take them both in, you'll scare away Nasrallah. You have to let me help, or the entire chain will fall apart."

"You are playing in an area that you aren't competent by training; besides, you aren't fully informed regarding the facts. Just let us handle it, James. That's an order," Jerk said. I could tell that his anger was just below the surface and would head my way soon.

"Without question, on both counts you are right, but I'm not going to back off. You need me, and I need to be sure that Julie isn't sacrificed just to close a case file."

"Listen, James. All the people involved on our side, and on theirs, are professionals. Don't count on anything you hear or see being true. It's a play, and we are all actors, but the climax and closing scenes will be conducted with weapons drawn and blood on the floor. You are only a pawn and pawns shouldn't die. Remember what we told you…don't die for nothing."

Grey's tone was final, but I wasn't yet convinced. "What if the Taliban staged Mike's death? What if he is the real McCoy? You could turn him, spy on them using Mike. If, by amazing chance, the story he told me is true, then he should be given a chance to redeem himself. Prison perhaps, but not death."

"There isn't a chance in Hell that this Mike is real. If I could see him in person, I would know instantly if it's him. We served together for months before he disappeared."

"A suggestion, Grey. If I can have your word to let me be part of this, I'll try to get a photo of Mike. That means that if Mike and I meet again, I expect you to let me handle it and not swoop in and grab him. If he turns out to be the Marine you remember, then we try my suggestion. Turn him to our side."

"We can see that you just don't know how dangerous this is for you, James. You are blinded by love and feeling your way along a tiny trail on the side of a high mountain. You are going up when you should be going down. One more time, James, Jerk and I take orders, obey orders without question and say sir a lot. The only thing we can do is to send it up for the brass to consider. We don't make decisions at our level."

"There is something else you should know," Jerk said. "Julie. There is more to her than you have seen. Open your love-struck eyes and look around." Grey shot him a dirty look after he spoke.

He had let something out of the bag…a gift to me, or a warning?

Grey wiped his hands and stood up, looking down at me as if I were in the first grade. "One last question, James. Did this Mike believe you when you told him that Julie was a ringer?"

"No. He said that she had been certified, whatever that means."

After we parted, I made my way slowly back to the dorm, thinking over what they and I had exchanged. I had promised Mike that I wouldn't disclose who he was, and I had done exactly that. From now forward, the Colonel's men would be looking for him and know precisely whom they were looking for. It struck me that the only way they could find him would be if he was actually the Marine who defected, otherwise he was an unknown face and could be anybody. And then there was Carol. She planned to make me pay for help, and her payment would cost me the affections of the girl I wanted most in this life. I couldn't betray Julie to save Julie. It wasn't in my DNA. What an incredible mess.

Who was Julie? I couldn't make myself believe that she was an actress pretending to love me and pretending be Julie Frank. Deep inside, I still believed her story, especially when I was with her, also I believed Mike. I was just dumb enough to believe everybody, even Carol. It was hopeless for me to sort out. Either everybody is lying or nobody is lying, and it was possible that just some are lying. Rats!

"Scout Sniper Platoon, Alpha Company, 1st Battalion, Grey had said. Snipers. All of them, including Mike…if Mike was telling the truth," I said out loud to myself as I made my way back to my room. Just before I turned the handle, I realized the implications. Mike was the perfect assassin to take Julie out. He had training, motivation and was in position to do it. I might have protested that Julie was a ringer to the wrong person. Mike likely expected that I would make a plea, an especially impassioned plea, if I believed that Julie was actually Julie Frank. Grey and Jerk were right again. I might have made the problem worse. Mike's real identity would have to be discovered and soon. He was dangerous if he wasn't the Marine defector, because he was lying to me. He was even more dangerous if he were telling the truth…a fully trained Marine sniper with a grudge. Sweat beads grew on my forehead, and my pulse went up.

"Hi, Rick," Howard said, looking up from his book. "I didn't know you were coming back this morning. Say, you feel all right?"

"No," I said and threw myself on the bed. A mistake, the gun ripping at my flesh because I forgot to take it out. I reached behind me, withdrawing it and tucking it under my pillow. Howard's eyes never left me.

"Why, exactly, are you carrying a big gun around with you?" he asked.

"None of your business, Howard. I can't talk about it."

"You're into drugs, aren't you? I figured since you know hookers and carried a gun, what else could it be."

"No!" I said angrily. "No drugs, no crime and I don't play with hookers, like some person I know."

"It was your idea, Rick. How can you infer that I'm some sort of despicable person because I get pleasure out of it? Didn't you want me to discover that part of myself?"

"I'm sorry Howard. I want you to be happy but please…no more questions and stop inferring anything about me for now. Please?"

"Sure, Rick. By the way, Carol really likes you, you should know."

"And, how do you know this?"

"She asks a lot of questions about you, and your girlfriend. She's interested in you. Perhaps you would like her if you got closer, if you know what I mean."

I rolled up to a sitting position and looked at him. Actually, I looked past his desk light and the large stack of books catching his one eye on me. "What, exactly, has she asked about?"

"Oh, she wanted to know how often you saw your girlfriend and where you usually went together, and…you won't like this next part. She asked if you were sleeping with her yet."

"And what did you tell her?"

"I couldn't tell her anything, because you never tell me anything."

"You didn't happen to tell her that I carried a gun did you?"

"Of course not!" His eye widened, and I saw his head emerge over the books. "The lady doth protest too much," popped into my head. I stood up also, my anger beginning to rise up like a sewer overflowing. Nothing much could stop it.

"Howard…you have to tell me the truth, dammit. I have to know if you told her." Howard's lower lip started to tremble, and it seemed that his chicken neck was longer than ever. He told her. He didn't have to admit it with words. He told Carol that I was carrying. I had to resist the urge to hurt him, to pound on him until he bled. "You promised. Why would you tell her that?" I demanded. He didn't have to answer, because the obvious truth was that Howard was as weak as they come. His head slowly sank beneath the cover of his books, his answer screaming noiselessly inside my head.

"You're not going to remain silent and get by with it Howard. You might have put my life at risk. You are going to tell me how the subject came up. Did she ask or did you just volunteer?" I moved around the desk and stood over him, watching the back of his head, his face in his hands. His shoulder sagged and trembled, but my sympathy was not with Howard at this moment. It was disgust, not empathy, that filled my soul, that and the gripping fear about the implications. I would no longer have surprise working in my favor. I pushed his shoulder roughly. "Talk," I commanded and pushed harder.

"She seems so nice. I never thought…." he mumbled into his hands.

I pushed him back to a sitting position and put my tight fist hard against his nose, feeling the wet running down the back of my hand. "So help me, Howard, you are going to tell me everything or else I'm going to beat on you until you do." It was no empty threat.

"She started asking during sex. My mind wasn't clear. I wasn't careful."

"How did she ask…How?"

"She asked if she could look through your things. I wasn't sure if your gun was with you or under your pillow. I stammered…. She started questioning my resistance to her question then promised to do something to me that I like a lot. I admitted to her that there was an item you wouldn't want her to see, that's all. She guessed that it was a gun. She said it, not me."

So they, I also include Carol in the conspiracy, suspected that I carried a gun, and now they know I do. Mike had seen me being trained and probably guessed. It was heads-up, a warning, for them. I might as well throw the gun in the trash, because I'll never get the chance to draw it. Was Sally also linked with them, and her two bad boys, were they also involved? I'd have to guess that they all were. My path up the mountain just got steeper and more narrow, and I still didn't know where I was headed. Grey and Jerk had to be told, and as soon as possible.

Chapter 26

Seductive Carol

The only way I can describe the sensation of walking around feeling as though you are in the crosshairs of a sniper is…well, creepy. My imagination was running away with me, and the anticipation of being suddenly, without warning, shot was wearing me down. Of course, I reasoned, they wouldn't shoot me first. It would bring national attention to this little city, and Julie would go to ground. No, they would either kill us both at the same time or even more likely, her first. This was not the best way to spend your sophomore year at college. I didn't like the feeling of helplessness that was weighting me down, the waiting for unseen enemies to strike first. There had to be another way. That's why I was waiting on Carol to keep her appointment with Howard. She would have to walk right past me on her way to the elevator.

If this was an old movie from the forties, I would lean against the wall, smoking a cigarette, my fedora pulled down low, one knee bent and bracing with my foot. Mean, I would look mean, the smoke curling up and flowing over the brim of my grey hat, eyes narrow and hard, my face a permanent dark stubble of hair. Instead, I just hung around in my blue hooded sweats, waiting anxiously, rehearsing what I was going to say to her. The more I thought it over, the more I felt that I had nothing to lose by trying to contact Mike again. After all, he could terminate me anytime he wanted…if…he was the sniper trained Marine he claimed to be. They had nothing to gain by getting rid of me just now and a lot to lose. Mostly, the element of suspense and surprise. The cat would crawl out of the bag, and all hell would cut loose.

Carol was walking toward me and in a hurry. As she went by, I noticed her tight, form-fitting skirt which clung to her abdomen and followed the natural arc toward her pubis, matching the parallel curve of her buttocks and the reverse curve of her lower spine. Natural, but also odd to see the female form like that, the tumblehome effect that it gave because of her rather ample curves. Her body's hourglass shape from the rear was strikingly sexual, in fact, advertised sex, a walking billboard of sex swaying just ahead of me.

"Carol!" I called and watched her turn toward me smiling.

"Well," she said. "I hoped I would see you tonight. Thought over my proposition?"

"Sure. Keeps me up at night thinking about you. Just the thought is arousing, but looking at your expression right now, it isn't a surprise. You know all that."

"I have that effect on men. Want to come upstairs with me and experience a little two on one?

"Ah, the *ménage à trois*. No thanks. I'm not being anywhere near Howard when he takes off his clothes."

"Afterward, then?"

"Not with any trace of Howard even in the air."

"Men! You all are so delicate, aren't you."

"I'm not delicate at all, Carol. I just don't associate my roommate with sex."

"Will you be here in an hour?"

"For you? Of course. Want to dine with me again on cafeteria food?"

"Not especially. What I want is to dine on you, but I'll take what

I can get."

"I'll be waiting. Howard told me that you are asking a lot of questions about me. Care to explain why?" Her pupils changed size briefly, and she looked around before answering.

"Just interested in you, anything wrong in that?" she coarsely whispered, showing exaggerated surprise.

"The other thing, Carol."

"The gun? Hey, you aren't the regular little college boy are you? Where I'm from, all the men are carrying. I'm a little proud of you, and to me it indicates that you are a mover not a follower. I like it."

"Tell anyone?"

"No. Whom would I tell?"

"Mike?"

"You got the wrong idea about me and Mike. I don't see Mike, except by accident. We don't engage. Get the idea?"

"Yet, you can get hold of him when you need to?"

"I leave a message at the bar. They give it to him. At least, I guess that they do. Mike scares me, there's something different about him. What do you think about Mike?"

"I don't think. I don't know."

"I don't understand. Isn't Mike your old buddy?"

"The honest answer is that I don't know who Mike really is, only what he tells me, and he tells different stories at different times. What do you think he's up to?"

"At least half the men down there are doing something illegal or, at least, immoral. Mike's no different. Sure, he's up to something. Aren't you?"

"I'm not up to anything, and I'm not doing anything illegal."

"Yet, you are carrying."

"For me, it's defensive only."

"Oh yeah? Defensive against whom or what?"

"Could be Mike." That stopped her, and she just looked at me, looking between my eyes like people do if they are trying to figure you out. I was starting to believe her, at least as far as Mike went. Perhaps Carol was just a good-looking hooker like she said. "I should try and meet with him again, want to help?" I asked.

"The pool hall again?" she suggested.

"That's what I was thinking."

"It's none of my business, Rick, but Mike seems, well, capable. You better watch yourself."

"So, you're sure you never told him about a gun? You know, a warning?"

"I'm sure. Haven't spoken to him face-to-face for a long time."

"One more question, then you better get upstairs before Howard explodes. You and Sally close?"

"We work together sometimes. You know that. Other than that, there's no friendship. Different circles."

"Do you know the two ex-cons she hangs out with?"

"I've seen them, and I wouldn't party with those two, either one of them. I don't know them, don't want to."

"Thanks. I'll be here when you come down," I said and gave her a quick embrace. In turn, she patted my butt and smiled. She was watching me as the elevator door slowly closed. It gave me an uneasy feeling, her level stare, the blank look on her face.

What did I accomplish with her? I still wasn't sure about anything, who the bad guys were and what was going to happen, or when. My gullibility was hanging from my face like an Appalachian beard.

"Do you know that woman?" a deep voice asked. I look behind me to see a uniformed campus guard looking sternly at me.

"The one who just got on the elevator?"

"That one. I've seen her before someplace, and the way she looks, she doesn't belong here. You know the rules, don't you?"

"Sure. No unescorted female visitors, don't close the door with female guests, out by ten. Those rules?"

"And the one about visitors are restricted to relatives and students only," he said.

"She's a student, officer, and I just escorted her, didn't you see? And I'm waiting for her to come down, and we're going to the cafeteria. There are no broken rules that I can see."

"She doesn't look like a college student to me, more like a streetwalker."

"You're just kidding, right? It's the new look, a bit trashy. They all do it nowadays." I laughed, but he didn't. He looked at the elevator door and then back at me. I waited for the question about which room she had gone to, and I could sense that he was about to ask when a noise made us turn. A scuffle had broken out between two male students, and one was lying on the floor. The guard forgot all about Carol and went off to face his new problem. I walked quietly away and settled into a dark corner chair, picking up my phone.

"Hi," I said when she answered, the murmur of her voice trickling deliciously into my ear.

"Hi, yourself. What are you doing right now?" Julie asked, the near whisper she used often on me was so personal, so intimate.

"I am sitting in a chair in the lobby of my dorm waiting on a hooker to finish off my roommate."

"You are kidding."

"Not."

"There are too many whys to know where to start asking. You first."

"There are too many answers to start answering. It's necessary, I started it, and it's all about a girl named Julie." She was silent on her end, chewing on that little tidbit for a time.

"I've got to hear about this in person. Come over and pick me up, and I'll make it worthwhile."

"Can you give me a couple of hours?" I asked.

"Do you get a turn with her also?" Julie asked, the last word in her sentence emphasized a bit.

"You don't have to ask that, do you?"

"I hope not. Men are men, though."

"Not this one. This one has found his mate, the one that no other woman could come between, the one he dreams about every night, the one who sets him on fire with the sound of her voice alone."

"You haven't seen fire yet."

"Then I'm going to die happy. How about shortly after seven?"

"I'll be waiting, lips puckered."

We exchanged our usual love you just before clicking off and without putting the phone away, I dialed another number I had stored. Sally's answering machine picked up.

"Hi Sally. This is Rick James. Call back, please," I said. Before I could get the phone back into my jeans, it rang.

"Sally, Rick. What can I do for you?"

"I'm not sure. Just a question for now. Your two con boyfriends. Are you still in contact with them?"

"As I remember, you thought you might like to hire them for a job. That it?"

"Maybe. I thought I would discuss something with them first."

"I'll have to let you know, Rick, but I can ask them. I'll get back to you."

"Thanks," I said, not meaning it. At the moment, I didn't have a plan or a reason for my call. It was just something spontaneous coming out of me, an irritation that I had to scratch. I slumped back in the soft chair and apparently dozed off.

Something was poking me, and I opened my eyes with a start. The first thing I saw was Carol's face smiling down at me. "You waited for me!" she said. "You waiting for the likes of me. It touches me, Rick." She leaned closer, putting her face against mine while she whispered into my ear. "I want you, Rick. You've got to let me show you how much."

I smiled back at her and caressed the back of her neck with my hand, kissing her cheek at the same time. "Ready to eat?" I struggled sleepily to my feet and looked at my watch. "You got finished early?"

"Don't worry, Howard got his money's worth tonight," she laughed and stood beside me, encircling my waist with her arm. When she did that, I knew that she could feel the weapon I always wore at my back, but she didn't comment on it.

We chose the same little table in the corner, next to the big window letting light out of the room instead of in. I was always amazed at how much food Carol could eat. She just wasn't heavy so I assumed that her sexual activity used a lot of calories, that and the late hours she kept.

"I love meeting you like this," she said between bites and brushed a long strand of hair out of her eyes. "You are my special friend, Rick, but not like a brother, more like an unfulfilled love of mine. There is an entirely other side of me, the side that is completely wild and uninhibited. The side that I want to show you."

"Carol, I like you. I enjoy meeting you and learning about you, but I told you that I have a girlfriend, and I'm loyal to her. I can't cheat on her."

"Pity. What's your girlfriend's name?"

"Why do you care? Anyway, I thought you knew her name already. Don't you?"

"Not that I remember. She must be very special. Sex with her what you expected, Rick?"

"It's good, but don't ask me any more about it."

"I'll bet she doesn't know what I know."

"It's enough for me."

"I've never been in love, at least I don't think so. What's it like, Rick, this love thing?" She leaned forward, reaching for a bun, and my eye was drawn to her deep cleavage. Her breast moved seductively as she pulled her arm back, and I envisioned her unclothed form without meaning to. She smiled slightly because she knew my thoughts but continued eating, her eyes flashing briefly at my face.

"Love is new to me, but I can tell you that I felt love for her before we actually spoke to one another. It's like I always knew her, like she is part of me, her brain and mine have the same thoughts at the same time. I think about her when we aren't together, dream about her, and when we are together, I don't want to part."

Carol nodded knowingly, watching my face. "So you think you know her completely, inside and out? You know everything about her…everything?"

The question made me uncomfortable. Carol had penetrated to the dark spot I chose not to open to myself. "No. I don't know everything about her, but love is also about trust. I don't need to know everything, just that she loves me too."

"But Rick, dear boy! You know what I do for a living. If you fell in love with me, it would be in spite of that knowledge. What if you discovered it later, though? Wouldn't that make a difference if you found out that I lived that sort of life before you knew me and then realized that I never told you?"

"There isn't anything like that with her."

"But, you don't know for sure, do you?"

"No."

"In fact, Rick, if you think about her right now, and you tell me the truth, you will admit that she has said or done things that make you wonder. Isn't that true?" Carol smiled, knowing that she had found some nails sticking proudly from the surface, ones that I had been avoiding.

"You're right, Carol. There are times that I think that there are things she is keeping from me. You can't ever know a person's thoughts, can you? You have to have respect for them and assume that there are things they can't tell you."

"Things that she doesn't want you to know, you mean. Things that, if you knew them, might alter your relationship, you mean. See my point now?"

"You have a point, but so what? I still love her."

"Rick, my bet is that your girlfriend is very attractive, even beautiful. Is that her?"

"Very much so."

"On this subject, I know more than you. The female shape, her voice, her scents are tailored by evolution to trigger desire in a man. When you experience the whole package for the first time, you are hooked. You think that desire and love are the same, and when you take parts of her in your mouth and she with you, you believe that it's nearly holy and made just for you. It isn't, Rick, it's just biology doing what it does to ensure reproduction of our species. What you have experienced is the human female, not just your girlfriend, but all of us. The opposite sex, Rick. You are a male, and you need the female to complete you. That's why I am more honest, why I understand the attraction better than you. You have been blinded by the female body, the female mannerisms, even the female hormones that you inhaled." She paused for a breath and observed me to discover if she was getting through.

"You know that most marriages eventually fade or fail, don't you? The reason is that there was never love, just physical attraction, and when we get older, the attraction isn't so strong any longer; the bond breaks. Girls like me can give you the physical part, and we also can whisper in your ear and make you feel special. We give you the same thing, exactly the same thing, as the woman you think you love, and you don't have to offer to die for us, because we don't expect it."

"I'm not experienced like you, Carol, so I can't dispute anything you said. This was my first sexual encounter, and I feel like it changed my life. This is the woman I want, the only woman I want or need."

"You find me at least attractive, don't you, Rick? I saw you looking at my chest just now, and I know you've seen my outline. Don't your sex organs react just a little when I show up?"

"Of course they do, Carol, but I am going to remain true to one woman."

"If I were astride you, my breasts bouncing against your cheeks, you would find me just as exciting as her, possibly more. It's about sex, Rick, not love, and if you give me a chance, I will prove it to you."

"I know you are right, Carol, at least at some level. Let me pose a question, though. If you find the man you really want, really love, would you still go to bed with others, even for money?"

"I might be true to one man in the future, Rick, and I will expect the same from him. Let me remind you though, that I am experienced regarding sex, and I can tell the difference between love and sex when I find it. You can't. You need to find out if it's real, and I'm offering you the only way." She paused for a moment, and I saw a twinkle in her eye, and as my eyes followed her neck to her chest, I had an image of her body in my hands, her nipples erect, her pubis pressed against me. I pushed my chair away from the table and looked around for an escape route. I was too close to this woman for comfort.

"That won't work, Rick, because you will start to think about me now, imagining what it would be like. You won't be able to just walk away and forget me." She laughed, throwing her head back and showing her perfect teeth. The tender trap nearly had me in its spider's grasp.

"Carol, I need to know if I can trust you."

"I'll never talk about what we do, Rick. You can trust me."

I don't mean about sex. It's the other thing. I have to know if you are part of a plan to commit murder. Is anyone paying you to be here?"

"I don't murder, Rick. The only pay I get is what Howard paid me tonight. I don't understand what you are talking about." Unless Carol was a consummate actress, I couldn't help but believe her. She was complicated, seductive and intelligent but not a killer. I could see no possibility that she was a link in the terrorist chain. Perhaps Mike was also on the level; I had to find out.

"Tell Mike same time, same place. Tomorrow."

"I'll leave a note. You be careful, you hear? I claim you as mine, you'll see."

Chapter 27

Julie my Julie

*J*ulie waved when she saw me and smiled broadly as I started across the street. I gave her a little wave in return, and then watched as her hands went to her mouth, a shock registering on her face, the car coming at me finally exploding into my consciousness. My peripheral vision saved me, that and my youthful reflexes, and I dove toward the curb just as it brushed my back, accelerating sharply down the road. It was an old car, and it smoked, the oil vapor still hanging in the air as the sound of its harsh motor grew fainter. It happened so fast that I didn't get a look at it or its driver, and I pushed off of the pavement, stood, and brushed myself off.

"I think he tried to hit you, Rick," Julie said, still covering her mouth. "Are you all right?"

"He missed," I smiled, trying not to show that I was rattled. After all, you aren't expecting to be killed outside of a war zone, and even less so, intentionally. I looked down the street again, but the car was gone. In a college town, there are always inconsiderate and aggressive young drivers who create mayhem with their father's car. It might not have been intentional at all. Or it might have been.

"Ready to do something exciting tonight?" I asked her, trying very hard to act normally.

"Have something in mind?" she said coyly and kissed my cheek wetly.

"Oh, I thought we might go back up the mountain tonight? Want to?"

"I do! It's a great idea, but sorry, we can't." She patted my arm in mock sympathy. Of course I realized the absurdity of my suggestion, but it was a way to tell her what was on my mind. It was her, especially after having proximity moments ago with the provocative Carol. I searched my brain for a quiet substitute location, but the fate of a student living in a dormitory is that there are few places for the practice of amore.

"Dancing?"

"Not tonight."

"Dinner?"

"Eaten already and so have you."

"Study together in the basement of the library?"

"Perfect."

We found our little booth, still too small for two but just right for our current needs, and we crammed in together, my arm around her neck. She leaned into me and kissed me passionately, arousing every male piece of protoplasm I possessed. We smeared our faces together and clutched as if one of us was destined to leave and never return. Carol was right and wrong. Sex for sure but also love, deep, lasting, overwhelming love. We were inhibited by our location but not by our emotions. Each of us knew the other person's body intimately, and both of us were comfortable with our passion, knew that our desires were reciprocal, making our encounter all that more intense.

"Julie, I love you," I said and dove into her lips again before she could answer. I knew that she was about to say the same thing, knew what she felt when she looked into my eyes. Likely, we were about to get carried away, showing no restraint, when we heard footsteps moving among the old book stacks. My ears strained to perceive any threat, and I became aware of the large handgun at my back. It signaled me that it was there and ready. The footsteps eventually faded, but our embrace ended for the moment.

'My, my, Rick. We need to find a quiet place. You are in serious need of attention," she said. The compact from her purse clicked, and she began reassembling her makeup, intermittently watching me. "So, now is the time to tell me the obviously interesting story of your involvement with prostitutes. I am dying to know what you have gotten yourself into." She snapped the purse closed and looked at me with her big innocent eyes.

"It started with the gun that I wear. You know about that, I'm sure."

"I've seen it. I was there when my father gave it to you."

"College boys don't carry guns, especially to class. I was afraid of what Howard might think and, especially, what he might do. I hired a hooker, actually two of them, so that I could hold it over his head, buying silence with the threat of disclosure."

"Is it working?"

"Not at all as I planned. Howard was unconcerned about my gun, but he is addicted to paid for sex. Now one of them is a regular visitor."

"So, you met with one of them for over an hour?" Her voice was even, controlled, but rang alarm bells in my head.

"I take her to dinner at the dorm cafeteria. There is a good reason."

"And the reason?"

"This isn't fair, you know. You can plot with your father and his men and think nothing of not keeping me informed, but you want to know every detail of what I am working on. All I get is ridicule from them every time I stick my neck out."

"You are a novice. I worry about you and don't want to see you at risk. You can understand how I feel, can't you?"

"And you. Are you a novice like me?" The question was at the root of the issue. Julie was part of the team, the bait for sure, but possibly a lot more. It was time that she told me the truth, but I could see it on her face when I asked. There was no way she was going to tell me what I wanted and needed to know.

"They, and you, are trying to protect me. I appreciate you the most, because you have no part in this. You are in this because of your feelings for me, and because of that, I am responsible for you."

"From what I was told and what I have gathered, Julie, there are some dangerous people who are assembling and who mean you harm. I am willing to die with you or in place of you or do whatever it takes, and I understand that I am putting my life on the line. Since we are lovers, some day to be husband and wife, I deserve to know all the facts."

"Yes, I can see it from your point of view. But the facts wouldn't help you and might make for an unfavorable position for us. You know what you need to know at the moment. Now please tell me about the girl you mentioned." There was no surprise that I was still being kept ignorant, not really. They didn't trust me, that's all. Either I was too rank an amateur to be trusted or they were using me as the bait, not Julie. Would she do that to me, I wondered? Looking at her beautiful, lovely face swept away all doubts, but deep in my head was Carol's insight. I was blinded by love and lust, captivated by Julie's feminine presence. I couldn't think straight around her. Blindfolded on the high trail and heading up.

"The girl's name is Carol, and I have become friends with her for a reason. She is the link to Mike, the only link. I am using her to contact him and set up a meeting."

"Is she trying to seduce you?" Julie asked softly.

"Yes. It isn't working."

"Are you sure? Aren't you attracted to her just a little?"

"She is designed by nature to attract men, and she understands the process very well. Given enough time she could induce almost any man to frolic with her. But not this one. I belong to you, and you have nothing to worry about." My answer compelled another satisfying kiss from Julie, with both her hands around my neck increasing the pressure from her lips. Our breaths mingled as we breathed in and out through open mouths locked together. Could some evil force end this paradise I had found? Surely God wouldn't let that happen, I prayed, as my tears lubricated our thrusting faces.

"Julie, Julie, what are we doing here? We have each other and the prospect of a lifetime of happiness, but what are we doing with it?…we are waiting for killers to strike taking one or both of our lives. Whatever the reason, it's not worth it."

Julie pushed away and looked me in the face, her jaw set and her lips tight, "Yes, it's worth it. They cut my mother to shreds, and she never harmed a soul in her life. And they will do the same to me if we don't stop this forever. I can't hide, have children, a husband, a life, knowing that one day, out of the blue, a savage killer might grab me from the shadows, or my children. We are going to end this and soon."

There was no arguing with her, and I was along for the ride, like it or not. "At least tell me who are the suspects, how are they going to come after you?"

"I won't be shot from a distance. No, Nasrallah wants personal revenge for his daughter's death. He has sworn to kill me himself, in person." Her eyes were far away, her thoughts as well, as her mind summoned both the past and a possible future. Until this was over, neither one of us could ever have peace. She was right, it had to be finished once and for all time.

"Tell me, Julie, is Biggs part of the plan to kill you? Yes or no."

"Biggs is a person of interest."

"That's it? That's all I get?"

"Haven't you heard that you are not to be told everything for your own good?"

"Enough that I'm sick of hearing it. It doesn't make sense either. I'm involved, I'm carrying a loaded gun. I've spent weeks of training to get ready. And you want to know the most important reason?" Her face was blank. She definitely wasn't interested in the list of reasons.

"I'll tell you anyway. You, my dear. I can't lose you," I said.

Julie's face softened, and she leaned into my waiting arms. I held this wonderful creation close to me, compressing her into me, trying to wrap myself around her like some type of shield against harm or worry. Nothing in life, not riches, power nor possessions can ever be as valuable as someone you love and nothing can be lost so easily.

Chapter 28

Close call

$\mathcal{T}$he pool hall was in sight, and I was on time. There was no way to tell if Mike got my message or if he would show, but I would be there just in case. I pushed my way past the crowd congregated in the eating area and entered the pool hall, standing there, waiting for my eyes to adjust to the dark. Several tables were in use, but the one I had used before was still unoccupied, and after selecting my pool cue, I settled in and started shooting. One eye was on the ball and the other was scanning the room. After two racks and twenty minutes, Mike was still a no-show. Well, it was a gamble, and it made me more convinced than ever that he was involved, an active participant. I decided to wait a full hour and racked another set of balls and concentrated on my playing, forgetting Mike Flannigan for a moment.

The doors pushed open, allowing the noise from the outside crowd to enter and causing me to look up expectantly. Two large men were entering, their shoulders blocking the light. They stood and looked around slowly, and one of them removed his sunglasses, looking right at me. As they moved in my direction, it slowly dawned on me that these were the ex-cons of Sally's. How did they know I was here just at this time? Obviously, Carol was more connected than she admitted.

The one in the lead was wearing his usual filthy denim jacket, set off nicely by his even more grubby, regulation black undershirt. A large gleaming belt buckle caught the light menacingly. His ragged hair was partially covered by a black cap, the sort worn by the Confederate Forces of the South, but in a dingier brown shade. His partner was similarly dressed but additionally adorned by a large beer gut hanging over his belt.

"You Rick?" he said hoarsely and picked up a nearby cue, weighing and testing its balance.

"Yes. What do you want?"

"No man, it's you who did the wanting. We're here to make some money, you know, the green stuff."

"You two have names?" I asked.

"We don't need names, man. Names just get in the way. You got something for us?"

"There is a house I am interested in. I want to find out who lives there. Something you can do?"

"Why don't you just knock on the door and ask?" They both laughed a guttural coughing laugh.

"I was thinking more of waiting until the house was empty and just, you know, breaking in and looking around."

"Why can't you do it yourself?"

"Seemed to me that it was more in your line of work."

"Might be, but what's in it for us?"

"Two hundred and anything you find there of value."

"And what do you get out of it?"

"You'll tell me what you find."

"Likely, we'll find an empty house. Isn't that the point of waiting until they leave?"

"There is a possibility of someone living there who doesn't want to be seen."

"Who lives there, man?"

"Are you agreeing to do the job?"

"You got to pay us two bills each…in advance…before we will discuss it."

'How do I know you will do the job?"

"You don't."

"That doesn't sound like you are really interested. I don't think we have a deal," I said.

The fitter one moved close to me, obviously implying a threat, his stench wafting up to me. "You carrying any money with you, man?" he asked, showing his bad teeth.

"Not that much."

"We'll take a down payment. Fork it over," he growled, moving even closer to me. We were back at the moment Grey had described. Kill or be killed. I started to twist in the direction which would allow a quick extraction of my weapon, but I needed some front room before going for it. He was too close. As I saw it, I had two choices, give them all the money I had and chance being searched, or pull my gun. If I managed to get it in my hand, I could be forced to use it to stop them, and the results of a shooting would be huge. We stood defiantly in place, and I detected the other patrons moving away from our table, sensing a row.

"How would you like me to blow a big hole in your head?" a voice said, accompanied by the click of a pistol hammer being cocked. The newcomer was behind the fat one and in shadow. The voice seemed slightly familiar but also menacing, in control. Light glinted off of the dark muzzle of the gun which was being held behind the ear of the fat man. The muscular arm holding it was in the light and a tattoo was visible on the forearm. It was the circle and crosshairs of the sniper platoon. I had seen the same markings on both Jerk and Grey.

"Hey, you got this wrong, man. We're old friends here," the muscular one said, turning to face the newcomer.

"You got fifteen seconds to clear this room. If I see your grimy ass when I come outside, you both are dead men." The voice had its intended effect, but both men remained smiling grimly as if it were an inside joke. "One, two, three…," the newcomer counted.

"Sure, man, We're going, but we'll see you both again. Better grow eyes in the back of your heads," the first one said, and they turned around sullenly and sauntered for the door, frequently looking over their shoulder at us.

"What the hell, Rick?" Mike said angrily. "What in the world brings you to try to deal with that bunch? You'll eventually have to kill them, you know. They have your number, and you can expect them to pop up again when you least expect it."

"I am an amateur, haven't you heard? I make stupid mistakes over and over, and I'm in over my head." My whole body was shaking a bit, either from anger or fear, and I felt my temporal area pulsating. "You were right in the nick of time, Mike. I owe you one."

Mike slapped me on the shoulder and smiled. I could tell that the incident didn't stress him in the least. "I was in the corner watching you the entire time. It's always wise not to rush into things."

"Your tattoo. You were a sniper?"

"My entire platoon. Does it make you believe my story?"

"I always believed your story. Your problem is that Grey and Jerk don't. They want to see your photo first, because as far as they are concerned, you have been declared dead."

"So that's who they sent…Jurkowitz and Graham." He looked at the ceiling, remembering, recalling the violent action they all had been part of. "Those two were the best…killers from birth. They enjoyed it, reveled in it and wanted more and more. I'm surprised they ever left the theater."

"Well, they are out there right now and want to find you. You would be wise to let me help you prove who you are and how you can help them stop Nasrallah. Personally, I also want you to help, mostly to save Julie from harm, but also to save you, to restore you to what you were."

"Me? I was never worth much. Barely finished high school. The only thing I ever did of any value was to shoot well, so they trained me to be a killer also. Not much to be proud of, Rick, to be able to sum your entire life in a short sentence. The only thing I've ever done wrong was to fall in love with a beautiful girl. Same as you, Rick. You are into something right now that's similar, and you are going to wreck your life because you are in love. You'll end up killing or being killed for a kiss from tempting lips. You advised me to run away and now I'm advising you to do the same. Run, Rick. Get away as far as you can. Find another woman who excites you, there are plenty of them around. If you don't, you will end up just like us, a gun in your hand, a human being in your sights."

"You didn't run, Mike, and neither can I. Tell me what I can do to help."

"Frankly, Rick, I don't know. Likely they have already had me in their crosshairs, and there is evidently some reason they didn't pull the trigger. They are waiting for something to happen, some event which will turn them loose, and then the killing will start. Grey and Jerk look on me as a traitor, not just a defector. In their minds, I died when I left the platoon, so they won't be a bit sorry to turn my switch off, and you can be sure there will be no remorse about it."

"What do you know about the people you report to? Have you met this Nasrallah in person?"

"They communicate with me electronically. I never met any of them in person, and I wouldn't know Nasrallah from Santa Claus."

"Then you can't really help," I realized out loud.

He seemed to think about my question for a moment before answering. I could see him turning over all possibilities in his mind. "No, there isn't anything I can do. I was directed to determine if the woman calling herself Julie was a legitimate target and I did that. Until I get other orders, I am to wait around."

"I told you last time that Julie is a double, and I still think that."

"So, you believe Julie and the others are lying to you and yet you stick by her?"

"Love is a strong pull, Mike, as you know."

"Forget that drivel, that double talk. She's the real McCoy all right, and you are standing in harm's way. Whatever is to happen will happen soon."

"Thanks again, Mike. You better get out of here while you can. I'll stay and play pool for awhile so we won't be seen together."

"Sure you can handle yourself if those two boys are waiting outside for you?"

"I think so."

"You seem well-armed. Know how to use that piece?"

"How did you know I am carrying?"

Mike laughed, "The bulge when you lean over. I can almost read the serial number."

"So Carol didn't tell you about the gun?"

"We don't talk, Rick. You can count on her, though. She's just a good girl gone bad."

Mike gave me a last approving nod and slipped into the shadows of the pool hall, disappearing like a ghost, leaving me alone with my thoughts and the pool balls. Not really concentrating, I hammered away for another fifteen minutes until I was sure Mike had time to leave. Evening had started descending, and the patrons in the deli area were mostly gone. I exited the sagging entry way and cautiously looked both directions. The street was empty, and I started walking toward the dorm, roughly a mile away. Each time a car passed, I moved closer to the buildings at my right, but when I approached the alleyways, I moved toward the street. Yes, I screwed up again and now had to avoid ex-cons as well as Middle

Eastern terrorists. What a life, and why am I living this way? I'm not actually that useful, more in the way. Even Julie won't trust me fully. I kicked at a stray paper in anger, forgetting for a moment even where I was headed. Somewhere in the distance, a sound was growing louder, though familiar, not quite recognizable. It was a car, an old one, and getting closer. Suddenly, I recalled the same sound after my close call with a similar car. It was the very car that nearly hit me, and again it was rapidly heading toward me. I had just enough time to draw my pistol and move back toward the bricks as it came up on the sidewalk, the old motor roaring loudly, intending to scrape me off the wall. The kill or be killed moment had arrived, and I started firing at the driver as the old machine hurtled right at me like a demonic meteor. The third bullet penetrated the windshield causing the car to veer left, lightly scraping my leg. I had a glimpse of the two ex-cons glaring at me, looking at me with wild, evil eyes, just as the car passed. I pushed out from the wall, swiveled and emptied the gun at the rapidly receding car. It fishtailed harshly but recovered and smoked its way into the distance, the sound diminishing as it disappeared. Eight big, finger-sized rounds were fired from my weapon, and some of them hit, I knew they did. My legs were trembling, making me brace against the wall as I tried to recover my bearings. The gun was empty, and I wasn't carrying the additional magazine…a mistake. If they returned I wouldn't stand a chance. I sprinted for the nearest alleyway, one that I knew connected with a parallel street. With hesitation and trepidation, I entered the dark alley, listening cautiously for the return of the loathsome car and its dangerous occupants. I was attempting to be quiet, stealthy, but I ran directly into an assortment of trash cans, making an enormous amount of noise as they clattered to the pavement. Other than a few rodents scurrying around, I was the only occupant of the alley, and I continued to creep forward with my arms extended, heading toward the dim exit. A ragged sound, the old car sound, returned and was growing louder, making the hair on my neck stand up. I plastered myself against the wall just as a pair of yellow headlights lit up the alley. The car idled roughly, panting like a predator and protruding into the opening toward which I had been going. Several seconds went by while the car pulsated, ready to pounce, its lights probing the narrow alley as I faced the other way, hiding my face but holding my position until I had no choice except to run. At last, slowly, reluctantly, it backed out, roaring off down the street. It was my chance to get away, and I moved as rapidly as possible toward the exit, figuring that they would leave to search other streets. When I reached the opening, I carefully looked around and listened, hearing their car in the distance, still searching, relentlessly looking for me. Quickly, I crossed the street at a run and took another alley heading away from my tormentors. Several blocks later, I reached a busy street and sprinted toward the dorm and safety. While I was running, I realized how much my training had helped, most certainly saving my life. Next time we met, I resolved, those two would catch slugs, there was no longer any choice.

Chapter 29

The proposition

The first problem was my lack of sleep. My nights were spent churning over and over about the shooting, my firing into the receding car on a city street. Were the police about to show up and question or even arrest me? And did I actually hit one of the two thugs in the car? And did Carol sell me out? I liked it better when my head was only full of Julie, her face, her voice and her body. I did learn from the incident, though, and I carried an extra magazine like I was instructed to. There was no use in telling Grey or Jerk about the incident, because I could foresee their anger at my incompetence. Nor did I feel compelled to tell them what Mike had said, because likely, they didn't care. My biggest concern was why the two thugs have made a point of trying to harm or kill me? What did they have to gain by it? Clearly, there were factors at play that I didn't understand, which was the reason I was at this moment waiting on Carol to enter the dorm on her way to satisfying the lusts of my roommate. She had sold me out, and she was going to have to answer why.

No matter how many times I checked my watch, it didn't speed up the passage of time, or alter it. She was forty-five minutes late, unlike her previous visits. My pacing around the entry halls didn't do anything but make me noticed by other people, especially the campus policeman who was watching me out of the corner of his eye. Did she know I was waiting for her, and angry at her? It seemed the only explanation possible. I sighed, expelling my frustration, and started upstairs to tell the disappointed and horny Howard. From the elevator bank, you can see the outside doors, the ones leading to the street. After I punched the up button, something caught my eye, and I turned. It was Carol, and she was waving at me with her arm and hand low, discrete, meant only for my eyes.

As I walked toward the door, she ducked out of sight which made me suddenly alert to danger. Was she drawing me out so that the cons could grab me? I kept walking, but slower, tense, intent on spotting any peril before anything happened. I was prepared to shoot them on sight, no matter what the consequences.

Carol was hiding in the shadow of one of the pillars of the entry way, and nervously looking around when she saw me come out. I noticed her dark sunglasses and the shawl, a new style for her.

"Carol?" I questioned.

"Come out here, we need to talk." She looked both ways and then waved me toward her instead. As I complied, she removed the sunglasses and dropped the shawl, showing bruises around her eyes and neck. She had been beaten and choked, rather severely, it appeared.

"How did this happen to you?" I asked, touching her neck lightly.

"Rick! I am so glad to see you. I thought I would never see you again." She hugged me, burying her face into my cheek, sobbing in a heartfelt way.

I put my arms around her and pulled her close. "Who beat you, Carol. Was it a customer?" I asked.

"No. It was those two friends of Sally. They wanted to find you, Rick. They didn't tell my why, but they beat me until I told them everything I knew. Did they…?

"Yes, they did. Twice I was almost killed by them. I still don't know why they would do that, what motive they would have. Unless someone hired them. Do you know?"

"No Rick, I have been told nothing at all. Sally must have told them where I was. We haven't been living together for months, but she knows my haunts, and that's where they found me."

My mind raced with the possibilities. Mike saved me from them so it wasn't agents of the terrorists who wanted me out of the way. It must be some completely other reason still connected to Julie, but I couldn't fathom what it could be or who wanted it done. I was unimportant, nearly useless, who would gain by my death? There was only one other person who disliked me. Biggs. I had invaded his privacy, stalked his home, spotted his lover. He was the only possibility out of a very short list. It had to be Biggs. Only problem is that I couldn't see the delicate, refined Professor Biggs associating or dealing with the low life ex-convicts. It didn't seem possible.

"Carol, are you here to see me or Howard?" It was a question I had to ask, because this girl didn't look ready for entertainment tonight.

"Both, Rick, just like usual. I'm glad you're not angry with me and that you didn't get hurt on account of me."

"I was angry before I saw your face. Now I'm sorry that you were beaten on account of me. The way you look, I can't let Howard paw all over you tonight, it was an effort for you just to come over here."

"I have to see Howard, I promised, and I need the money," she said.

"Absolutely not. I'll tell him you were sick, and it will be the truth. What has he been paying you?"

"A hundred. I deserve more though."

"I'm sure you do. Come out to eat with me tonight, and I'll

supply the hundred, How's that sound."

"Don't you want anything in exchange for your money?"

"No, Carol. I owe it to you, I don't want anything, you know that."

"Rick, you are the greatest guy I've ever met. If there is ever anything I can do for you…well, you'll tell me, won't you?"

"What you can do is to come with me so we can find a cozy quiet cafe to eat and talk. I think I know just the place."

Students, like me, seek out those little places which serve a good cheap meal at the expense of surroundings. We simply don't care to have fancy, only good food, friendship and, if possible, good music, and I knew the perfect spot, one that I had never taken Julie, and it was within walking distance, another requirement.

We were in a tall booth, a modern rendition of a jukebox projecting from the inner wall and a red and white checkered tablecloth covering the plywood table. The place was dark and old with creaking wooden floors and a few dents and scraps here and there, but it had a comfortable well-worn feel about it, like generations of college students had hung out, their lingering conversations still faintly audible. Carol felt comfortable enough to take off her wrap, and by candlelight, I could make out finger-shaped bruises around her neck. Her voice was also altered, giving a rather husky sound which would be appealing if it hadn't come from nearly being strangled to death. Both eyes were red with blood staining the conjunctiva.

"Poor baby. They really did work you over," I whispered so that only she could hear me.

"I've been beaten before, Rick. It'll heal in a few days, and I'll get my confidence back. That's why I need the money. I've not been working lately."

"If you need any more money, let me know," I told her.

"One more hundred, and I'll be okay. Can you do that?" When

she asked, she cocked her head to the side and gave me an endearing little smile.

"Of course."

"How did they try to kill you, Rick?"

"Both times with a car. They tried to run me down but missed."

"You should have shot them."

"I tried. I guess I also missed. Our friend, Mike, saved me in the pool hall. He pulled a gun, and I think he was willing to blow them away right there."

"I told you that he seemed like a serious man, a capable one."

"He is an ex-Marine sniper. Did you know that?"

"I don't know anything about him, but I'm a good judge of men; I have to be. Do you want to know what I think of you, Rick?"

"I'm afraid to ask. Hope it's good."

"You have to understand that I'm prejudiced toward you. That's how you get when you're in love. You get starry-eyed about someone. Ever felt that way yourself?"

"Carol, don't tell me that you are in love with me, please. We've only had a few conversations, you just don't know me that well."

"Yes, I know you, Rick James, and I love you. Don't bother to try and change my mind about it. I told you, I'm a good judge of character, and you are the best man I have ever met."

"Carol, I am humbled that you love me, but I already have a girl that I love and who loves me."

"It doesn't matter, Rick. I can wait for you, however long it takes. You go ahead and enjoy this girl, get your fill of her and then, when you are ready, come find me and I'll show you what you were missing." I'm not sure what I was feeling about Carol at that moment. Pity, perhaps, compassion, for sure, but also attraction. Physical, sexual attraction. She grew on me. It might have been the brief hug that we had exchanged, but I was feeling drawn to her. I wanted to protect her, and yet I knew protecting a professional sex worker was a foolish endeavor indeed.

"Thank you Carol. You know, in another life, I think you and I would have made sweethearts. There is something about you that fits me, something familiar, something that clicks."

"There is a thing I want to ask you, Rick, and I want you to listen and to take it seriously. Please?" I nodded that I would, that she could ask. "This business you and Mike are in. I don't even want to know what it's about, but it's dangerous, and you could get hurt or worse. We both need to pack it up and leave…together…start new someplace else. Become new people. We need to leave this city, Rick, before it's too late for either of us. I will make you happy, Rick, put this life I'm leading behind me and become the woman you want to stay with. How about it, Rick, will you go with me?" At the moment she finished her request, I realized that someday I would regret refusing her. Somewhere in my thoughts was the fear that no matter how hard I tried or cared this whole thing was going to turn out bad for all of us. Without speaking, I looked at Carol's face thinking about what she had just offered. It was a real chance, her offer, and I knew that she was sincere about it. Julie's essence came floating through my brain, her magical hold of me had not dissipated. Live or die here, I belonged to Julie, body and soul, for as long as I could draw a breath. I simply could not leave her. Every time I was with her reinforced my passion and my obligation to her. Julie was what I wanted most in life and nothing else mattered.

"I have a duty, Carol. The woman I love is in some danger. I simply can't leave her and go with you, but I want you to know something. Part of me wants to go with you. It's a great offer you have given me, and one that I will forever treasure. Something tells me that I will look back on this moment as one of the paths I should have chosen but didn't. Thank you from the bottom of my heart."

Carol started to cry. The tough street girl with a heart was crying, and it tore at me to watch her. "You big sap," she sputtered, wiping her face with the back of her hand. "You've rejected my love, my body and my entire future and still I love you. You are sitting across the table from me, and you might as well be a hundred miles away. I can't show you how I feel, you won't let me, and by not going, not escaping with me, you have condemned both of us. Instead of being happy together and forgetting the past, we will be crushed by the present. This might be the last chance for either one of us. If only I could have made love to you, I might have convinced you, but you are loyal to that girl even though she would never find out, so we both lost what could have been." I wanted to leap across the table and take her In my arms, kissing away the tears and the foulness of her present life. But I didn't. Julie kept me from doing anything but sitting there a hundred miles away and just watching, bereft of words.

The Green Scarf

Chapter 30

Gunplay

"Why do you guys have to drive so hard?" I yelled from the back seat while holding my arms against both back doors. Without an answer, the car jerked suddenly around another corner, flinging me against the driver's side, in spite of my seatbelt, currently cutting me in half. "Come on Grey, slow down!" I pleaded. He glanced over his shoulder and grinned.

"Are you afraid, James, or just weak?" he said, and they both laughed as the car screeched around to the other side. Thank goodness we were almost there, and ahead, I could see the old warehouse and its decrepit metal garage door. The car stopped violently, bobbing up and down on its springs, also glad to stop for a breather.

"Out, James. He's waiting for you.," Jerk said and opened the back door. I stood limply and straightened my clothes, giving them a dirty look, not that they cared what I thought. We went up the creaking stairs together, and it occurred to me to worry how much weight these old stairs could handle at one time. Jerk pushed me through the open door, as usual, and I stumbled clumsily into the room. Colonel Frank was behind his desk, his arms folded in front of him, staring at me as if I were a private who was captured AWOL.

"James. You wanted to see me?" he asked. Since I was intimate with his daughter, in mutual love with her in fact, and that I had committed endless hours of painful training for her protection, a normal person would expect a tad more friendliness. It was hopeless. Colonel Frank had been in the field too long and had become a marionette, a military robototron.

"Sir. Thank you for seeing me, sir. I wanted to give you an update on my situation and seek your advice." I figured I might as well tell him about the attempts on my life and the shooting, the beating of poor Carol, the meeting with Mike. The whole works. I had to get it off my chest to somebody. His Marine units didn't care, and I didn't want to trouble Julie with any bad news. The Colonel was the only one I could talk to.

"If you are here to cry about the dangers of living in a big city, you can stuff it," he remarked and studied his papers.

"I thought you would be interested that I had to empty the gun you gave me at a car recently."

"Didn't hit them, did you?" he said, still not looking at me.

"I don't know, do you?"

"You didn't. I guess our training wasn't adequate, or that you weren't up to the task."

"Do your informants also know who hired them to knock me off?"

"I think there is guilt by association. As I've been told, you sought them out. Isn't that true?" He looked up to fix my face in his hard glare.

"I was trying to find out who Biggs has in his house. My butt is not the only one at risk here, you remember." At that, Colonel Franks stood up, his fists hard against the table surface.

"You were told to leave that issue alone, James. Can't you take an order, any order?"

"No, sir. I'm not under your command. Rick James is a free citizen who decides his own fate. Perhaps if you told me more, I would feel part of a plan rather than like a dumb kid with a gun."

"You have become more of a liability, James, than an asset. We have built a steel cage for our uninvited guests, and they are creeping toward the trigger. You are the weak link, the only weak link, and you are here because Julie thinks she is in love with you."

"Thinks? You doubt it?" I demanded. This was my sore spot, my flammable fluid, and I burst into flames on the spot.

"Yes, thinks. If you left tomorrow, she would find someone else to drape over and try and protect. It might only take a week."

"How do you mean, protect? Do you imagine that she is protecting me?"

"Of course she is. By far, she is the more reliable and the better trained. You don't even know the real woman, the one you imagine you love so much. But if things continue like they are, you might be the one who is responsible for her death. How does that make you feel?"

"Creepy," I admitted. "Can you at least explain it for me?"

"We can't, James. You have proven yourself not be a team player. This is a battle between hardened ruthless people and the good guys...us...and I am playing for keeps. Our side will win if we don't get weak."

"Why can't you people just kick Bigg's door down and arrest Nasrallah? What is so hard about that?"

"You fool, you stupid kid. That's probably what he wants us to do. He's smarter than you think."

"What if you're wrong, that it is that simple? He's hiding right in front of you, and you don't believe your eyes. That's the trick...there is no trick!"

"Get out of here, James, and don't come back until you are requested." He signaled his troops that the conversation was over, and I felt two big hands lift me off the floor and spin me around. Jerk shoved me toward the door.

"Wait!" I shouted. "What about the two thugs who are trying to kill me. Don't I get any help or are you going to let them do it?"

"You have a gun. Defend yourself," the Colonel said just before his door closed.

We stood in the courtyard looking at each other without conversation. I realized that they weren't about to take me back in the car. "What, no ferocious ride back to the dorm?"

"It's only eight or so miles. A walk will give you time to think. It'll be good for you," Grey said.

"Can you at least give me some more ammo?" I asked. Grey reached into his pocket and took out two filled magazines for my weapon and handed them to me without comment. They stood watching me, waiting for me to get the message and leave. I was on my own, from now forward. They weren't going to lift a finger to help me any longer, and the Colonel didn't care at all if I was out of the picture permanently. With a last look at my former buddies, I stuffed the hardware in my pockets and headed out into the fading evening light. Eight miles to go.

By this time, I knew my way from the warehouse to my dorm, and I strode forward with determination to travel as rapidly as possible. I had run a similar distance many times, but had infrequently walked that far at one time. My calculations estimated a travel time of under two hours. The cafeteria should still be open, and I would likely be ravenously hungry. The first part of the trip was through a seedy post-industrial part of the city with few street lights and fewer strollers. Going past the long buildings, with their broken windows gaping like open mouths with bad teeth, made me want to quickly transit the area. The fractured pavement, heaving in spots, required a slower pace, and I nervously watched over my shoulder each time I slowed to feel my way over the humps. In the distance, I could hear occasional angry shouting coming from the nearby clustered tenements, just now out of sight. My journey was occupied by my thoughts, of what awaited me and Julie, and how I could stop this madness. Her father, if he is her father, suggested that Julie was more than a mere soft girl, beautiful to the eyes and marvelous to behold. She was trained, whatever that meant. I had seen no sign of it other than an occasional, flickering hard look occasionally pass over her face. She was the same age as I was and there had been no time for training in my life.

In the distance, I heard a sound that gave me goose bumps. It was too far away to be certain and the sound faded in and out, just out of reach, but I was becoming sure that it was my old friends again. The sound of the old car was definitely getting closer, only three or four streets away, and I started casting around for a possible hiding place in case it came down the street I was using. The only way the car would be searching for me is because someone told them where I was and where I was headed. That included exactly three people. One of them or all of them were trying to get me killed, to take me out of the picture. Someone, likely me, was going to die before this night was over. The sound was only a block away now and moving south. All it had to do is to turn north at the next block, and it would be on top of my position. I had to hide and quickly. Beside the sidewalk ran a high linked wire fence topped by barbed wire. The enclosure surrounded an abandoned weed-filled parking lot adjacent to a vacant and rusted steel building, lit by one vapor light mounted at the entrance. The fence opening was on the other side, a block away, so I decided to climb the fence and started pulling myself up. As I was fighting my way over the rusted barbed wire, the old car sound grew louder and closer. They had turned up my street and were closing the distance rapidly. I jumped off, flattening myself against the rotted pavement, being partially hidden by the weeds proliferating inside the fence. Slowly, the old car crept by, seemingly alive and perceiving that I was in proximity. The yellow headlights streamed through the weeds, and the old car stopped, watching, listening for my breathing, not fifteen feet from where I lay. I held my breath and willed it to drive away, forced it using my mental power alone. The thought crossed my mind that if I suddenly opened up on them I would catch them by surprise, even possibly taking one of them out. The urge to act became stronger the longer the moment lasted. I rehearsed in my mind pulling my weapon and firing through the fence at the drivers side. Surly it would work. My muscles tensed with the coming effort just as the car slowly, defiantly puffed away continuing the search farther away and leaving me panting with the mental effort of inaction.

I slowly, cautiously, rose to my feet, listening for the return of the car. I could hear it in the distance, covering the area methodically street by street. It knew for sure that I was around. I felt sweat trickling down my back, the odor of stress arising from my body. There was a particularly dark area near the building and I sought it out and sat down, trying to get my legs back under me. I tried to remember my training, what the experienced Marines had taught me. It wasn't only about firing a weapon, it was about strategy, bringing the fight to the enemy, doing the unexpected. They expected me to hide, run and fire my gun only as a last resort and only then for defense. A plan formed in my head, and I realized what I had to do. I stood up and took out my gun and checked the magazine. The prey becomes the hunter.

The sound echoed around the abandoned buildings and reflected from the walls creating an ominous guttural rumble. It was still cruising about three blocks from me and I was confident that it would continue searching. I climbed over the fence again and dropped to the street, beginning a sprint toward the car, feeling for my extra magazines as I ran. Two more blocks. It had stopped moving again and was idling, looking and waiting for me. I was coming, they didn't have to worry. As I turned the next corner, I saw the taillights come off and on as they jerked forward and braked again. Behind them, I was hidden by the night and the lack of street lights and because they were looking forward using their dim headlights. I had to get close enough to shoot before they were aware what was happening. They must have seen something interesting, and the backup lights went on, meaning at least the driver was looking backward. An entryway was nearby, and I moved into its shadow, watching as the car moved backward close to my position. Instead of feeling fear, I was relaxed, watching dispassionately as my quarry came to me. It wasn't hatred that I felt, nor excitement. I felt detached, methodical, like a scientist in his lab or a housewife killing roaches. The car idled again and was only two lengths away, the old motor roughly turning over. My pistol hung loosely at my side as I moved away from the building and into the street and walked forward behind the car. Inside the vehicle, there was no light but as I came closer, I could make out two heads, big heads, in silhouette, outlined by the forward headlights against the street. They were moving back and forth looking into every crevice, knowing I was there. The front windshield had three large holes and a spider web of cracks where my previous rounds had struck. I walked directly toward the rear of the car, confident that this was the last place they would look. I raised my weapon and without hesitation, opened fire.

There was a brief acceleration of the car which veered sharply to the right, jumping the curb and striking a building with some force, the hood popping up at an odd angle. The old motor continued its throbbing rough idle as I came toward it from the driver's side. I raised the pistol again and fired five more rounds at the men in the front seat, the light from the explosions lighting their faces in an instant, frozen expression of death. It was over. I put my weapon away and walked slowly away, hidden by the night and no longer in a hurry to return to my former life.

"You did good tonight," he said, stopping me in my tracks. I drew my gun and crouched, listening for the source of the voice which was nearby.

"Grey?" I asked, sure that it was him.

"Yeah, it's me. Put down your gun." He emerged as a faint shadow, separating from the building just ahead of me like a specter, a large one. My gun went back into its place.

"Give me the gun, James. It's evidence, and you don't want it on you any longer," he said, and I saw his arm extend forward, waiting for it. Reluctantly, I handed it over, grip first. He walked back the short distance to the idling car, wiping the gun down before he arrived, then tossed it in with the bodies.

"Want a ride now?" he asked.

My thinking was clouded; I was walking like a robot with any direction coming from Grey, not myself. He herded me along to his waiting car, and I got in the front beside him.

After the car started moving again, he patted me on the shoulder. "I knew your training would take hold eventually. You're one of us now, James, you can be trusted."

It dawned on my fuzzy brain what he was telling me. "Grey, was that a test? You had me kill those men to prove myself to you?"

"No, James. You had to kill them, or they would have killed you. We just wanted it to happen in controlled circumstances where you had backup. You handled it just like I would have, or any other highly trained soldier would. Never let your enemy dictate terms to you and you didn't. I'm so proud of you I could pop."

"Thanks, Grey, but now I have blood on my hands. I just murdered two people, and I'll have to live with it forever." My grief had just started with the realization of what I had done. I knew that my mind would replay this event over and over the rest of my life.

"Get over it, James. Those two were never going to do anything in life but more crime and violence. You didn't pick this fight with them, and it's not your fault that it had to end this way. Trust me, it was better here where no one could see what happened than right outside the dorm or when you were with Julie. This was the only way, James."

Grey was right. This was the only conclusion which left me able to continue my life. There would be no questions asked about their deaths, especially down here in no-man's-land where this sort of crime was common. The Colonel and his men were skillful manipulators for certain, and they were good judges of character, both the dead men's and mine. They foresaw accurately what was going to happen and were there to watch, supervise and likely take charge if things went wrong. Still, it was a test, a brutal, deathly, unremorseful test of Rick James, junior Marine.

Grey drove back to the warehouse, taking his time and turning the corners smoothly. I let the world slip by, my mind blank and limp, barely aware that the car had arrived at it's destination. Jerk opened my door, standing there grinning at me like some big happy chimpanzee.

"You the man, James!" he shouted and picked me up in his bear arms, squeezing until I coughed.

"Put me down you big lug!" I protested. "Don't congratulate me on being a murderer."

"Upstairs, James. He's waiting." Grey said, leading the familiar way up. And so he was, pacing the floor as usual, looking down at his polished shoes as the door opened. His eyes were different, softer, more compassionate than I had ever seen. He walked toward me with concern, his arms extended for an embrace of men. I felt like crying, like confessing to my father figure that I was frightened, had done something horribly wrong and grateful that he was here to comfort me and to make me feel safe.

"You proved yourself tonight, both to us and to you, James. You have what it takes. We could always see it. That's why we spent so much time with you, forging you into what we knew you needed to become. The only thing which would make me more happy is for you to join us, join the U.S. Marine Corps. I would be delighted to call you a fellow Marine."

"And I would be happy to call you father," I said, pushing back and getting a good look at him. "Tell me, Colonel, did you tell those two to kill me?"

"No, James. I had nothing to do with that. Others may have or perhaps it was their idea all along. The first I heard about it was their first attempt outside the woman's dorm. Julie told me. We knew that it was going to be inevitable from then. We told them where you were tonight so you could do exactly what you did."

I looked around for a chair, feeling faint, and one was thrust under my rear by one of his boys, and I sat heavily into it. The three of them stood around solicitously, probably recalling their own first experience with killing another human being.

"What's next?" I asked weakly.

"Nasrallah," the Colonel answered.

"You expect me to shoot him also?"

"I wouldn't mind, but we have other plans. We're still not positive of where he is, not sure enough to act yet."

"He's hiding in Biggs house, even I know that."

"That's what he wants us to think. Maybe true, maybe not. Could be that the person there is just another of Professor Biggs' lovers, not a dangerous terrorist. We are watching that house closely, but so far, there isn't enough information to act or even get a warrant. We have to wait a bit longer. Some mistake will be made that will tell us when to start moving. We can't let him slip away this time."

"What do you want me to do?"

"Keep Julie happy and safe. Keep your eyes and ears open and be ready."

"Sir, tell me what I need to know about Julie. There is a lot about her that I haven't been told. She is hiding something from me."

"It'll have to come from her, son. I feel as strongly about her as you do. We protect her and love her above all others, don't we?"

"Yes, sir."

"One more thing, James, then I'll have Grey drive you back." He bent over his desk and withdrew another gun, this one glossy and new. "I got this for you. Should shoot just like the old one, and you can keep this one forever. You've earned it." He handed me the new Colt pistol, "45 Caliber" engraved on its slide. I turned it over then put it in my usual place at my spine, then just stood there and looked around. Finally, I was on the team.

Chapter 31

The trap

After a couple of days, my nervousness dissipated, and I was finally able to get a full night's sleep. Back to the routine of daily college life. Arise early, study, eat fast, study, go to class. Like that. I felt like a student again, even in Biggs' class. He was careful to avoid my eyes which were always on him wondering if he was the one who wanted me dead. You can always tell if someone is watching you, and I was watching Biggs, every breath he took, but there was no response, no flicker that he was aware or even cared. If he was acting, he was very good.

And the gorgeous girl wearing the green scarf was there waiting for my eyes to feast on her. I could see the whole picture, the warm loving, exciting girl of my dreams who would occasionally turn her head to be sure I was aware of her, and I was, I certainly was. She was too far away to get a whiff of her perfume, but nevertheless I could still smell it, and it still aroused me, even just the memory of it. She never spoke of the episode with the cons, but I was certain that they told her, that she knew her father was pleased with me. I couldn't tell any difference in her attitude toward me, even in the depths of her eyes. It was something that she always knew I would do, just part of who I am. Each time class ended and she walked away, toward her other appointments, my heart sank. Not nearly as much as when I left her at night and the woman's dorm door closed behind her, and she, with one last look over her shoulder, told me goodnight with her eyes and then disappeared. It was agony.

And I had no word from Carol, who had dropped Howard from her list of appointments, to his everlasting dissipation. It was all he talked about, and his grades suffered from his unfulfilled needs. I was certain that Carol no longer wanted to see me, since begging and pleading her lost cause that night. Part of me was sorry that we had lost contact, but the more intelligent part realized that no good could come of it, and it was time both of us moved on. And so it went.

One day I went to the woman's store again to find a nice gift for Julie. Not that I was looking for anything in particular, but I figured I would recognize it if I saw it. Thanks to my anonymous donor, I had enough money to feel comfortable in buying a gift for her, some little, but very nice token of my love.

One push and I was back to a familiar but still exclusionary place. The world-of-women kind of store where men were as comfortable as a finely dressed woman in an auto parts store. Their money was always welcome but a man's motives for frequenting such a temple of womanhood were suspect. After all, what reason would a man have to enter such an establishment? In the staff's eyes, the first and most likely reason was that he had done some major injustice or wrong to a woman, and he was trying to buy back her affections. Striking her, seeing another woman? All equally horrible and the reason he felt particularly sneaky being in there. They had to watch such a man very closely, because his morals were definitely lacking. And in I walked, young and green about the ways of women, obviously still infatuated with the superficial and definitely insincere about my intentions.

"What may I help you with?" she asked with a stiff smile. I noticed the lack of a sir attached to the end of her sentence. Of course, I didn't warrant the use of sir, nor did I expect it. But it would have been nice.

"I'm not sure. Just here to look around, perhaps buy a gift for my girlfriend." I didn't understand that the proper description would have been lady friend. My designation seemed so juvenile, so very much indicating a poverty of both money and wisdom.

"Yes, feel free to look around, and let us know if you need help," she said and turned quickly away so as not to help at all. I strolled through the aisles looking over attire that Julie would never put on, even for me. I did find the sweaters interesting and found a white one that was really appealing…until I looked at the tags. Cashmere, Italy, $350 dollars, flashed in front of my eyes, and I put it quickly down. The shoe selections pulled me in, and I picked several up for close inspection. Flimsy for the price, I realized.

"Size? What size does she wear?" a clerk asked, eyebrows raised.

"I'm not sure," I admitted. "She's about so tall," and I held up my arm, palm down trying to recall her exact height.

"That simply won't do. You must know her exact shoe size. What about bringing her in for measurement?" she suggested.

"A surprise."

"Find another gift would be my advice. Women are picky about shoes anyway." She walked away because, in her eyes, I was beyond help. I surveyed the store from my position. The only possible item, other than jewelry, was the sweater I had spotted, so I made my way through the narrow isles again. The money I would use for the purchase was from an unknown source, for unknown reasons, and I didn't feel possessive of it. Julie was worth it.

Now the matter of size again and the unexpected categories of petite, small, full as well as numbered sizes, even age related sizes, or style of fit. It was numbing, and I felt lost again and looked around for help. They saw me, I was certain, but not one came to find out what I wanted. I found a bell and rang it several times and stood waiting.

"Yes?" she said as she closed the distance. Her tone was dismissive even before she heard what I wanted.

I handed her the sweater and asked, "How do I determine the correct size?"

"You don't know her size?"

"That's what I mean, I don't."

"Well, is she tall or short, plump or thin?"

"None of those. She is what I would call ideal, perfect." The clerk rolled her eyes as she shook her head.

"Really, young man, do you think you should be doing this alone? Don't you think you should bring her with you?"

"Look, I know her height and weight, isn't that enough?"

"Not enough. It's also about arm length, bust size and personal preference regarding style."

I looked her over before speaking. "What size would you wear?"

"Me? Well, I would take a large. Is she my size?"

"No. I'll take a medium, and your promise that she can return it if she doesn't like it."

"Want it wrapped?"

"Yes, please, and I already know that it's extra."

I left exhausted from the effort but with a beautifully wrapped bundle under my arm and a burning desire to see Julie's face when I gave it to her. Not able to wait a moment longer than I had to, I gave her a call as I was walking.

"Hi!" she said in her breathless way.

"Have any plans for tonight?" I asked.

"Sure. I'm going to spend the evening with a wonderful guy. Jealous?"

"Absolutely. What kind of food appeals to you right now?"

"Anything you pick will be fine."

"There is a small restaurant just ahead of me that we haven't tried. Looks like a Greek place. It's about a mile from where you are. Want me to come get you?"

"No. You grab a seat, and after I change, I'll be right over. You can wait for me, and I'll show my appreciation. What's the name of the place?"

"Jimmy's. On Fourth street."

"I'll be there. You wait now, promise?"

"Promise."

The place was clean on the outside, and I entered still clutching my gift. The waitress showed me to a quiet booth, and I put the package on the opposite bench where Julie was sure to find it. I sat there drumming my fingers and checking my watch. There was still two hours until sunset, and the street was busy with people. There was no risk in Julie coming alone to this area, but the thought grew on me that I should have gone over to the dorm before I called.

"That package for me?" Mike asked, catching me by surprise. I looked up to see him standing beside the table, smiling and casual.

"Hi, Mike. You are the last person I would expect to see here."

"You waiting for Julie?" he asked, then sat down opposite me.

"Do you expect me to answer?"

"I heard that the two fellows I rousted in the pool hall were killed. That your work?"

"I'm no killer, Mike, but I'm not sorry to hear about it. How were they killed?"

"By gunshot. Multiple gunshots. A pro job. Don't you know who did it?"

"No idea. That all you want Mike?"

"No Rick. I want the pistol you are carrying. Use two fingers only and put it on the table."

"And why would I do that?" I answered, feeling my blood pressure start climbing.

"Because I'm pointing my pistol at your abdomen right now,

and I'm not asking again."

You could easily see it in his eyes. They were dead flat with no emotion. It was a job to him, and friendship or talk wouldn't change anything. If he was telling me the truth, then he had the drop on me and given his history and his predicament, he had nothing to lose. The problem for him and for me is that we couldn't be sure that the Colonel's men weren't out there someplace with their rifles aimed right at his ear, waiting for the best moment to blow his head off.

"They'll kill you, Mike. This isn't the way out."

"I've been dead for years, but you haven't been dead yet. Want to see what it's like?"

"No, I don't."

"Then do what I said, or I'll shoot you right here."

"What do you want me for, or should I ask, who wants me?"

"The party just wants to talk to you, that's all. I was ordered to bring you or shoot you, your choice. Ten seconds, Rick." His eyes were steady and didn't even blink. He was prepared to shoot, I could feel it.

"Where are we going?"

"Five seconds left."

I took the gun out, put it on the table and watched as he slowly pulled it toward him without looking away from my eyes. "Now get up slowly and we'll go out the back way. One slight unexpected move from you and I won't hesitate."

The waitress took that moment to show up with her big smile. "Can I bring you two fellows something to drink?"

"We have to leave for a moment, but I'll be right back. Could you see that the lady gets the package I left on the seat?"

"Why, yes I will!" she said pertly and walked away with her hips swaying for our benefit. I got up at the same time Mike did, and I saw that he wasn't bluffing about the gun. It was pointed directly at me, waist height. I turned, going deeper into the cafe with Mike behind me far enough that I couldn't risk spinning and grabbing the gun. He was experienced and well-trained.

We emerged into the alley mingling with overflowing garbage cans and litter. "That car…you are driving," he said. The only car in sight was a smaller white Mercedes. It was the car that I had seen Biggs driving when I tracked him.

"So it's Biggs. He was the one," I said.

"Shut up," Mike warned.

The door was unlocked, and I got in first, looking for the keys hoping to drive away before he got in. Mike had it well-planned, because there were no keys in the ignition. He got in the other side with his gun still pointed at me.

"Listen up, Rick. I was only told to bring you, not shoot you. I assume that they only want to talk to you or else I would have been given the order to kill you. Play it safe and let's get there in one piece and see what they want." He was urging me to avoid a desperate act such as crashing the car.

"Guess we aren't friends then?"

"My mission always comes first. Didn't they teach you that?"

"No. I'm not a Marine, just a trusting college student."

"That's a mistake on your part. Now drive to Biggs' house. I understand that you know where it is." He tossed me the keys and kept his eyes and his pistol on me. There wasn't much choice, and I could always hope that a sniper would zero in on his head before we arrived. But that didn't happen. The trip was uneventful, and I pulled into Biggs' driveway, and the garage door opened as if we were expected. I had a sinking feeling watching the door go down behind the car.

"Out, hands up," Mike barked. I got out and stood there in garage of the very house that I wanted to burgle or at least to have someone else burgle. This part of it was ordinary, with yard tools hung neatly along the wall just as an orderly and organized man like Biggs would do. Mike pointed with his gun at the door to the house, and I started in with some anticipation. We passed through the well-appointed kitchen into the living room where they were waiting. Both of them.

"Well, Mr. James!" the dapper man in the large chair said. He was the same one I had seen outside the restaurant with Biggs that night. He had a dark complexion and a well-trimmed beard and looked distinguished as if he were also a college professor. I chose not to answer and instead looked at Biggs who stood beside the chair, a small grin on his face. He had me where he wanted this time. I wondered if he realized that I was capable of killing him in cold blood if I got the chance. And there was no doubt that I would, given the slightest opportunity. In my mind, I could see my hands around his thin neck, his expression one of desperation instead of gloating as he was doing right now.

"Why was I brought here?" I asked them. "What do you want from me?"

"Why nothing at all, my fine young lad. You are unimportant except as bait," the Lebanese man said.

"Bait? Bait for what?"

"Why your dear Julie! You are the other sides' weak link. She will come looking for you, you realize."

"So you are Nasrallah, the one they have been looking for." I always knew it was him, they wouldn't listen. Nasrallah was hiding right in the open, right in front of their noses.

"I don't answer to you. You are going to be kept alive long enough to see your Julie one last time and for that you should be grateful. You also owe us a debt for having Mike save your life in the pool hall. Yes, that was our doing. We didn't want any harm coming to our bait, you see."

"So you didn't tell those two thugs to get rid of me?" I asked.

"Not at all, the opposite in fact. Was that your bullets found in their heads?"

"I'm no killer."

"Of course you are, lad," Nasrallah said and then grinned as if he knew what had happened.

"You're not so smart now, Rick James, are you?" Biggs asked, the smirk still on his face.

"And how do you think you are going to survive this, Biggs? You and your lover are doomed, and what did you get out of it? I wouldn't be grinning if I were you." I said. Biggs' smile faded, his brain was coming to reality. This was no longer a game between lovers. There were going to be deaths, lots of them.

"Whatever happens to you, James, you will richly deserve. For your information, I'm retiring to the Mideast, and I'm sure to be happy there without the likes of you."

"Bet you never make it, and you will richly deserve whatever happens to you, Biggs."

"Enough!" Nasrallah barked. "Tie this man up in the basement, and put him where he can be seen through the doorway." Mike nodded that he would comply and pointed his gun at me and the other hand toward the door leading down. Two heavily armed men emerged from somewhere in the house, their distinctive appearance was if they had just emerged out of a fractured building in Beirut. They leaned against the far wall with their machine guns at the ready, positioned for trouble when it came.

I went down first, looking hard for some object I could use for defense. If I could get the gun away from Mike, I might have a chance. "Forget it, Rick. I know what you are thinking. Don't risk it, this thing isn't over yet." He sounded almost sympathetic, and it caught me by surprise. I looked at his face trying to discern what he was thinking, but there was nothing there. He kicked a chair into position and pushed me into it. Deftly, he put the restraints on which were nothing more than large zip ties, but there was no way of getting out of them or breaking them. He did the same with my feet and attached both to the chair. I was immobilized except for my mouth.

"How are you going to get Julie here? You know they will be watching her, don't you?" I asked.

"Yes, we know. I'll have Carol tell her where you are, and the rest will take care of itself. Those two have wanted to get together, and now they get the chance, thanks to you."

"Mike, listen to reason. You can't get away. Switch sides before it's too late," I pleaded.

"This is all worked out, Rick, and you have a ringside seat." Without another word, Mike bounded upstairs and out of sight. I had time, lots of time, to think and put this together. It was carefully planned by both sides all along. Nasrallah wanted Julie to come to him so that he could do to her what he or his men did to her mother, and this time, right in front of her father, right under his nose. Julie and the Colonel's men wanted this to happen, because they would finally get their hands on Nasrallah. I understood all that, it was simple, except the part where Nasrallah obviously knew that there were hard men watching him. How could he even hope to get away? Even if this simplistic plan was going to work then Nasrallah, Mike, and Biggs would face the wrath of the Colonel's men. To be sure, not one of them would survive. And, there was always the chance that Julie wouldn't come, that she was part of the Colonel's plan to use me as bait. With or without Julie, her father's men would be coming, because this trigger was what they were waiting for. I was expendable to both sides, simply a dangling piece of mutual bait.

My wrists hurt, and the more I moved, the more I could feel the trickle of blood from the cuts made by the sharp plastic. Nasrallah was supposed to be so smart. Would he accept death just to kill

Julie? It didn't make sense. Was I the only one to reason it out so clearly? There was more to this story, and I hoped I would live to see the rest.

The minutes came and went, and I lost track of time. My hands were full of blood, some of it dried and the rest sticky. I couldn't sit here much longer, something had to happen. Occasionally, I saw movement at the head of the stairs, and I looked up wanting to see Julie's face but also not wanting to see her. Would Julie play into their hands so easily? This whole thing was upside down, and my brain struggled to get in and sort the parts. Then it dawned on me. Nasrallah was too smart to do it this way. The man upstairs couldn't be Nasrallah, but no one seemed to understand that except me. There was a secondary plot, one deeper and more sinister than even this one. If Julie came, so would the troops, if not to rescue me, then to protect her. They simply weren't going to let anything happen to Julie. The thought gave me some peace of mind, but what was Mike's angle? Surely he would be the first to be killed, and he had to know it. The one comment he made to me twirled around like a dervish. Mike was also not what he seemed. Grey told me long ago that they were all professionals, and truth was never to be found on the surface.

There was scuffling upstairs. Feet moving about quickly and low murmured voices. Something was happening. "Bring him up," Nasrallah shouted. Soon I heard Mike coming down toward me. He unclipped me from the chair but left my hands tied behind me.

"You need to be upstairs now," he said and pushed me toward the staircase. We went up with me in the lead, and just as we made the landing, I heard a soft knock at the door.

"It's her," Biggs giggled. "It's the one you wanted!" he said to Nasrallah.

"Well, Biggs, let her in," Nasrallah said, pointing to the door. Mike eased me back against the wall, drawing his gun and pointing it at my head, the cold barrel against my temple. Nasrallah backed into the room and stood in the middle of the floor. The armed guerrillas pointed their weapons at the door. They were all ready for whatever came in. I felt Mike's grip tighten as if he expected a rush of troops into the room.

The door swung open, and there was Julie, dressed in her pure white sweater, a green scarf around her neck. She was alone and looked so small and fragile, her big eyes darting back and forth until she spotted me and Mike's gun at my head.

"Run!" I shrieked before Mike's big hand instantly covered my mouth, pushing my head roughly back against the wall. I could still see what was happening and helplessly watched as my precious Julie came into the room alone, and the door closed behind her. My neck was straining with the effort, and my eyes were bulging out, looking at the event unfolding that everything in me wanted to prevent. Julie was about to die because of me, and I was going to be forced to watch.

"So, Julie Frank, in person," Nasrallah said graciously as if she was a favored and honored guest, one to be feted and treated with respect. "I had the privilege of meeting your mother some time ago. It was a joyous occasion, especially for me." He laughed deeply, smiling at her. She didn't respond but briefly looked around the room, taking it all in, then moved gracefully toward Nasrallah, fixing him with her eyes.

"And your name is Nasrallah, I understand," she said just loud enough to hear, getting closer with each step.

"Yes, you may call me that," he said unconvincingly.

"You will let Rick James go," she said without looking at me.

"Kill him, Mike. Do it now so she can watch," Nasrallah ordered, grinning more broadly. I noticed Biggs' head swivel my way, delighted to be able to watch the event himself.

"No," Mike shouted and let his hand fall from over my mouth. I felt all the heads in the room turn and look at us.

"Julie, it's a trick! He's not Nasrallah!" I screamed. It was no use, because she was still moving toward him, nearly there. Nasrallah's eyes went between Julie and Mike, back and forth, trying to understand how the situation had changed. The tide had turned against him just at the wrong moment. I could see his face when he knew what was about to happen, his eyes suddenly widened and his mouth came open as if to protest. Mike let me go and fell to the floor, rapidly firing at the two men against the wall, flinging them backward by the force of his bullets. There was a click just before I saw the flash of a long blade open in Julie's hand, and in a move too quick to comprehend, I saw Nasrallah being lifted off of his feet, his head falling backward in agony with this small girl in front of him, looking up at his face. Her arm jerked forcibly upward completing the cut she had started in his belly, and as he fell backward, I saw a rush of blood and intestines pushing out of the gaping hole she had made. He didn't die at first, there was a moment when he looked down as piles of his intestines coiled on top of him, spilling to one side. Julie spat at him and threw the knife across the room. The deed was done exactly as planned. Revenge, was it sweet? From where I stood it wasn't anything but gory. The odor of Nasrallah's open abdomen filled the room.

At that moment, the door burst open, and Grey and Jerk entered, armed with deadly looking machine pistols and wearing body armor.

"Got him, I see," Grey commented dryly, observing the still quivering mass on the floor, and the two dead men slumped against the far wall. I slid, my back against the wall, down to a sitting position, too weak to support myself any longer. "And you," he said to Mike who was still on the floor. "You finally got it right. Welcome back to the world." Mike got up and exchanged hugs with Grey and Jerk. Old, valued and regained friendship. Mike was always on their side, he just didn't know it until he was forced to make a choice.

I felt a soft hand on my forehead, and she pushed my head back to look into my eyes. "Rick. I'm so sorry that you had to be involved in all of this, so so sorry my dear." She leaned down and kissed my sweating forehead in such a tender familiar way that I nearly forgot all the violence I had just witnessed.

"You have blood on your new sweater," I commented, loosing my grip on reality for a moment.

"Yes," she answered and patted my neck. Mike came over and handed her a small clipper which she used to free my hands and with their support, I pushed myself back to a standing position.

"What happened to Biggs?" I asked, just as a burst of machine gunfire erupted from deep within the house, shaking the walls with the power unleashed. For a moment, there was profound silence broken only by the ringing sound in my ears. Something fell heavily nearby, and I turned to see Biggs curled in a fetal position on the floor with Jerk standing over him.

"They were trying to use the escape tunnel," he said. He kicked Biggs hard in the back and pushed him farther into the room. I could hear Biggs weeping through his hands, his fine clothing in tatters from being forced upstairs by Jerk.

"We need to talk, Rick. There are things I need you to know now that it's over," Julie said lowly to me, her big eyes soft and inviting as if nothing at all had happened. She led and assisted me into the dining room, and we sat down, her hands clasping mine in a tender way.

"One question first," I said. "Are you really Julie Frank?"

"Yes, Rick. I really am. But...," she hesitated, not really wanting to reveal the rest, the lies.

"But you have lied to me," I suggested.

"Deceived. But for a good cause. I am older than you by a

couple of years. After they killed my mother, dad sent me to be trained by the CIA. I'm one of their field operatives, and I never told you about it because I couldn't. You were never in danger because Mike, Jerk and Grey were always nearby. We had to let Nasrallah believe that you were the one person whom I loved so much that I would throw away caution and come to him. He and his team had prepared an exit tunnel for a mysterious departure, but we always knew about it."

"So you used me to catch the prize."

"I didn't want you involved, none of us did. You persisted, and I fell in love with you. That part was and is true. I love you just as much as you thought and as much as I said. You are my one and only love. But I can understand if you will never look at me the same way again. Remember when I said that I might do things that you would find hard to accept? Now you understand."

"Why did you have to cut him open? Couldn't you arrest him or simply shoot him?"

"It's what he deserved, and it's what I wanted. Call it revenge, because that's what it was."

"This is going to take me awhile to understand, Julie."

"Can you still love me, Rick? If you can, I'll be what you want me to be. There is only room for you in my heart and I'll do anything to keep you."

"Love you? Don't be thinking that I could ever not love you, Julie. You are part of my soul, everything I've ever wanted, and life without you is unthinkable." She stood and leaned over the table and found my lips with hers. It was an act of love, but at that moment, my ability to fully appreciate her touch was not at full capacity. I was spent, physically and emotionally, and I didn't want to grapple with hard facts and brutal details any longer.

"We still have to clean up here and be sure there are no surprises, Rick. Grey and I will take you back to the dorm shortly, if that is what you want," Julie said in my ear.

"Dorm? No Julie. You and I are together from now on. I don't care where I sleep as long as it's with you. For a moment, I was sure that you were going to be killed right in front of me. To have you back, to be able to touch you and hear your voice, is like a dream come true. We are going to make love for hours and hours and get this ugly business behind us."

"I was hoping you would feel that way. By the way, this isn't the sweater that you bought me. That one is still in its bag, and I'll wear it for you in the morning." She gave me a smile and once again had me completely captured. She pulled away the scarf from her neck and put it around mine, tying it just so. "Keep this for me tonight, but I want it back in the morning!" she said and stood up and looked around, probably for Grey.

"Julie?" I asked, getting her attention back. "Something is bothering me about this affair."

"Of course, Rick. It all happened so quickly from your point of view."

"No, that's not it. Nasrallah was supposed to be so smart and crafty, yet you tricked him so easily. I'm sure that the one you killed was a double. The real Nasrallah is still out there and may be outwitting you."

"No, Rick. We got him. This has been in the works for months, and we've had time to study every angle. It's over, and you and I can relax." She was so confidant, so sure that she nearly had me believing, but not quite. I still remembered that Nasrallah had hesitated admitting that was his name. Why would he do that? Wouldn't he want her to know who was about to cut her open?

I got up and followed her into the room of dead bodies. Mike gave me a wink, the plot now open and exposed for me to see. They had to make me believe just to be sure that Nasrallah believed also. A closely choreographed play or dance, detailed and executed perfectly by everyone including the ignorant me. I walked aimlessly around, thinking that I should go to the basement and see the tunnel but then realized that it was full of more bodies, thanks to the machine gun work by Jerk. For a moment, I just stood in one place, trying to get my thoughts together, not noticing that Biggs was now standing up not far away and looking at me.

"It's all your fault!" he shrieked, banshee-like, and before I could act defensively, he was rushing at me, arms extended, his face contorted with rage. He ran into me with everything he could muster and together we fell into the abyss through the basement door, my back and head taking the brunt of the fall. I seem to remember the pain of the stairs hitting me and the body of Biggs enclosing me when the explosion occurred, and my world was torn away from me forever.

Chapter 32

Colonel father

Another volley of rounds started impacting stone at the crest of the hill, raining down a mist of rock chips and dirt. "You guys get your head down!" I shouted and watched them hunker down, sliding slightly downward from their firing positions. It usually only lasted ten seconds at a time and we could see the tracers coming across the little valley as soon as the enemy opened fire. I knew there couldn't be more than a dozen of them over there nestled in the big rocks. Very hard to target them adequately from here, I knew, and too small a target to call in an air strike. The last round made a whizzing sound as the bullet tumbled after striking something. Silence. "OK, let them have a burst," I said, and the men started shooting again. This was going to go on all day. Trouble was, I just didn't have the hardware to project enough firepower over there to silence them. The convoy was due soon, and the exchange would grow more intense.

"Sarge!" It was Conroy, scrambling up the hill toward our position. Seeing the messenger coming from the command tent was never good. We would be called on to take on more risk or chastised for poor results. Conroy got close enough, and panting for breath, said "Colonel wants to see you, ASAP," then headed back down, half sliding, his foot braced against the sand, before I could respond. What was I going to say? Sorry, can't come right now, maybe later Conroy. Nope, that's not how it works. I pulled on my canteen and looked around at the men, wiping my lips with my sleeve.

"Listen up!" I shouted. Several heads turned toward me to hear their instructions. "Gotta go down the hill for a bit. While I'm gone, take turns returning fire to keep their heads down. The convoy should come into sight soon. As soon as you see it, put a few RPG's into those rocks, then hit them with sustained fire. I'll be back before it's over." A couple nodded that they understood, and I patted Corporal Jones on the shoulder to indicate he was to take charge and carry out my commands.

The tent was sand-brown, nearly matching the typical colors up here in the mountains, and had all the flaps rolled up because of the heat. I could see several of the staff hunched over tables amid a collection of communications gear and maps. Colonel Frank was walking between the isles with his hands on his hips, ever impatient. Some things never change. He saw me coming and came toward me.

"You're still getting fire?"

"They are dug in, sir. We'll need to blast them out. Any chance of some air support?"

"Not for two hours. See the convoy yet?"

"Not yet. Soon."

"Need anything up there?"

"They're not hitting us, but I'm not sure we are hitting them either. Best we can do right now, sir."

Colonel Frank gave me a long look. I knew that he wanted to say something personal, but he wasn't a man given to softness, not even between us, not even after the years we had known each other. Instead he just nodded to me, giving me at least that acknowledgment of our bond. I did the same to him, and we stood there for a moment remembering.

"Sergeant James. Think you can get a squad in behind them?"

"They'll have to cross the valley where they can be seen. There won't be an element of surprise, and we don't know if any fighters are behind that bunch waiting for us to do just that. If this were night, then yes."

"Yes, that's the consensus. Just thought I'd get your point of view."

From up at the firing positions, we heard the scale of gunfire ramp up until every man was shooting. "They've seen something. I should go back up," I said, waiting to be dismissed.

"Go ahead, Sergeant. Don't get hit, that's an order." He squinted at me, and I could feel that he wanted to physically touch me, but he didn't. I saluted sloppily and started running up the loose rock and sand back toward my men, then paused as a thought occurred to me.

"Conroy!" I yelled and saw him looking at me from inside the command tent. I waved him over and he came at his usual sprint. "The gear of Sergeant Adams. Is it still here?"

"Sure, Sergeant. Nothing's been shipped out yet. Something you want?"

"Yeah. Find his rifle, the big one, and some ammo and bring it up the hill. Do it fast. Got that?" Conroy looked back at the command tent, deciding if he would be allowed to do what I had asked.

"Now, Conroy. We need that gun, I'm counting on you." I waited until he sprinted away then continued my climb, working my way through the rocks and sand. The other side was firing back vigorously, and some of the men had moved out of position, their hands covering their face from the rock spray. I worked my way to Jones who was blasting away and tapped him on his back.

"Hi, Sarge. The first trucks are in sight, and they are already under heavy fire. There's a Bradley stopped, and I can't tell if it's been disabled or just returning fire. There's a lot more of them that we figured." We couldn't let the Taliban take out the convoy. It was carrying our own food and supplies, and the loss would jeopardize our entire flank. I turned, looking back down the hill and saw Conroy heading up carrying a long sack and a metal canister.

"Jones, go down and help Conroy bring that rifle up, and take it to that rock up there. I pointed to a large outcropping somewhat above us. A good high-firing platform for a fifty caliber sniper rifle. Adams had been our company sniper and was expert with the 50 cal. I was not his equal, but I had more training than anyone else on this hill. I popped my head up quickly, spotting my target. There wasn't any problem finding it because of the quantity of tracer fire streaming from the rock formation about 1200 meters from us. Multiple positions were firing, most at the coming convoy, still in the distance. Jones was right, there were quite a few Taliban over there. I saw Jones signaling me, and Conroy already skidding back down the hill. My turn.

The rifle was long and heavy and needed to be fired from a prone position. Jones had found an ideal spot with a slot between two boulders and a nearly flat area behind. The rifle was already set up on its tripod when I arrived. "You spot," I told Jones and got into position. Jones raised his field glasses and took a long look.

"I can see movement but no clear targets. You won't have much to shoot at Sarge."

"All this thing needs to do is to touch them," I said and began loading the weapon with explosive ordinance. No tracers this time because we were going to fire by optics alone. I squinted through the eyepiece and focused the scope on my target. There was movement. An arm then a head would appear. Sometimes a rifle with hands. All of the sightings were brief. My mental calculations told me that my bullet flight time was nearly two seconds. Too long to hit a moving target, especially a briefly exposed moving target. I settled in, looking around with the telescope, trying to pick my first shot. For some unconscious reason, I kept being drawn to a certain area. There was something between the rocks, something green, and it wasn't moving. Since there was no living vegetation in sight, the item must be part of the gear or supplies of the enemy. I kept looking, thinking it over when I saw a man leaning over the spot, retrieving some object. Then it dawned on me what I was looking at. Their ammo supply was positioned where they could get at it easily, and I was looking right at it. The opening on the other side of the valley that my bullet would past through was no more than one foot wide. A small target for such a distance, and especially for the first shot using a borrowed rifle. It was a lot to ask, but I was going to ask. "Please," I offered to whomever was listening, if there was anyone listening.

"I have a target, but it's a small one. If I miss, they might figure out what the target is and move it. We might only get two shots," I told Jones.

"Shoot at something else, Sarge. Sight it in first." It was a very good idea. Save the important target for later. Yes, I agreed. I moved the crosshairs around and found another spot where tracer fire was originating. It was about the same size opening but nearly fifty meters away from the ammo dump.

"Keep your eye on the targets, Jones. You won't have any problem seeing where this round hits." I squeezed the trigger slowly as I had been taught and expected the gun to wallop my shoulder with the recoil. The muzzle flash and resulting report were enormous, much larger than I expected, but the recoil was light, very light.

"Wow," Jones remarked. "You took the whole side of the boulder off, Sarge. That thing is a cannon!" I looked again and could see the area of impact clearly. Ten inches off, not bad. I adjusted the scope and found the target again, this time firing quickly. Even I could see the explosion erupt from the behind the rock. Dead on. I moved the crosshairs back to the green box deep behind the crack and held my breath as I pulled the trigger. This time, we all could feel the resulting explosion as a large fireball rose like a mushroom, twisting and coiling flames mixed with rock and smoke, rising high in the dry air and resonating among the cliffs. Firing from the other side stopped suddenly, and the Bradley started moving again, the column right behind it. We had won, at least for today.

We left two spotters on the cliff with night glasses, just in case, but the rest of us came down for food and a little rest. Our convoy arrived safely with only a few dents, no injuries. I sat down on a comfortable rock and started opening an MRE, chicken and rice it said. I could smell coffee brewing from nearby. We had to rest up, because a platoon was heading across the valley tonight, looking for stragglers, and I was leading it.

"Sarge," Conroy said. "Colonel's waiting for you. He said to bring your food with you."

Reluctantly, stiffly, I got to my feet and followed Conroy, eating while we walked.

"What's it about this time, Conroy?"

"He didn't tell me Sergeant, but he's in a good mood." He should be, I thought. One lucky round and the supplies and men made it through without a hitch. Doesn't get any better than that. We entered a plush double-walled tent, dark on the outside but brightly lit inside. Colonel Frank was sitting at a table, a MRE open in front of him.

"Ah, the man of the hour. Come on in and eat with me Sergeant. You saved the day I understand. Good work, Sergeant James."

"Thank you, sir. It was a luck shot. I wasn't sure what I was seeing through that little crack."

"Nonsense, James. Took a lot of skill to pull that one off. You can expect a commendation shortly." He seemed to have difficulty talking about what we both knew he wanted to talk about. He wasn't a man who could easily show emotion, and he was getting older and grayer by the day. I heard that the only reason he was still in the field was by his own personal request, and I wondered if it had anything to do with me. Being close to me, I reflected, was that what he actually wanted?

"James, you know I've never called you by your first name. Would it be permissible to you if I did, at least for tonight?"

"Certainly, sir. I would like that."

"Well then, Rick, here we are, alone in the middle of nowhere, fighting a persistent enemy together. Who would have thought that would happen?"

"For me, sir, I'm very grateful to still have you around. We're always afraid that we will hear about your retiring or your transfer back home."

"You won't hear that, Rick. There is nothing back home for me. I would like to die here like a true soldier rather than in a nursing home bed back in the States. Besides, you are here." I looked at him when he said that, trying to understand what he meant.

"You are like a son to me, Rick. You are all I have left." For a moment, I thought there were going to be tears from him, but thankfully, he remained dry eyed. I often wondered if he had cried when Julie was killed, but it was never a question I could bring myself to ask. They were very close, those two, and I feel sure that he did, at least in private.

"We never caught him, you know," he said and looked far away into an imaginary distance, probably trying to bring up the image of a man that he never saw.

"You mean Nasrallah."

"Of course. He was right there, but we never even got close. He was smarter than all of us. We still can't find him, and believe me, we've turned over every rock in the world looking for him.

"Yes." I refused to expound on how I tried in vain to convince everyone that the wrong man had been killed that night. It wouldn't bring any of them back, not one of them. I was the only survivor, and it took three days for rescuers to find me buried under the house that had collapsed into the basement. Biggs had unwillingly saved my life with his dead body. The memory of having his corpse against me for three days had given me problems ever since. Julie and the others were torn to bits by the explosion, not even enough left to bury. The details about it were read to me by an orderly in the hospital when I came out of my coma. I didn't even get to attend her funeral, much less tell her goodbye one last time. Mostly, I tried not to think about it, any of it. When I did think about her, it gave me crippling pain, and I couldn't function, sometimes couldn't even stand on my own two feet. No, I couldn't think about Julie if I wanted to survive this war. I needed to concentrate on keeping my men alive to go home to their loved ones.

"I wish things had turned out differently Rick. You could have been my real son, even given me a grandson by now. We were cheated, Rick. It shouldn't have been like this."

"No, sir." We ate our MREs in silence, washed down by hot black coffee. A soldier's meal appropriate for two soldiers eating together, separated by age but bound together for life by the memory of a young beautiful woman that they both loved more than their own lives.

"Sir, I want to thank you for the privilege of sharing a meal with you, but my men will be assembling by now. We have a night mission to carry out."

"I understand, James. That's a very dangerous mission you boys will encounter tonight. You'll be careful, won't you?"

"We will, sir. Thank you for your concern. May I ask you one question before I go?"

"Anything."

"Who was it that ordered those two cons to kill me back then. Do you know?"

Colonel Frank wiped his chin and looked at me without blinking. "It was me. I figured that if they were able to take you out then you weren't worth having around. That, and you were the weak link. I realized that Julie would have to go rescue you at her peril. Just what Nasrallah wanted her to do. If you were out of the picture, it would foul his plans."

"Then it wasn't part of the plan for her to come to my rescue?"

"Too dangerous. No, it was her idea. She couldn't bear to have you in Nasrallah's hands. She put herself at risk for you, and you know what happened next."

"Nasrallah blew us all up. That's what he wanted all along."

"That's right." We stood and looked at each other for a long time. I had a feeling that I wasn't going to see Colonel Frank again, at least in this life.

"Goodbye, sir, and thanks again."

"Good luck, son. Be safe."

I went outside into the cool night and looked up at the stars. At least there was no moon tonight, I thought. As I walked toward the assembly area, I opened the flap on my shirt pocket and gently pulled out the green scarf, holding it to my nose, desperately trying to get one more lingering scent of Julie, then carefully folded it and put it safely away again.

258

The End